DEADLY DEFENSE

A Cass Leary Legal Thriller

ROBIN JAMES

Deadly Defense

A Cass Leary Legal Thriller

By

Robin James

Chapter 1

"It's bad luck!" one of the shower guests shouted. "Every time you break a ribbon it means you're going to have another baby."

My fingers froze. I balanced the giant gift-wrapped box on my lap, poised to rip the bow off the top.

"Having babies isn't bad luck," my sister Vangie said. She sat next to me, holding a pen and paper in her hand, marking down the contents of every gift and who it was from. On my other side, Tori, the bride-to-be, held up the cherry-wood salad bowl Miranda had picked up from her trip to Holland, Michigan, a month ago. It came with matching utensils.

Tori smiled. "I think that particular horse is out of the barn." True enough, her son, my two-year-old nephew Sean, toddled out from the kitchen, his face covered in pink frosting from the cupcake he'd purloined off the table.

"Let 'er rip, Cass," Tori said. She looked radiant in a pink halter dress, her hair expertly styled, cascading down her back. She was strong, healthy, and vibrant. That hadn't always been the case over the last couple of years, ever since Tori had been injured in a horrific car crash. Now, she and my brother Matty finally felt they could move forward with their lives.

"Fine," I said. "But can anybody confirm if the bow-breaking baby curse can transfer to the maid of honor?"

"I think you're safe," Jeanie Mills yelled from the kitchen. She'd been little Sean's accomplice in the cupcake thievery. She popped the last bite of her own treat in her mouth. Jeanie was the closest thing we had to a mother of the groom today. She'd taken my brother and the rest of us under her wing years ago after our actual mother died. Steady, stalwart Jeanie. I didn't know what any of us would do without her.

"Fine," I said. I broke through the ribbon and handed the package to Tori. The box contained the attachments to a mixer Tori had listed on her registry.

Twenty minutes later, with the gifts all opened and stacked in the corner of my living room, Tori's guests made their way out to the side yard where we'd set up tables under two big tents overlooking the lake. I watched in awe as Tori navigated my stone pavers, only catching her balance once on the porch railing.

"She looks good," Vangie said. "It wasn't so long ago I didn't think she'd ever walk without a cane again."

"She's a miracle," I agreed. And so was Sean. He raced out of the back door. I scooped him up before he could get off the porch. Tossing him up, I blew a raspberry into his belly, making him chortle.

"What's the rule, Turbo?" I asked him.

"Wife jacket," he answered.

"Yep." I kept his life jacket on a hook near the back door. Little man wasn't allowed to step foot outside without wearing the thing. My house sat nestled on several wooded acres with several hundred feet of lakefront just a few steps off the back porch. Even though the sandy bottom was only three feet until the drop-off, we took no chances with Sean.

"I've got him." My niece Jessa appeared. Nearing her fourteenth birthday, she'd grown taller than me in the last few months. She grabbed Sean's jacket and helped him put it on. Then she took his hand and led him to the table with the cocktail wieners and meatballs.

"I love her with him," Vangie said.

"They're adorable."

Jeanie came to join us on the porch, followed by Miranda Sulier, my office manager and another of my most trusted humans.

"You did a nice job," Miranda said. "Is she going to have the reception here?"

"I offered," I said. "But no. Matty got some kind of deal at the lodge downtown. With their date so late in the fall, they're worried if it's really cold."

"No predicting a Michigan fall," Jeanie agreed.

We stood there, Vangie, me, Jeanie, and Miranda, watching as Jessa helped fill Sean's plate. Then Tori took his hand and the two of them made their way to one of the tables surrounded by some of Tori's friends from college.

My other niece, Emma, came out to the porch to join us. For the last few months, she'd been interning in my law office. She had plans to start law school next fall. I hadn't yet been successful in talking her out of it.

Something distracted her today. She'd been on her phone more than usual. Even now, she stared at her screen with a frown as she made her way down the porch to stand next to Jeanie. It was subtle. I don't think either Jeanie or Emma meant for me to see it. But Emma tilted her phone screen so Jeanie could read whatever was on it. Jeanie nodded, then made a slight downward gesture with her hand, as if to tell Emma to put the thing away.

"What's going on?" Vangie asked, picking up the same signals I did.

Emma and Jeanie passed a look. "Nothing," Emma answered. "Just a meme I thought Jeanie would think was funny."

Miranda caught my eye. Then she turned to Jeanie. "A meme? Jeanie doesn't know what a meme is. You're both lousy liars. What's going on? You two have been plotting something all afternoon."

"It's nothing," Emma insisted. "Nothing that can't wait until Monday."

"Really?" I said.

Emma bit her lip. She looked at Jeanie. Jeanie shrugged. "You might as well tell 'em. She's gonna find out soon enough."

"Mom!" Jessa shouted from the lawn. Sean had managed to roll a sauce-covered meatball down the front of his white shirt.

"On it," Vangie said. "Oy. That's gonna stain. I should have thought to put a bib on that little guy."

Vangie bounded off the porch and made a beeline for Jessa and Sean, just as Sean slapped a sauce-covered hand on Jessa's dress.

Tori looked up from her conversation and saw the carnage. As she moved to join the clean-up effort, Vangie waved her off. Shaking her head, Tori came to join the rest of us on the porch.

"I told Matty we should just wrap him in plastic the day of the wedding. The odds of him keeping his little tux clean are zero."

"He only has to wear it for the ceremony," Miranda said. "Then we'll get him changed. Don't worry about it. That's what Sean's nanas are for."

I smiled at the word. Sean didn't have any biological grandmothers. But he had Jeanie and Miranda and they were just as good.

Emma's text tone went off again. She frowned as she looked at the screen, then quickly pocketed it.

"What's going on with you?" Tori said. "You and Jeanie have been plotting something all morning."

"It's nothing!" both Emma and Jeanie said in unison.

"Right," I said. "I think it's time for you to share it with the class."

Out on the lawn, Tori's college friends tried to wave her over. She waved back but didn't move.

"I miss them," she said. "But I'm beginning to remember why I like them in small doses."

I tried not to laugh. They were nice enough women. But Tori didn't really seem to fit in with them. She was the only one of her friend group who had a kid. One of the only ones who was about to get married. The rest of them were all in their late twenties and still trying to figure out what they wanted to do with the rest of their lives. Tori had a son. She'd found the love of her life in my brother. And she'd survived something horrible and fought her way back from it. I could understand why she felt disconnected from women who seemed more carefree to her.

That ... and she was one of us now.

"Come on," Tori said. "Spit it out, Jeanie. What plot are the two of you hatching and why are you trying to keep it such a secret?"

"Let's go inside," Jeanie said.

I looked back. The house was empty now. It seemed a little rude to leave all of Tori's shower guests out in the yard without us. At the same time, none of them were paying attention to anything but the food and mimosa table. It didn't seem like that big of a deal to steal away for five minutes.

Miranda held the door open as the women of the Leary Law Group made their way to my kitchen.

"All right," Jeanie said to Emma. "Fill them in. But let me preface this by saying I think this is a horrible idea. No good will come of it. But I know your Aunt Cass well enough to know this is exactly the kind of shit sandwich she can't help herself from biting into."

"Well, thanks," I said.

Emma took a breath. "I got a phone call from a lady I used to babysit for. Over in the Eden's Edge neighborhood."

"Ohh," Miranda said. "Swanky." Eden's Edge was on the west side of town. The *rich* side. The subdivision had been put in about fifty years ago, catering to those with a minimum high six-figure incomes.

"I used to nanny her daughter Elyse for the summer," Emma continued. "The Bakers. It was a while ago. You were still living in Chicago, Aunt Cass."

"Okay?" I said, dubious.

"Well, the Bakers live through the woods and behind the Karls. It sounds like they got to talking. Kim Baker knows I've been working for you. So she suggested maybe she could break the ice. You know, using me."

"Break the ice for what?" None of these names rang any sort of bell for me. I didn't know the Bakers or the Karls.

"Dahlia Karl," Emma said, exasperated.

"Ooooooh crap," Tori said. Clearly, the name had meaning to her.

"Who's Dahlia Karl?"

Jeanie had her own phone out. She typed something into it and turned the screen toward me. A news article popped up. The headline read:

Taney County Sheriff's Deputy Slain by Married Lover

"Wait a minute," I said, my pulse starting to ratchet up.

"Megan Lewis," Miranda said, filling in the blanks my brain was trying to close as well.

"Detective Megan Lewis," I said. Lewis used to work for the Delphi Police Department. Years ago, she'd gotten demoted after I brought to light some mistakes she'd made in a murder investigation. She'd left the department shortly after.

"Deputy Lewis was beaten to death last June," Jeanie said. "Dahlia Karl is married to the man who did it."

"Okay. So what's this all about?"

"She wants to meet with you," Emma said.

"Wait a minute. Her husband was sleeping with Megan Lewis. He killed her. Now his wife wants to talk to me? Why?"

Emma and Jeanie exchanged that look again.

"Oh man," Tori said. "Does she want to hire us? For him?"

"We really shouldn't talk about this here," I said. "Tori, it's your day. Your bridal shower. Why don't we just get back to the party and talk about all of this on Monday?"

"She wants you to come to Dahlia's house and meet with her," Emma said. "Kim Baker ... her friend. The one I babysat for. She's really worried about Dahlia's mental health. This whole thing has taken a toll on her."

"I would imagine."

"Trust me," Tori said. "This is way more interesting than what's going out on the lawn. We could use another juicy case, Cass."

"What? I was hoping we could maybe coast on some mundane, boring real estate closings for a while."

Jeanie, Miranda, and Tori all burst into laughter together.

"It's just a meeting," Emma said. "That's all she's asking for. Maybe an hour of your time. If you don't want to get involved ... and trust me ... you probably shouldn't ... at least you'll have given Mrs. Karl the time of day and we move on."

"She's got money?" Miranda asked.

"No," I said. "No way. Don't start."

Miranda shrugged. "I'm just saying. From what I've read in the news so far, the Karls can probably afford to pay for a top-tier defense."

"Megan Lewis was a cop," I said. "Which makes Dahlia Karl's husband a cop killer. Even if ..."

"It's a meeting," Jeanie said. "One meeting. See what the woman has to say. I'll admit. I'm curious. That's all."

Laughter reached us from the yard. Vangie had Tori's guests playing a shower game, making veils out of crepe paper and plastic plates.

"What do we know?" I asked.

"Not much more than what's been in the news," Jeanie said. "Deputy Lewis was bludgeoned to death in her own bed. Reed Karl confessed to killing her. They'd been having an affair for a while."

I winced at the description. There would be crime scene photos if I agreed to get involved. Awful ones.

"Then I don't get it," I said. "Why does your friend Kim Baker think I can be any help at all?"

"She says Reed refused to talk to any lawyers. But Kim seems to think Dahlia ... that's the wife ... has something to say."

"She ought to cut her losses," Jeanie said. "Sounds like Reed Karl ... I'm sorry. The name even puts me off. Never trust a man who's got a last name for a first name and a first name for a last name."

"I'll keep that in mind." I smiled.

"What do you want me to tell her?" Emma asked.

I knew I should have told her no. The victim, Megan Lewis, had been very well liked by the Delphi Police Department. I was certain she had the same reputation in Taney County. But Jeanie's words rang true for me too.

I was curious. That's all. And I knew the old saying about what curiosity does to cats.

"Set it up," I told Emma. Then I resisted the urge to meow.

Chapter 2

When I was a kid, I never came to places like the Eden's Edge neighborhood. Learys were east-side trash. Eden's Edge was decidedly west side with its stately, two-story homes, manicured lawns, and pools. Doctors lived here. Professors. Every major business owner. Even now, nearly half a century after these luxury homes went up, it still felt odd for me to be here. Things you think about yourself ... or things other people tell you about yourself when you're a kid ... can be hard to shake.

The Karls' home was unique even for this neighborhood. Tucked back in the southernmost corner of the subdivision, on a cul-de-sac, they had only one neighbor to their east. The home abutted the woods. Through those woods, their friends, the Bakers, presumably lived. It was about as private as you could get and still live in a platted subdivision.

Emma got out before me. The Karls' next-door neighbor was an older gentleman, mid-sixties with a shock of white hair. He stood on his porch, sweeping off some fallen leaves. He gave us a wave and stopped for a moment, curious as to who we might be.

Dahlia Karl had a wooden welcome sign propped up against her yellow-painted front door. The door swung open and a pretty, red-haired woman greeted us with a wide smile.

"Emma!" she beamed. "Look at you!" She rushed forward and enveloped Emma in a hug.

"Aunt Cass," Emma said. "This is Kim Baker. I used to babysit Elyse, her daughter. Is she here?"

"She's at volleyball practice," Kim answered. "She's an eighth grader. Can you believe that? I think that's about the age you were when you first started working for us."

"Wow," Emma said. "Well, tell her I said hello."

"She's going to be so sorry she missed you. Come on in. Dahlia's in the back bedroom."

Kim Baker's smile faded a bit as she said it. She led us down a long, slate-tiled foyer and into the kitchen.

We weren't alone. A young girl with long blonde hair tied back in a loose bun stood at the kitchen sink. She wore a red apron and busied herself drying dishes and putting them on a wooden rack. She had earbuds in and didn't hear us come in.

The kitchen itself gleamed. I couldn't see so much as a single fingerprint on any of the stainless steel appliances. Something delicious was baking in the oven.

"Clara!" Kim shouted. She stepped forward and put a hand on the girl's arm. She jumped back and pulled out one of her earbuds. She gave us an unsure smile.

"Clara, this is Cass Leary. And maybe you remember her niece? Emma? She used to stay with Elyse for us when she was little."

"Oh, hi," Clara said.

"Clara is Dahlia and Reed's daughter," she said. "She and Elyse are pretty close. Sisters from another mister."

Clara strode forward. She shook my hand with the confidence and maturity of a twenty-five-year-old, not a kid of maybe thirteen or fourteen that she clearly was. For a moment, I felt a kind of déjà vu. Clara was washing dishes. Cooking. Cleaning the house. Her father was in jail. Her mother, by all accounts, was a wreck. Who was looking after Clara? I knew the answer before I even asked the question. Nobody. Clara Karl had no choice but to grow up fast. She probably didn't feel like she could rely on any of the adults in her life right now. The same thing had happened to me at roughly the same age when my mother died and my father couldn't drag himself away from a bottle of whiskey.

"Mom's still getting dressed," Clara said. "I told her you were coming. Let me go check on her."

Clara took her earbuds out and set them on the counter. She slipped the apron off her neck and hung it on a hook as she disappeared down another first floor hallway.

"She's been a trooper," Kim said. "Dahlia wouldn't have made it this far without Clara. I do what I can to help out, but I work full time."

"Is there any other family?" I asked.

"No," Kim said. "Both Dahlia and Reed are only children. Their parents are long gone. Dahlia's from England. Just outside of London, I think. Clara and Reed are the only family she has in the States."

It was hard to fathom. I had my brother, Joe. Though I'd taken on the role of a de facto mother to my two younger siblings, I'd never felt completely alone.

"Clara's been doing everything," Kim said. "She's making her own doctors' appointments. She's making them for Dahlia, too. The other day, she had me take her to the grocery store to do the weekly shopping. I mean, Dahlia gives her money, but she's just been so out of it the last few weeks. I'm trying to step in where I can. Clara knows she's welcome at our house anytime. We're just through the woods behind their house. Dean and Reed cut a path for the girls when they were little. Clara just doesn't come over as much anymore. She's afraid to leave her mother now. But Clara helped me convince Dahlia to get in touch with you."

"How awful," Emma said. "I hope there's something we can do to help."

Clara reappeared. "She's okay. She forgot to take her morning pills."

Clara went over to the counter. There were pill bottles lined up along the wall. Clara took one pill from two different bottles and carried them back down the hall. A moment later, she reappeared along with her mother.

Clara Karl resembled her mother. Dahlia too was tall and blonde. She wore no makeup and practically blended into the wall as her daughter gently pushed her forward. It almost seemed like she was holding her up. Dahlia looked like she'd dried fresh tears on the way out. She was pretty. Beautiful, actually. She had big, almond-shaped eyes, high cheekbones, and a slender, well-muscled frame.

"Hello," she said in a voice so breathy she sounded like Jackie Kennedy.

"Thanks for coming out here on a Sunday and with such short notice," Kim said. "Dahlia's just been beside herself. I don't know if you can help, but she has to talk to somebody. This is just too big for her to handle all by herself."

"She's not by herself," Clara said. "I'm here, Mom. It's going to be okay."

Dahlia looked absently at her daughter. She smiled, then kissed her. "Honey. It's okay. Why don't you go up to your room for a while?"

"I can stay," Clara said. "If you need anything ..."

"Clara, it's okay. You've been working yourself to the bone all morning. I'm not an invalid." Dahlia Karl was indeed English. She sounded like the former Queen herself.

Clara looked unsure. But finally, she relented. She gave her mother a hug and went upstairs, hopefully out of earshot.

"She's been amazing," Dahlia said. "What kind of teenager has to be encouraged to go play on a screen for a while?"

"Clara's a good kid," Kim agreed.

"We can talk in the living room," Dahlia said. We followed her back toward the front of the house. She had a large, coved-ceiling living room with a grand piano in one corner and two couches and two chairs arranged facing the center of the room.

Emma and I sat together on one couch. Dahlia took the other couch. Emma pulled out a notepad and poised her pen over it.

"I'm going to just be outside," Kim said. "Some of those flower beds out front need some attention. Dahlia, if you need anything, you just give a shout."

"I'll be fine," Dahlia said. Kim said a hasty goodbye. Flower beds in October? It was a weak excuse for an exit, but Dahlia didn't seem to pick up on it.

"Mrs. Karl," I said, cutting right to it. "Are you looking for legal representation for yourself? Is there something ..."

"No," she said. "Not for me. But Reed ... I was hoping you could talk to him. He's all alone in that jail cell. He's terrified even though he won't say it. He won't let me visit him. He won't let me anywhere near him."

"He's confessed to killing Megan Lewis. I'm not sure what help I could be."

Dahlia had a handkerchief in her hand. She twisted it between her fingers. "What happened ... it's not ... it's not like it's been portrayed in the press. Or on social media. I know what people are saying about Reed. But he needs someone to help him get his story out."

"It seems like he did a pretty good job of that all by himself. He gave a detailed statement to the police as I understand it."

Dahlia shook her head. "The last few months have been a nightmare, Ms. Leary."

"I'm sure they have. And it's Cass."

She nodded. "I'm not saying I condone what Reed did. But I understand why he did it."

"Okay," I said. "So why did he do it?"

She took a great, heaving breath. "I know how this will make me sound. I know what happened to Megan Lewis was unspeakable. Awful. But she isn't the person people think she was. She ... Ms. Leary ... er ... Cass ... Megan made our lives a living hell for months. She terrorized my family. And nobody is going to believe it ... they won't even know about it if you don't help my husband."

Emma caught my eye, then she quickly went back to her note-taking.

"Ms. Karl, maybe you better start at the beginning."

She nodded, then blew her nose into her handkerchief. "It's just us. Just the three of us. Me. Reed. Clara. She's just fourteen. I'm so worried about her. She's missed so much school."

"That has to be so hard," I said.

"I know what you're probably thinking. That I should be furious with my husband. And I am. Believe me. Part of me hates him for what he brought into our lives. I try not to. But I'm a human being."

"Did you know your husband was having an affair?" I asked.

She nodded. "Not at first. But then you start to notice things. You worry. Things have been so difficult between us for a very long time and that's my fault."

"Why is it your fault?" Emma blurted, with all the indignation of her generation.

Dahlia Karl's entire posture changed. Her shoulders slumped and she made herself very small. "I haven't been an active participant in my marriage for a very long time. I wasn't there when my husband needed me."

I could see Emma bristle beside me. I understood what she was thinking. I was thinking it too. What kind of number had Reed Karl done on his wife to get her to think his cheating was justified?

"What do you mean?" I asked.

"I've tried," she said. "But mostly for Clara. Whatever energy I have left, I've given to her. Making sure she has everything she needs for school. Helping her with her homework. Driving her where she needs to go. Making sure she eats three meals a day. Being a mum. When it comes to Reed, I just ... I haven't been there for him. And I see the way you're looking at me."

I tried to make my face neutral. So far, what I'd seen was the exact opposite of what this woman was saying. Kim Baker had just said *she* was the one taking Clara to the store. I could still smell whatever meal Clara was cooking in the oven.

"I'm not looking at you any way," I said. "I'm just trying to understand ..."

"I don't think I deserved to have my husband cheat on me," she blurted. "That's not the point I'm trying to make. I just mean ... I understand how he fell into it all. Up until a year ago, Reed was the best husband I could have asked for. And a wonderful father. God. Clara is Daddy's girl for sure. He adores her. This whole thing has just destroyed her. And that's why I'm here. Not for me. For my daughter. I couldn't live with myself if I didn't at least try to do something to make sure Reed's rights are being protected."

"Okay," I said. "That I can understand. But you said something about Megan Lewis. You said she terrorized your family. What do you mean?"

Dahlia looked out the window. "Reed was going to leave me for her. He doesn't want me to know that. But I do. I felt it in my heart. Maybe if I'd have just let him go, none of this would have happened. The thing is … Cass … I still love Reed. In spite of all of it. I love him. I love his mind. I love his passion. I love the kind father he is. And I don't know who I'd be without him. Even now."

"Tell me about Megan Lewis," I pressed her again.

Her eyelids fluttered. "She wasn't … she's not … she was not a good person. She did things. Horrible things. I'm not saying she deserved to die because of them. But the jury needs to hear about it. They need to know all the facts before they decide what Reed is guilty of."

"What things did she do?"

Dahlia met my eyes. "Megan Lewis was obsessed with my husband. And she believed I was the thing keeping him from being with her fully. So she tried to get me out of the way."

Her tone had dropped and gone flat. I got the sense this might be the first time she'd spoken those words out loud.

"Okay," I said. "Mrs. Karl …"

"Dahlia," she said.

"Dahlia. I need to be clear on something. If I were to agree to get involved in this case, I wouldn't be your lawyer. I'd be your husband's. If that is indeed what you're asking me."

"It is."

"So … whatever you tell me here. It wouldn't be protected by attorney–client privilege. Do you understand that?"

"I do."

"All right. So what do you mean Megan Lewis tried to get rid of you?"

"There were a series of things. First, I had this sensation of being followed home from the grocery store. I would find little notes on my windshield. Typed letters calling me bad names. Names I'd rather not repeat. And the neighbors saw her. She would drive by the house. All hours of the day and night."

"You're saying Megan did all of this? You have proof of that?"

"The police must have proof of it," she said. "They searched Megan's phone and computer."

Emma took furious notes. I crossed my legs. "Dahlia, did Megan Lewis directly threaten your life?"

"Things were escalating. The police know all of this. But they don't care because she's one of them. They were protecting her. They didn't care what she did. She knew she could get away with it. And then she ..."

Dahlia let out a sob.

"And then she what?" I asked.

"She broke into my home," she said. "She ... she took Ian's things. She destroyed them. She laid them out where she knew I would find them."

"Ian?" Emma and I said it together.

"Reed was so angry. He swore to me he would make sure nothing bad happened to me. That he'd end it with Megan once and for all. I believed him for a while. I don't know. Maybe he did. But then she broke in here."

"Who is Ian?" I asked.

Dahlia broke down in tears, burying her face in her hands.

"Ian was my brother."

The voice came from the hallway. Clara stood there, her face ashen. Emma and I exchanged a look. Clara came into the room and put her hands on her mother's shoulders.

"Ian was my little brother," she said again. "He passed away a few years ago. My mom's talking about his toys. We had a break-in a few months ago. Before ... everything else happened. Someone took Ian's toys. His favorite stuffed bear. Mom found them hanging from the ceiling in her bedroom."

"How awful," Emma said. "I'm so sorry that happened to you."

"Clara, please," Dahlia said. "Honey, I'm okay. It's okay. I can talk to these ladies. You don't have to take care of me."

"Clara," Emma said. "I think whatever you've got in the oven might be starting to burn. Why don't we go check?"

Clara was reluctant to leave her mother's side, but Emma was able to guide her away.

Dahlia wiped her nose with her tissue. "I was terrified. Clara was devastated. We filed a police report. They were just starting to look into it when ... Look. I don't know what happened to Megan Lewis. What led up to it? That's something you'll have to ask Reed if you decide to help us. But I am telling you. What Reed did, he did because he was trying to protect us. I don't know how much further that woman would have taken things. But what kind of person rips open a dead child's toys? Clara saw! Megan could have done anything she wanted to me. But Clara is completely innocent in this. She's my baby. Reed was only trying to protect us. He took it too far. I won't deny that. It's just ... there are mitigating circumstances and people need to know."

I had far more questions than answers. But Dahlia collapsed into a fit of tears. A moment later, Kim Baker walked back in. She went to her friend and gathered her into her arms.

"Will you talk to him?" Dahlia asked through sobs. "Will you at least go see him? I know my husband. For all his faults, he thinks he's being noble or chivalrous or something. I told you, I don't condone what he did. He's going to go to jail for it. I know that. He has to. But he isn't just some cold-blooded killer."

Dahlia stood straight up, shrugging off Kim's embrace. "I can't breathe," she said. "I need air."

Before Kim or anyone could stop her, she bolted down the hallway, back to what I assumed was the primary bedroom.

"I'm sorry," Kim said. "She's been a mess. She blames herself. Which is nuts. I know. But Dahlia's very fragile. Even before all of this. We almost lost her about a year ago."

"What do you mean?" I asked.

"Dahlia's been depressed. She and Reed lost their son a few years ago. Ian was only four years old. She hasn't been the same since. That's why she thinks Reed sought comfort in another woman. I hate him for it. I'd like to scratch his damn eyes out for putting her through all of this. But Dahlia isn't wrong. I saw the notes Megan Lewis left on her car. I know how frightened she was. And listen ... they can afford to pay you. Reed has money. Lots of it. He invented this app people use to find used car parts. He sold it for millions a few years ago. I know you're one of the best defense lawyers in the state, Ms. Leary."

"I'll talk to him." I said the words almost before I formed the thought. Kim's shoulders sagged with relief.

"I'll tell Dahlia," Kim said. Then she crossed the room and actually hugged me.

Emma came back to the living room. She'd managed to distract Clara and keep her in the kitchen so now it was just the grown-ups.

"Thank you for everything," Kim said to Emma, then hugged her again. She showed us out the front door.

For a moment, I didn't know what to say. I couldn't stop looking at the Karls' house. I put the car in gear and backed out of the driveway. For a moment, Eden's Edge didn't seem luxurious. It seemed oppressive.

Neither Emma nor I said anything as we drove back to my house. I made my way down the driveway into the woods. As I hit the garage door opener, Emma finally broke the silence.

"Well," she said. "Miranda's going to be thrilled about the size of the retainer the Karls can afford to pay. But what are you going to do about the bigger problem?"

"Which one?" I asked. Just as I said it, another car pulled in behind me with my bigger problem behind the wheel.

Chapter 3

ERIC WRAY HAD SPENT ALMOST twenty years as a detective for the Delphi Police Department. He was my best friend, my closest confidant, the person whose opinion mattered most in the world to me, and lately, the love of my life. He stared at me in that way he had. Those dark eyes, that scowl that was downright sinful, hands on his hips. Even as I knew he was about to get really pissed at me, I couldn't help having a wicked thought or two.

"Hear me out," I said.

No sooner had I gotten those words out before Emma bailed on me, slinking out of my house like a rat from a sinking ship.

"Cass ..."

"Sit," I said. I went to him. I expected steam to come out of Eric's ears as he stood there, nostrils flared, immovable as a hunk of marble. I reached up and put my hands flat on either side of his face. A muscle jumped in his jaw. He settled a bit under my touch. Then, reluctantly, with his muscles coiled, he followed me out to the porch.

"I went to see Dahlia Karl today," I explained. "She's asking for my help. I haven't fully decided whether I want to give it yet."

"Dahlia Karl."

"Yes. Her husband is Reed Karl."

Eric made a noise low in his throat. I knew he understood the implication, but I said it anyway. "Reed Karl is accused of murdering Megan Lewis."

"Accused? He confessed. He did it, Cass. He killed her."

"I know."

"And you're telling me you're considering defending him in court?"

"I'm telling you I plan to have a conversation with him."

"Why?"

I took a breath, ready to launch into a speech I'd prepared in my head before he even walked in the door. But that simple question threw me off guard.

"Why?" he repeated.

"I'm not sure." It was as honest an answer as I could give him.

"Money? Word is Karl's loaded."

"I won't say that's not a factor. A small factor. Though if you asked Miranda, it's everything."

"Miranda doesn't dictate the clients you bring into your office."

"No. She doesn't. Listen, this came to me through Emma. Dahlia Karl is a friend of a friend of hers. She just asked me to listen. So I did. And I have to tell you, I came away from that meeting with more questions than answers. Enough that I'd like to at least talk to Reed Karl about what happened. I know exactly how you might feel about this. She was a cop. You're a cop. I get ..."

"Do you?" he asked. "I'm not so sure. This isn't just a knee-jerk reaction on my part because Reed Karl is a confessed cop killer. Which he is. Megan Lewis ... she was a friend of mine. Christ, I mentored her. She would have made a good detective for Delphi until ..."

"Until I cross-examined her and ruined her life. I know that's what she thought. But you and I both know that's not fair."

It was Eric's turn to take a breath as if he were about to launch into a tirade. He didn't though. Instead, he checked himself. Took another breath.

"You didn't ruin Megan's life. I don't think that, no. I can't speak to whether or not she did. She wasn't your number one fan, that's true."

"She made a mistake. One I had every right to exploit when she was in that witness box. I did my job. She didn't do hers."

"I know that."

"And this isn't even about that. That was years ago. She had a different life."

"She didn't have a choice. She couldn't stay at DPD after her demotion. She was toast as far as any type of meaningful advancement. She knew that. Cass, I'm the one who told her she'd be better off starting over somewhere else."

"Okay. May I ask when's the last time you spoke to her?"

Eric made a face. "What's that supposed to mean?"

"It's not an accusation. It's a legitimate question. How long has it been since you talked to Lewis? There's a real reason I'm asking."

He turned his palms over. "I don't know. It had been a few years. She started over in field ops for Taney County. That's what I heard. She got promoted a while ago and was starting to work some property crimes. They liked her in Taney County. She was a solid cop, despite your opinion of her."

"I didn't have a poor opinion of her at all. It was just one case where I had a problem with her detective work. So did you as I recall."

"She's dead, Cass. What difference does any of that make now?"

"The past doesn't. And I'm glad she landed somewhere that appreciated her. I truly am. It's just ... I think maybe Megan's personal life didn't really mirror what was going on in her professional life. I think maybe she was struggling."

"Because of whatever Dahlia Karl said?"

"She was sleeping with Dahlia's husband. A married man. Does that sound like the Megan Lewis you used to know?"

Eric sat back. He shook his head. "No," he admitted. "No, it doesn't. And I don't have a good answer for you as to what was going on. Like I told you, it had been a few years since I talked to her. I thought she was doing fine."

"I don't think she was. Eric, Dahlia had some pretty disturbing things to say about her. She believes her husband was acting to protect his family."

"From Megan?"

"Yes. Dahlia described a series of troubling incidents in the weeks leading up to Megan's murder. Threats she made. And then ... there's some question as to whether Megan might have broken into the Karls' home. Dahlia's experience was that Megan was trying to force her and Reed apart."

"Dahlia says. Cass, why should anyone believe her? Her husband, her meal ticket, is sitting in the county jail. Dahlia has every reason to say whatever she can to save his skin."

"Maybe. Only ... it really felt to me like she was telling the truth. She was terrified of Megan. It got ugly."

"Ya think?" Eric said, incredulous. "Cass ... we're using words like killed. Murdered. They're not even appropriate for what happened to Megan. I've talked to some of the guys from the sheriff's office. He caved her skull in. She was no threat to him. She was sleeping in her damn bed. She was bludgeoned so badly, she wasn't recognizable as a human being from the neck up. They couldn't even use dental records to identify her. They had to use DNA."

"That's awful."

"That's what you want to defend?"

I had no answer for him. Not yet.

"He admits to doing it," Eric said. "Full stop. This isn't some case where maybe they got the wrong guy. If it were that, I'd almost understand. But it's not that. Karl admitted to killing her. He wants to pay for what he did. So let him. Don't get involved in this one."

"It's only a conversation. If what Dahlia says is true ... if it's probably true ... well, then a jury should hear it. Don't you think?"

He shook his head. "I'm sorry. I can't hear this. Don't start lecturing me about how the system works. How everyone deserves a defense in court."

"They do, don't they? You, of all people, should know that."

Eric curled his fists. It was a low blow, maybe. Not so very long ago, he had been the one needing a defense in court. He understood that not every bad deed was created equally.

"I can't do this," he quietly said. "If you decide you want to get involved in Reed Karl's case, I can't be part of it."

Losing Eric's skills as my private investigator would be a blow. But one I expected.

"I get it," I said. "I just need to know that you'll trust my judgment."

"What do you mean?"

"I mean, if after I talk to Reed, I think I can help him. That I want to help him, you won't hate me for it."

Eric's eyes flickered. His face fell. "Hate you?"

"You know what I mean."

"I can't hate you. I can hate what you do. There's a difference."

"I know. And I love you."

He grunted, but his expression softened. "I love you too. But trust me. It kills me that the reason you want to look into this ... as much as I hate it ... is one of the things I love about you."

Warmth spread through me. I put a hand on his knee. "I'm sorry."

"You're so damn righteous."

"I know." I smiled.

"It doesn't mean you're always right."

"I know that too."

"I mean it though. I can't go down this road with you if you choose to take it."

"You're loyal," I said. "Eric, don't you get it? That's one of the reasons I love you. And if ... well ... after I get Reed's story. If I want to do this. If you really feel ..."

He put a hand up. "Stop. Don't say that. I'm not going to ask you not to pursue something you feel that strongly about for me. That's not my style."

"I know. I'm just saying, if you did ..."

He looked at me. The intensity of his gaze burned through me. "If I asked you not to do this ... for me. You'd change your mind?"

I leaned in and kissed him. "I love you."

"I love you too. You drive me crazy, but I love you, too."

"It's just a meeting, Eric."

He smiled and kissed me on the forehead. "It's never just a meeting, Cass. I know you too well."

Chapter 4

I WAITED in the attorney's room of the Woodbridge County jail. The looks I got from some of the deputies told me my reason for being here hadn't gone unnoticed or appreciated. Some met me with blatant scowls, others just refused to meet my eyes at all. Everything Eric said had been right. Megan Lewis had been well liked. There were plenty out there who still blamed me for her downfall with the Delphi P.D.

But none of that mattered as Reed Karl was led into the room in his jumpsuit and cuffs. Deputy Jake Bunton, a man I'd known since high school, didn't meet my eyes as Karl took the chair at the table where I sat.

"Are the cuffs really necessary?" I asked. I knew they weren't.

"It's okay," Karl said. "It doesn't bother me."

I scanned his face. I'd seen pictures of Reed Karl on social media. He was handsome. Athletic. He sported a full head of thick, dark hair. He peered at me from under an unkempt lock, his bright-green eyes searching mine.

Deputy Bunton moved off. He would stand guard just outside the door. He knew I knew the drill. He could have recited it anyway, but Bunton seemed as if he wanted as little to do with me as possible. I realized then he was engaging in his own form of self-preservation, probably. He didn't want to be seen as fraternizing with the enemy. Even just to exchange a pleasantry or two.

I waited until Bunton left the room. Karl lifted both cuffed hands and smoothed his errant lock of hair out of his eyes.

"Do you know who I am?" I asked.

"My wife told me you were coming," he answered. "I told her not to spend the money."

"The charges against you are pretty serious. Your wife wants to make sure you're afforded the opportunity to defend yourself. You're entitled to that, you know. I understand you've so far refused even a public defender."

"There's nothing to defend," he said. "I told everyone what happened. I just want this to be over."

"Over how? You understand this isn't the end of anything. It's just the beginning. You'll face life in prison without the opportunity for parole. You're what. Thirty-eight, thirty-nine? You could be looking at fifty years of hard time. If you survive."

"Why do you care?"

"Because your wife asked me to talk to you. Despite everything that's happened, she wants you to have a fair trial. She wants to be able to tell your daughter she did everything she could for you."

At the mention of his daughter, Reed Karl flinched. He blinked rapidly, staving off tears.

"How is she?" he asked.

"Dahlia?"

He shook his head. "Clara."

"She's a fourteen-year-old girl who doesn't get to have a childhood anymore. She's taking care of your wife more than your wife is taking care of her. She should be in school. She should be with her friends."

"I don't know what she thinks about me," Reed said. "God. She must hate me."

"Well, your wife doesn't. I can't speak to how your daughter feels."

"Dahlia and Clara need to feel safe. They need to *be* safe."

"Is that what you thought you were doing? Keeping them safe? Do you want to tell me about that?"

He wouldn't meet my eyes. I wasn't sure what I thought of Reed Karl just yet. He didn't walk in here with any sort of bravado. He seemed dispassionate. Almost disinterested. So I decided to push him into an area he might feel uncomfortable about.

"Dahlia is terrified," I said. "She's not eating. Not sleeping. Kim is very worried. That's why she pressed the issue and asked me to see her. I have to be honest. I can't figure it out. You cheated on her. You're not denying that you and Megan Lewis were having an affair."

Nothing. No response.

"I mean, if it were me, the inclination to just leave you to your own devices in here would be pretty strong. You brought Megan Lewis into her life. Right? Now she's facing raising your daughter all by herself. How's she going to do that, Reed?"

"She's going to be okay. I told you. Dahlia's safe."

"Because you made her safe? That's what she thinks. She thinks you killed Megan Lewis to keep her from hurting her. Is that true?"

He stared at the wall. "I made my confession. I told the police everything they needed to know. They recorded my statement."

"I'm sure they did. I haven't asked to review your confession. I wanted to talk to you first."

"Why?" He finally met my eyes again.

I had something in mind to say, but didn't. Instead, I told him the truth. "I'm not sure yet. If I do agree to get involved in your case, it's going to piss off a lot of people. People I care about."

"Seems like your answer is pretty clear then."

"It would be. Only ... your wife still believes in you. That's the thing I can't figure out. I mean, I really can't. You cheated on her. You brought what appears to be an unstable influence into your family's life. I don't know what happened. Did you try to end it? Did you drive Megan Lewis over the edge? You could have just broken up with her once Dahlia found out. If you cared that much about Dahlia's well-being, I can think of a half a dozen better choices you could have made. I mean, the way she was killed. I haven't even seen the crime scene photos yet, but I've heard about them. This isn't looking like some heat-of-the-moment event. It was brutal. Megan Lewis wasn't just killed. She was destroyed. Anyone who could do that had to have been so angry. The fury. The rage it must have taken ..."

Reed closed his eyes. Was he imagining those last moments of Megan Lewis's life? When he opened them again, he stared straight through me.

"She'll be okay. Dahlia and Clara will be okay. She has friends. She has Kim Baker. I've provided for them. There's money. Enough to send Clara to any college she wants to go to. The house is paid off. If Dahlia doesn't spend extravagantly, she'll be fine."

"Mr. Karl," I said. "You've admitted to killing Megan Lewis. Do you understand what that means? Megan Lewis still has family out there. Next of kin. Someday soon, someone is going to advise them to file a wrongful death claim against you. In all likelihood, they'll win it. Then they'll go after every asset you have. Dahlia and Clara are not fine. They're not safe. Not financially. From what I understand, your wife hasn't worked since before she gave birth to your daughter. What is that? Going on fifteen years?"

"They can't do that!" he snapped. "That's Dahlia and Clara's money. It's for them."

"Not if it's in your name."

He buried his head in his hands, then slammed his fists to the table. His cuffs banged loudly against the wood. I couldn't stop myself from flinching.

"Are you really here to help me? Are you really going to agree to be my lawyer if I want you to be?"

I took a breath. "Maybe."

"What about here? Now? If I tell you things ... is it confidential?"

"Yes," I said. "I'm here for an initial consultation. Our communication is protected by privilege unless you're planning to commit another crime or hurt somebody else."

He shook his head.

"Okay. So why'd you do it?" I asked. "Why did you kill Megan Lewis?"

He pressed his thumbs against his eyelids. "I already told you. I already told everybody. She was ... she wasn't ... Megan wanted to hurt my family. She was trying to drive Dahlia out of her mind. By the time I realized what was going on, it was too late. She'd gone too far. I'm sorry. I'm so sorry. I didn't want it to come to this. But Dahlia wasn't safe. It was my job to keep her safe."

"Dahlia said there were letters. Threats. Tell me about that?"

Karl nodded. "I tried to keep Dahlia from seeing those. I tore one off the front door. I swear. If I'd have known sooner, I would have ended things sooner. I don't know if that would have made a difference. Megan was ... God. When I first met her, she was so different from Dahlia. She was strong. Confident. She was like this superwoman. She seemed like she could do anything. Dahlia was ... you have to understand. She was so fragile. I tried. For years, I tried to get her help. You can't imagine what it is to lose a child."

"Your son," I said. "Ian."

"Ian," he said. "He was four. Clara and Dahlia begged me to put that pool in. I would have done anything for them. I've tried to. Dahlia just struggled so much after Ian was born. It took her years to get over her depression. And then ... Ian just slipped away. Clara was at a friend's house. Ian was taking a nap. And Dahlia just dozed off. It happened so fast. When she went outside, Ian was at the bottom of the pool."

"That's awful," I said.

"I thought I was going to lose her then. Dahlia blames herself. It was an accident. We did everything we were supposed to do. The locks. The alarm. But Ian died anyway. Dahlia wanted to die, too. I'll admit. So did I. If it weren't for Clara, I might have just driven us both off a cliff one afternoon. But we got through it. I thought we did. It's just been so hard these last couple of years and Megan was so different."

"Strong," I said. "Capable."

"Yes," he said, burying his face in his hands again. "And for a while, it felt so good to be with her. I loved her. I didn't mean to. I'm so sorry for that. But Dahlia just wouldn't look at me anymore. She said I reminded her too much of Ian. People used to call him my mini-me. Clara looks more like Dahlia. But Ian was all me. All Karl."

"What happened, Reed?" I asked.

"I don't know. Megan wanted more than I could give. She wanted me to leave Dahlia. I hate this about myself. But for a while, I was thinking about it. Dahlia was so unhappy. And if I reminded her of Ian, I thought maybe it would be good for both of us to make a clean break. I just couldn't do it in the end. Because I do love my wife. I know how that makes me sound. I know I'm the villain here. Believe me. I don't want anyone's sympathy. I don't deserve it. But that's the truth. My truth. I loved my wife and in the end, maybe I just came to my senses. I tried to break things off with Megan."

"She didn't take that well?"

"She did not," he said. "She got so angry with me. She could turn on the dime. All of a sudden, the things I admired about Megan became the things that made her difficult. She got violent. She would hit. Claw. Scratch. She threw a heavy stapler at my head once. If I hadn't ducked, she might have broken my jaw. I told her it was over. She threatened to tell Dahlia. I called her bluff. I told her I'd tell her myself, but that I wouldn't leave Dahlia for Megan."

"Did you? Did you tell Dahlia?"

He shook his head. "Not at first. But then Megan started really losing it. Dahlia called me when I was off on a business trip. She kept getting these little notes left on her windshield."

"What did the notes say?"

"He's mine," he said. "Leave him or else. A few of them called her the B word and then the C word. When I got home, that's when I told Dahlia the truth. I confessed that I'd been sleeping with someone. I didn't tell her who. Not then."

"How did she react?"

Reed shrugged. "She just kind of accepted it. That's what was so hard. Maddening. She just shrugged it off and went back into the house. There wasn't even an argument."

"Then what happened?"

He pursed his lips. "I went back to Megan. I confronted her. She denied leaving the notes and I wanted to believe her. I'm an idiot. I know all of that now. But Dahlia gave me nothing and Megan was at least passionate. That was the end of it though. That weekend. It was the last time I slept with Megan. When I left, I told her we were done. For good. She acted like she understood. I know now she was only playing me."

"Why do you know that?"

"Things escalated," he said. "Dahlia got more notes. She didn't tell me at first. More on her windshield. In the mailbox without postage. Different places. Later ... after the break-in."

"Tell me about the break-in."

"Of all the things Megan did, that was the worst. She came inside our home. Violated it. After Ian died, Dahlia just couldn't bring herself to deal with Ian's things. She left his room locked for years. But finally, I convinced her we had to go through it once and for all. It was painstaking. Horrible. But one by one, we donated Ian's clothes. Got rid of most of his furniture. We kept a few things. Things that were special to him. His favorite teddy bear. Some other stuffed animals he loved. Some of his blankets. Dahlia thought they still smelled like him. I couldn't smell it. But I wasn't going to argue with her. We put them in a chest in the closet of his room and shut the door. Well, a week or two after I broke things off with Megan, I took Dahlia out to dinner. I was trying to start over. Trying to make things right. Clara was at a sleepover and Dahlia and I were alone. That night ... it was like Dahlia had some of her spark back. She was laughing. Happy. I knew we had a long way to go. I knew we might not even make it back. But that night, I had hope. When we came home, I knew someone had been in the house. The back door was wide open. We walked into the bedroom and four of Ian's stuffed animals were hanging from these makeshift nooses on the blades of our ceiling fan. Their eyes were plucked out and their throats were slashed. I didn't think Dahlia would ever stop screaming."

"Did you call the cops?"

"Yes. But they didn't find anything. No fingerprints. No sign that anyone broke in. When I told them about Megan, I could just tell by their expressions. She's one of their own. They were never going to seriously pursue anything against her. I don't even know if they questioned her. But that was it. Dahlia was just ... gone. I know my wife. Seeing those toys like that ... it just sent her to a very dark place. I thought I was going to lose her. I thought she was going to try to kill herself again. So ... I did what I had to do. I protected my family."

"You think killing Megan was how to protect your family?"

"They wouldn't believe me! I know how it looked. I was the bastard. The cheater. She was the cop. You've seen how these deputies look at me. At you for even talking to me. They weren't going to help. And Megan was too far gone. She was going to hurt Dahlia. Or she was going to drive her to do something terrible."

"You believed Megan Lewis was either going to kill Dahlia or drive her into taking her own life?"

He got quiet. Reed Karl withdrew into himself.

"Did you say any of this when you confessed to killing her?"

"I tried to."

"The point is, your wife believes there are mitigating circumstances. Look, what you did is reprehensible. You took a life. If Megan Lewis was all the things you say she was ... she needed help not ... death."

A shudder went through him. "I'm sorry," he whispered. "For all of it. I wish I could take it all back. I can't."

42

"That's meaningless."

"I know."

"The rest of your life," I said. "Your wife still thinks you're worth fighting for."

"Do you?" he asked.

"I don't know."

"Dahlia is worth fighting for… And Clara. Is there … do you think the jury could be made to understand?"

"I don't know," I kept repeating.

"I didn't know what I was going to say to you when you came here today. But … Ms. Leary, my daughter needs to know. She's too young to understand now. When she's older. When she's an adult. I don't know if I'll ever see her again. I don't want her to see me here. Not this place. But … if you'll help me."

"How do you think I can help you?"

"Clara. If I tell my story to a jury, then it'll be out there. Forever. Someday, Clara will know what happened. She may never forgive me, but she'll know. I don't expect to ever get out of here. I'm willing to spend the rest of my life in jail for what happened. But if I could get up there and tell people what happened, that's all I'm asking for."

"You'd be crucified on cross-examination. It's almost never a good idea for a criminal defendant to testify."

"What difference does it make? I confessed? I'm not saying I didn't do this thing. I just want the chance to say why. You can help give me that chance. We're not going to win. I know that."

"You're telling me you acted in what you thought was the defense of your family? If these things you say Megan did can be proven ... then ..."

"Just put me on the stand. That's the only thing I ask. If you do that, I'm prepared to pay whatever fee you set. Double. The money doesn't matter. My wife ... my daughter. They're the only things that matter. I want Clara to know. I want a record made. I want to tell people what happened. Not to save my own skin. But just so Clara knows. You can do that for me. You can make sure I get to testify. Will you?"

One more time, I said, "I don't know. Yet."

It was the best I could do. I knew I should probably just walk away from Reed Karl and never look back. But I thought about Dahlia and Clara. If Dahlia was as fragile as Reed said she was ... and Kim Baker seemed to think so too ... then Clara Karl was facing an uncertain future too. One not unlike my own. My own mother had died when I was close to Clara's age. My brother and I had been left to more or less fend for ourselves. I had a champion then in Jeanie Mills.

Who did Clara have?

I knew the answer. It came to me as a whisper. Then a roar inside my head.

Me. She would have me. If I were willing to pay the price.

Chapter 5

RAFE JOHNSON HAD a huge smile on his face when I walked into his office the following Monday morning.

"You act like you're not surprised to see me," I said. Rafe had served as the prosecuting attorney for Woodbridge County for the past few years. He'd been a worthy adversary in a number of murder cases I'd taken on. But we weren't friends. Not really.

"I'm very surprised," he said. "Just not shocked. The Karl case seems like just the kind of lost cause you love sinking your teeth into."

"Very funny," I said. There was something different about Rafe's office. I'd only been inside it a few times, but where he normally hung paintings from local artists, the walls were bare.

"Redecorating?" I asked.

"Have a seat, Cass," he said. "I've been meaning to have a conversation with you outside of any work-related topics for a while."

"Oh? That sounds a little ominous. Everything's okay with you, I hope. And with Seena?" I'd only met Rafe's wife Seena a few times at various functions for the local bar. She was kind, though quiet and aloof. Rumor was, she hadn't wanted Rafe to take the job in what she considered a town too small for her liking.

"Seena's fine. At least ... I hear she's fine."

"Oh," I said, my tone dropping. "I didn't realize you two were separated."

"I haven't told a lot of people. It's still pretty recent. She's in Chicago, staying with her sister. As for me ... well, this isn't for public knowledge yet. But I trust you to keep it under your hat."

"Of course."

"At the end of the year, the governor is going to announce my appointment to fill a seat in Oakland County. One of the District Court judges is set to retire for health reasons."

"You don't live in Oakland County."

"I still have a house there," he said.

"Well, I'm glad for you if that's what you want. But I'm sorry for Woodbridge County."

Rafe smiled. "Are you sure about that?"

"I'm very sure," I said. "Professional adversaries doesn't mean enemies, Rafe. I know the difference, and so do you."

"I do. So you're here about Reed Karl. Will you be filing an appearance?"

"I'm not sure. Maybe. Probably. I'm at least going to get involved enough to decide whether I can help him."

"You understand there's no plea deal on the table, Cass. I can't do it. He confessed. Megan Lewis was a well-liked, mostly well-respected member of this community. I've got law enforcement breathing down my neck about it. He killed her. It's not even a question."

"I know. And I'm not here asking for a plea deal. At least not yet. But I am curious. If you're halfway out the door, why are you letting pressure from local law enforcement get to you?"

Rafe picked up a tablet on his desk. He swiped it open, then turned it so I could see the screen. What I saw there jarred me. I wasn't quite prepared.

It was Megan Lewis. At least, what was left of her. She lay on her back in her own bed. Blood soaked her white sheets and splattered all over her headboard. She had no face.

"Sorry," he said. "But if you're serious about walking into this particular arena, you ought to know what the lions are capable of."

"It's bad," I said. "I know that. Nobody is saying Megan Lewis deserved that."

"Is your client looking to change his not guilty plea?"

I stopped myself from correcting him. No. I hadn't filed a formal appearance yet. But I knew I probably would. Unless there was something in that discovery file that drastically changed my view of the case.

"No," I said.

Rafe nodded. "He wants to go to trial?"

I didn't answer. I really couldn't. Rafe regarded me, then gave me a slow nod.

"You sure you want to do this? I mean, are you really sure? You're gonna drag that poor woman through the mud. That's the only strategy you have."

"How about you let me worry about my own strategy?"

Rafe smiled. He put his tablet down and picked up a picture frame that had been lying face down on the credenza behind him. He turned it so I could see it. It was a picture of Rafe with Seena. They were happy. Laughing. Dressed in formal wear at a wedding or some other event.

"I can't imagine Wray's too happy you're entertaining the idea of defending a cop killer."

My first instinct was to admonish him to let me worry about my own love life as well as my defense strategy. But I realized he wasn't coming from a condescending place at all. His eyes filled with sadness.

"Take it from me, Cass," he said. "The job's not worth everything."

"Then why are you going to Oakland County instead of Chicago?"

He huffed a laugh. "It's a simple question with a complicated answer."

"Is it?"

"Seena made her choice. I have to make mine."

"And I have to make mine."

"Well, for your sake, I hope it's the right one. This can be a lonely career. But ... I for one will be selfishly glad if you do throw your hat into the ring. Even if I do think it's a dumb decision for your personal life."

I laughed. "Thanks for that."

"I mean it. Nothing would make me happier than to face off with you one more time before I take the bench."

"You'll have to run to keep your seat," I said. "The voters of Oakland County might have a different plan next November."

"I like my chances."

"Well, they'd be fools not to elect you in your own right. You'll make a good judge, Rafe. And I meant what I said. It'll be Woodbridge County's loss."

He opened a desk drawer and pulled out a flash drive. He tossed it to me. I caught it just before it bounced off to the floor.

"Your mandatory disclosures," he said. "The full police report. Crime scene photos. Digital forensics. The whole nut. I hope you didn't have other plans this weekend."

"I appreciate that."

"I expect you to file your appearance before you head back to the office. Don't tell me you're still deciding. You wouldn't have walked in here if you weren't sure."

I was sure. Mostly. But I still wanted to take a look at Rafe's disclosures.

"Thanks for this," I said. I dropped the flash drive into my bag. Rafe rose to his feet and extended his hand to shake mine.

"Give Matty and Tori my congratulations. I hear you've got a big family wedding coming up. If anybody deserves to be happy, it's them."

"Thank you. I will."

Rafe was still staring at the picture he'd shown me of Seena as I walked out the door.

Chapter 6

It was one of the more brutal crime scenes I'd ever viewed. The photo Rafe had shown me wasn't even one of the worst. Megan Lewis had been pulverized in her own bed. The coroner's report indicated nearly every bone in her face had been shattered. Her jaw had been broken in three places.

The anger. The rage. Nothing about the man I met indicated he was capable of this kind of blind fury.

I thought about what he'd told me. The fear he had for Dahlia's safety and sanity. The broken woman I'd encountered curled up in her bedroom, her fourteen-year-old daughter trying desperately to run the house in her stead.

I paged through the coroner's report. One small blessing appeared. Dr. Trainor believed the force of the initial blows would have quickly rendered Megan Lewis unconscious. There was at least a chance she never knew what hit her.

What did hit her? The police hadn't retrieved a murder weapon. The detective and Rafe Johnson would argue Karl had brought something with him. I knew Rafe's trial strategy would depend on this. If Reed came to that house with a weapon in hand, it would prove premeditation. Planning. First degree murder.

I hadn't asked Reed any of these questions. Not yet. I hadn't pressed him to tell me exactly what he did that night. I wanted to see all the evidence they had against him first. I would give him a chance to lie to me. If he did, we were done. The decision would be easy.

A knock on my conference room door jarred me. Emma walked in.

"What time is it?" I asked.

"Late," she said. "Eight thirty."

"You should head home," I said. "You don't have to stay here as long as I do."

"I know. I was kinda hoping you'd let me help you sort through some of this."

I'd printed out the most damning aspects of the file on Reed Karl. Emma picked up one of the crime scene photos. Only a tiny twitch in her jaw indicated the horror she might be feeling. She set the photo down.

"Anything usable here?" she asked.

"I don't know." I showed her the autopsy report. Pointed out the question of the murder weapon.

"Did you ask him?" she said. "Did Reed tell you what he used on her?"

"No. I didn't ask."

"He gave two separate statements to the police," Emma said, picking up the tabbed addenda to the police report. "Were they consistent?"

"In a way," I said. Emma skimmed over the first statement. There wasn't much to it. The police had come to his house a few hours after Megan's body was found. She'd not shown up for work or answered her phone. Another Taney County deputy had gone to check on her.

"His texts," Emma said. "Cass. Did you read through all of this?"

She showed me a portion of the cell phone forensics report. I'd leafed through it. In the days leading up to Megan's murder, her texts to Reed had grown increasingly desperate. He was trying to break it off with her. She begged him to come see her one last time. Two days before her murder, Reed had abruptly warned her not to contact him again.

"That's all consistent with his story," Emma said. "He was angry. She told Dahlia they were sleeping together."

"It is," I said. "There's just something that's bugging me about all of this."

"What?"

"They don't have anything. Before Reed confessed, the cops didn't have anything. Nothing physical."

"What do you mean? The crime scene lab found hair belonging to him in her bathroom. A partial print on her kitchen counter matched his."

"Right. But they were having an affair. That's not in dispute. He admitted that they mostly met up at her house. That's where they carried on the bulk of their affair. Adultery isn't a crime."

"Cass, you're talking like you're trying to prove somebody else committed this crime."

"No. No. I know. It's an old habit. It's just ... without Reed's confession, Rafe Johnson wouldn't have gotten a conviction. I think he knows that."

"You think there's a hook here?" Emma said. She pored through the police report. "He was Mirandized. He declined having a lawyer present."

"I know."

"This would have been a hell of a lot easier if Reed had called you right off the bat." She winced at her own poor word choice. In the coroner's summation, she theorized a baseball bat had been used to bludgeon Megan to death.

"Right," I said.

"Is Rafe offering a plea? I mean ... it feels like you can make second degree off what I'm seeing here. He doesn't admit to bringing a bat with him to her house. It doesn't feel like a stretch that this could have been in the heat of the moment. Except ... she was asleep. It only takes a split second to form a plan for first degree."

"You're learning," I said. "Does anything else bother you about the way this seems to have played out?"

She carefully combed through the pages of supplemental reports.

"That first time he was questioned," she said. "Reed insisted he had no idea what happened to Megan."

"He'll say he panicked. It's just …"

"Two days went by," she said. "Cass, they didn't have it. They had the forensics from his phone. But there's nothing putting Reed at the scene. Nobody saw him coming or going. They weren't going to arrest him."

"Not based on any of this," I said, picking up the supplemental file with reports on all the physical evidence.

"But he came forward anyway," she said. "Why?"

"Guilt? Panic?"

"Hmmm. What do you think?"

I surveyed the piles of evidence. The police report. The photographs. If a jury saw them, they would want to make someone pay. Megan Lewis didn't deserve this. Nobody did. And yet …

"Cass," Emma said. "If you can successfully argue second degree … I mean … you can. I just don't see a cut-and-dry case of premeditation here. Rafe Johnson has to know that. So why isn't he offering a plea deal?"

"Public pressure," I said. "And this will be his last case out the door. He wants to leave on a high. Or he feels like he's got nothing to lose."

"The things Reed said," Emma continued. "If he was truly in fear of what Megan would do to Dahlia. Can you prove any of that? What she did?"

"Her texts are damning. The notes Megan sent her. And then there's this."

I handed Emma a stack of photographs. They had been pulled off Megan Lewis's laptop.

Emma's eyes widened as she looked at them. "Is this for real? This was on her computer?"

There were three photographs of Dahlia on Megan Lewis's laptop. In each of them, Dahlia appeared to be asleep. Megan Lewis had gone into Dahlia's bedroom and photographed her without her knowledge.

"This is some pretty creepy, stalker-like stuff," Emma said. "I mean. Wow! Did Reed know she was doing this?"

"I'm not sure. But it tracks with what Dahlia said. She claims she felt she was being watched."

"But you'll have to kill her again," Emma said. "In court. You'll have to assassinate Megan Lewis. Are you sure you want to do that?"

"Do you doubt that it's true?"

Emma leafed through the forensics report on Megan's computer. She stopped again on the photographs of Dahlia, asleep in her bed. The photos were time stamped two weeks before Megan's murder.

"No," Emma said. "I don't doubt that it's true. Megan Lewis was disturbed. Maybe dangerous. But what is the winning outcome here, Cass?"

I put the photographs down. "I'm not sure. But I feel like I'm trying to save a family."

"Clara got to you."

"A little. Yeah."

"She's a sweet kid. She was always so polite when she'd come over to play with Elyse Baker. Those kids are so close. Mr. Karl and Mr. Baker cut a path through the woods between their houses so they could get to each other. I'm glad Clara has a friend like that. I'm glad junior high hasn't ruined it for them."

"I don't know," I said. "Reed Karl is going to go to prison for what he did. As he should. I just feel like his family is entitled to get the truth out. People need to know why he did what he did. His whole story."

"You sound like Tori." Emma smiled. "She told me almost the same thing."

Of all people, Tori understood what it was like to be the daughter of someone accused of murder. In her father's case, he'd been wrongfully accused. Reed Karl's case wasn't like that. But it was much more nuanced than what I knew Rafe wanted to present.

"I think we should do it," Emma said. "I'm not saying a whole trial. Maybe that wouldn't be good for anybody. And I'm also not saying Reed is some kind of hero. He's not. He is the bad guy in this. But ..."

"His punishment should truly fit his crime," I said. "That's all I'm contemplating."

"If he's convicted of second degree, he could be out in less than twenty years. Clara's fourteen."

"Right."

Emma turned to me. "Fathers sometimes have to do extraordinary things to protect their families."

My blood ran cold. It was something we never discussed. But not so long ago, her own father, my brother Joe, had to do something extraordinary to save Emma. I fought to keep my face neutral. Emma didn't know the truth. She couldn't. Could she?

"Will you let me work on this with you?" she asked. "If you take it on?"

I smiled. "Of course."

"Good."

She closed the flap on the file. Emma was quiet and pensive after that. I wouldn't ask the question. I truly didn't want to know what she knew about her own father. But as I looked back at the conference room table, at the mound of evidence against Reed Karl, I knew in my heart I could defend him. And I knew I could win.

Chapter 7

Three days later, Dahlia came to my office. She wasn't alone.

"They're here," Miranda said. She had that look on her face. Flushed cheeks. Her upper lip twitching. I knew what it meant. Sure enough, she held something in her right hand as she stood in my office doorway.

"She brought a check," I said.

Miranda looked down at her hand, almost absently. "Do you want to see it?"

I smiled. "I wouldn't want to take it away from you."

"Cass ... it's a lot of money."

"I'm aware."

"I mean ... a lot of money. We can finish the addition with this. Move you downstairs. Renovate this space. Expand the conference room. And if ... I don't want to plan too far ahead.

But if Emma does end up going to law school. And if she wants to land here when she's through. We can build her an office."

"Miranda, you are getting ahead of yourself," I said.

"I know. I know. It's just ... Cass, that little girl down there. She's terrified. And I get the sense she's holding everything together. We have to be able to give her some hope. That's what we do, isn't it? It's the whole point?"

"Let me talk to them. And don't you get *your* hopes up. This thing is a turd burger. Let's not pretend it's not. I've got a man charged with the first degree murder of a cop. And he's admitted to all of this. I don't have a lot of leverage."

"I know you. You thrive on cases like this," she said. I moved out from behind my desk. Miranda had set Dahlia and her daughter up in Jeanie's office. I wanted Jeanie in this meeting and I hated making her come up and down the stairs. She had new hips, but the rehab had been brutal.

"I've never handled a case like this," I reminded Miranda. She clutched that check to her chest, but I could see some of the zeroes in the amount box. It was the largest retainer I'd ever quoted. Part of me hoped Dahlia would balk at it. It would have made this a whole lot easier.

I heard Jeanie's laughter as we made our way downstairs. There was a dark cloud, too. Eric had just come in. He hung back near the kitchen. Though I wanted to ask him to be part of this meeting, I knew not to push my luck.

I put a hand on his chest. "We'll talk after," I whispered. "Will you be around?"

"I'll be upstairs," he said. He was coiled tight. His muscles felt like granite under my fingertips. I squeezed his arm as he brushed past me.

Jeanie swung the door to her office open. Dahlia sat on one of her couches, hands folded in her lap. She wore a pretty floral print dress, her hair pulled back in a bun. Clara sat beside her mother.

"Clara," Miranda said. "We just had some donuts delivered from the bakery downtown. You mind helping me put them on a plate?"

"Mom," Clara said. "I can stay with you. It's okay. I can handle it."

Clara really did look like her mother. The same stick-straight blonde hair. The same thin frame. But she was almost a head taller than her mother.

Dahlia shook her head. "It's okay. I need to talk to Ms. Leary alone. Go pick me out a donut. You know what I like."

"Good," Clara said. Then she turned to Jeanie and me. "She doesn't eat much. She'll forget unless I remind her."

"Clara, don't," Dahlia said. "These people don't need to know all of our business."

I resisted the urge to tell her that I absolutely did. If I were going to be able to help her husband, there could be no secrets of any kind.

"They're here to help us," Clara said, as if reading my mind. "They're on our side." She looked at me with expectant eyes. Again, I saw myself in her. But there was one big difference. Clara Karl wanted to trust the people in this room. When I was in her place thirty years ago, I didn't believe I could count on anyone but myself. Until Jeanie came along.

"Come on," Miranda said. She held a hand out for Clara. Clara smoothed her mother's hair back, then followed Miranda into the other room.

Jeanie took a chair near Dahlia. I shut the door and went to join them.

"You've seen him?" Dahlia said. "You've talked to Reed?"

"I have," I said.

"What did he say? He told me he doesn't want me to come down there anymore. He's worried about me. Everyone is worried about me. Clara puts up a brave front, but she's losing just as much weight as I am. I need to do better with the cooking."

"It's hard," I said. "I can't imagine the stress you're under. I do have to remind you, I can't share with you what I discussed with Reed. I can't discuss it with anyone."

"Right. Yes. You did warn me about that. I'm sorry. It's all right. But ... he was willing to meet with you. Can you share that much?"

"Yes," I said. "He was willing to meet with me."

"So you'll take the case? I'll pay up front. I worked it out with your bookkeeper. We're all set?"

"Ms. Karl, I need you to prepare yourself for what's in store. Your husband's legal options are limited in light of statements he's made to the police."

"Reed can't go to prison forever. He just can't. It would kill Clara. It might kill me."

"Your loyalty to him is honorable," I said. "And it may be one of the biggest things he has in his favor."

"He did what he had to do," she said. "That's what everyone needs to understand. That's why I'm here. Nobody else would even talk to me. Not after Reed confessed. Megan Lewis isn't who people think she is."

"We don't need to rehash all of that. But the way I see it, Reed's best outcome here is a plea bargain. One that's not currently on the table from the prosecutor's office."

"But you can turn that around. I know you can. Once they understand that you're Reed's lawyer."

I smiled. "I appreciate your confidence in me. But Rafe Johnson understands how strong a case he has. He's looking to make this the cherry on the top of his tenure as our county prosecutor. He's taking a judicial appointment in Oakland County at the end of the year."

"I see," she said. She took a shuddering sigh and her tears began to flow. "Is there no hope at all?"

"I didn't say that. I haven't even really started my investigation. I've only recently started digging into the state's discovery. I need a little more time."

"But do you think you can put some pressure on Mr. Johnson? Get him to reduce the charges against my husband?"

"I think it's possible. But there are no guarantees. And if he won't offer a deal, you need to understand what that will mean. Reed will face a brutal trial. Which means you will too."

She nodded. "And I'd have to take the stand? You'd make me testify?"

I exchanged a look with Jeanie. I had serious reservations about whether Dahlia Karl could withstand what would be a withering cross-examination from Rafe Johnson.

"You're Reed's wife," I said. "Because of that, you're biased."

"But I know what happened. I know that Reed did what he did because of me. Because of Clara. That woman was going to do something terrible. If the jury could be made to understand that ..."

"If I can prove it," I said. "It's not a given that I can. Rafe Johnson's a skillful litigator. He's going to fight hard to keep evidence of Megan's behavior out of evidence."

The door opened. Miranda and Clara came back in. Clara held a plate of donuts. Miranda carried a steaming coffee mug and set it in front of Dahlia.

"Sorry," Miranda said. "You probably prefer tea?"

Dahlia smiled. "I've been a convert for a very long time. Coffee is lovely, thank you."

She took a tentative sip. Clara sat next to her mother. "Ms. Leary was just deciding whether she thinks I'm capable of testifying if your father's case goes to trial."

I pursed my lips. I wasn't sure I liked the idea of Clara being involved in this conversation. She was still a child. Her parents had thrust her in the position of having to become a grown-up almost overnight.

Clara put her arms around her mother. "She'll be okay," Clara said. "She has to be. I'll make sure of it."

"Well," I said. "I have a lot of work to do. I appreciate you coming in. I just wanted to make sure you understood the scope of my representation. I'll be talking to the prosecutor's office again soon."

"And Reed," Dahlia said.

"Of course."

"Thank you," Dahlia said. "I really don't know what we would have done if you hadn't agreed to help Reed. And I do understand. You can't promise any miracles. But with you in my husband's corner, it gives me some peace of mind. Whatever happens, at least I know he's been given a fair chance to defend himself."

She rose. Clara moved with her. She kept an arm around her mother as the two of them headed for the lobby. Dahlia trembled so much I worried whether she was fit to get behind the wheel.

I watched through the window as the two of them climbed into Dahlia's Audi and drove away.

"She's fooling herself," Jeanie said. "Do you really think Johnson will come around with a plea deal?"

"That will depend on whether I can prove any of the things Dahlia and Reed have said about Megan Lewis."

It was then that Eric reappeared in the hallway. Just in time to hear what I'd just said. His scowl spoke volumes.

"Eric ..." I started. He held a hand up.

"Come on, Jeanie," Miranda said. "Let's let Cass and Eric chat alone for a minute."

Jeanie scooted out and followed Miranda into the reception area. Eric didn't look like he was going to move.

"I hate this," he said.

"I know."

"And I can't be a part of it."

"Eric ..."

"No. I get how this works, Cass. You're going to dig up every speck of dirt you have on Megan Lewis and vilify her. That's how you're going to back Johnson into a corner and get your plea deal. If you're lucky. But what if he doesn't?"

"He will."

"You can't be sure of that. He's under a hell of a lot of pressure to get the maximum against Karl. If I were still with DPD, I'd be one of the ones exerting that pressure. You can bet on it."

"I know."

"You can't ask me to work on this with you."

"I know that too."

"I will not be a party to investigating Megan Lewis."

"I understand."

He curled his fist and hit the wall.

"Eric," I started.

"I can't be here," he said.

"I won't ask you to be."

"No," he said. "You're not hearing me. I can't be here. At all. I cannot have my name on the letterhead. I can't draw a paycheck from this firm, Cass."

"You won't be working on the Karl case. We're on the same page."

He shook his head. "I'm out. All the way. I know you feel like you have to do this. I even understand why. But I also have to follow my own conscience."

"You're resigning," I said, my heart thundering.

He closed his eyes slowly, then opened them. "Yes."

I wanted to beg him not to. I wanted to apologize. I couldn't. We both knew why. Instead, I stood there as Eric came to me. He kissed me on the cheek. Then he walked right out the front door.

Chapter 8

I'D SPENT two weeks swimming in the horror that was Megan Lewis's murder. I'd viewed the crime scene photos so many times I became almost desensitized to them. Almost. I knew the moment the jury saw them, Reed's case might already be over.

I replayed his taped confession so many times I knew most of his words by heart. Megan had terrorized Dahlia. She had violated their home. The memory of their son. Clara, too, had been traumatized when she came home the next day.

The digital forensics against Megan was damning. She had routinely broken into the Karls' home. Stalked Dahlia. All of it awful. And yet ... I knew the one thing, the only thing that mattered. I sat in the lawyer's room of the county jail waiting for my client. Or what might become my client. I hadn't yet let Miranda cash that retainer check with all the zeroes. Not yet.

Reed came in. He looked thinner, more disheveled than our last meeting. I got the same dirty looks from every deputy as I checked in. I couldn't let that matter. Their feelings weren't my concern. Not now.

"Reed," I said as soon as the guard left to give us privacy.

"Dahlia said she came to your office again. Is she okay? How did she look?"

He didn't ask me if I would help him. He only asked about Dahlia. I found that comforting in its own way.

"She brought Clara with her," I said. Reed's face fell.

"I don't want her involved in this. I want her kept as far away from this as possible. Dahlia should have dropped her off at Kim's."

"I think Clara insisted on coming. She won't leave her mother's side."

"She must hate me."

"I don't think that's true. I think Clara is just trying to keep things together for both of your sakes."

Reed squeezed his eyes shut. "She's just a kid. It's not her job."

He was saying the right things. It seemed genuine. I watched him like I knew a jury would.

"I've reviewed the case against you," I said. "I have a lot of questions."

"Anything. I'll tell you anything."

I held a hand up. "I want you to tell me the truth. I also want you to get in the habit of *only* answering the questions I ask you. Nothing more. Nothing less. Because if we do this. If I agree to let you testify ..."

"You have to agree. Cass, I don't care what happens. I don't care how good a cross-examiner that prosecutor is. I don't care if he rips me to shreds. I only care that you let me get my story out. So people know why I did what I had to do."

"I'm not a facilitator, Reed. That's not my role. I'm a defense lawyer ..."

"You're on my side. I appreciate that."

"No," I said. "Actually, I'm not on your side. I'm on the system's side. There's a difference. I'm here to make sure you get the benefit of your right. That's all. It doesn't mean I think what you did was justified, Reed. What you need to understand is ... regardless of whether you take the stand ... that confession is going to play for the jury. I'll try, but I don't think there's much cause for the judge to suppress it. So assume it's coming in."

"Good," he said. "I want it to."

"You need it to. Because without it, I won't be able to talk about what they found on your phone. The pictures of what Megan did. Ian's toys."

"He didn't care," Reed said. "That detective didn't seem to care one bit about what Megan did to my family. The deputy who came out to the house after it happened didn't care either. This is what I'm trying to tell you, Cass. This is what everyone needs to know. They were all protecting Megan. They were going to keep protecting her. It was going to get worse. She was going to hurt Dahlia or Clara. I know it."

"Reed," I said. "There are no direct threats from Megan in any of the texts she sent you. Even the letter you say she taped to your door, it's more veiled. Ominous, yes. But ..."

"I'm not just saying she did it, Cass. She did it. The note was there. She was going after Dahlia."

"Okay," I said. "So why did you lie to the police?"

He jerked back.

"Don't answer me," I said. "Just listen. When Detective Patel asked you what you used to kill Megan with, you told him you used a lamp. But that's not what the forensics showed. The coroner thinks it was something more akin to a baseball bat. Only nobody ever found a weapon."

"I don't know," he said. "I was just ..."

"Stop," I said. "See, now you've already violated the first rule I told you. You're trying to answer something I didn't ask. I told you to listen. This is how Rafe Johnson will kill you on the witness stand."

"What do you want me to say?"

His question sent a chill through me. Was he asking to be coached? Or was he merely frustrated with my methods?

"The murder weapon is a problem," I said. "You admit to killing Megan, but you don't tell them how."

"What does it matter?"

"It matters because Johnson is going to hang you for that. He's going to pose the question. What did you do with the weapon? Did you walk into that house carrying it? Do you see what I'm saying? You never answered that question when Patel asked you."

"Because I can't," he said. "God. I swear to you, I didn't want to hurt Megan. I just wanted her to leave my family alone. I just wanted to protect Dahlia and Clara. That's all. That's everything. I just ... the whole night. It's just black to me. I was terrified. Panicked. I can't answer the questions you're asking me. I don't know how I could do what I did. I just ... did it. I just knew I had to make sure Dahlia and Clara were safe."

It felt like a lie. I knew it would kill him at trial if he took the stand. Only, he *had* to take the stand so he could explain his state of mind.

"Reed," I said. "How do you feel about Dahlia testifying instead of you?"

"No," he snapped. "Absolutely not. No way. It'll destroy her. It'll negate everything I've tried to do to protect her. You can't do it. Cass ... you know it won't just stop with what happened to Megan."

"What do you mean?"

"Come on. You know what I mean. If you put her on the stand, then she'll have to explain what happened to Ian. She'll be forced to relive it. You know that. She'll have to explain the context of those damn toys. She'll have to talk about why what Megan did was so hurtful."

"Why is that a bad thing? Reed, if ..."

"No!" he shouted. "I know what the prosecutor will do. So do you. He'll make Dahlia talk about the day Ian died. He'll make her admit in open court that it happened on her watch."

"Which is the truth," I said. "Look, I'm not saying it was her fault. Accidents happen."

"That's not how anybody is going to see it. You know what? Even if they do. That's not what I'm afraid of. Dahlia blames herself. She's nearly taken her life over her guilt. If you make her rehash all of that, it will trigger her in dangerous ways, Cass. I'll lose her. More importantly, Clara will lose her. I would rather lose this case. Spend the rest of my life in jail. But I will not expose my wife to this. I will not force her to sit there in front of a jury and talk about the worst day of her life. You might as well just kill her."

I wanted to argue with him. But I knew he was right. Rafe wasn't a monster. He would see Dahlia as another victim in this and coming at her hard could backfire. At the same time, Dahlia wasn't blameless. I meant what I said, accidents happen. But people would judge her for what happened to her son. It might make her even more sympathetic, but it could destroy her fragile mental health in the process.

"Please," Reed said. "Promise me you won't put Dahlia on the stand. You said my whole confession would have to be played. Well, I explained to Detective Patel why those stuffed animals had meaning to us. The way Ian died isn't relevant. I mean, what difference would it have made if he had a bad heart or died of cancer? Would that make what Megan did any more or less awful?"

"No," I said. "I suppose it wouldn't."

"Then we're agreed. Dahlia stays out of the witness box."

"I still don't think it's the best idea to put you on the stand, Reed."

"Then how will Clara ever know the truth? How will she ever know why I did what I did?"

"You could tell her," I said. "She could hear it from you."

He shook his head. "I want the chance to tell the world. Under oath. Make a record of it. Even if it means I go to jail forever. They'll believe me. They have to."

"The jury might believe you," I said. "But that's not the same thing as finding you not guilty."

"I know," I said. "I'm prepared for that."

"I'm not sure you really are. I'm not sure your nebulous answers on what happened that night are enough to get you out of this."

I stopped myself from asking the next logical question. I didn't want to know what Reed did with the murder weapon. I didn't want to know what was running through his head the night he killed Megan Lewis. It wouldn't help me. Wouldn't give me some clear path to victory.

"Cass," he said. "I know what I'm up against. I know they're probably going to convict me of first degree. I know this. But what you said ... about just making sure my rights are protected, that's enough. Okay? That's all I'm asking. I know my wife. I know my daughter. Especially my daughter. She may not understand it now. But someday, when she's an adult. Maybe if she has a family of her own. I think there's a glimmer of a chance she might be able to look at me and see me as something other than a murderer."

I sat back, folded my hands, and looked at him. Really looked at him. He didn't seem like a monster that day. He seemed human. Vulnerable. As honest as he could be. And yet the jury would see those pictures. Megan Lewis's final moments would be burned into their brains forever.

"We're going to try," I said. "That's all I can promise."

His shoulders sagged with relief. "I don't expect you to win, Cass."

"I know."

"I'm still a human being."

"I know that too."

"Just help me make sure my daughter knows it, too. That's all I ask. Just a chance to tell my story. To do the only thing I can to protect Dahlia and Clara. That's all."

"It's not much, Reed," I said.

"No," he whispered. "You don't understand. It's everything."

Chapter 9

As THE WEEKS went on and Reed Karl's trial date loomed, Rafe Johnson had gone radio silent. All communications from his office came through his assistant. He'd drawn a hard line in the sand. There would be no plea bargain unless I could come up with leverage.

Three days before Matty and Tori's wedding, I did something a little desperate. I showed up at a pee wee soccer game in the field behind Delphi Elementary School. Tori had given me the idea. She'd signed Sean up for a Community Education tumbling class and one of the other moms was a friend of a friend of Megan Lewis's. She'd come back with intel that Megan's friend's daughter played in this soccer league. Each time I'd tried to get her to talk to me, she'd hung up the phone.

Her name was Pamela Corso. She and her husband Gregg had recently divorced. I knew through the grapevine that they transferred custody every Wednesday evening after their daughter Ashlynn's game.

I waited until the game was over. All the little eight-year-olds ran for their snacks and juice boxes. Ashlynn Corso was easy to spot. She had a mass of red, curly hair and she flew into her father's arms. He was a redhead, too. I'd known him since he was just a kid. He'd been in Vangie's class. Pamela wasn't from Delphi originally. But she bought a house just down the street from Megan Lewis in the neighborhood adjacent to Eden's Edge. Her statement to the police was why I was here.

Pamela was just about ready to climb into her minivan when I approached. I called her name. She saw me, and her shoulders sank. Her face went hard.

"I knew you'd do this," she said, pulling her key out of the ignition. She'd thankfully parked in a spot far away from the other vehicles. I'd guessed she would want to make a clean getaway after Gregg took Ashlynn. This way, she wouldn't have to deal with any questions or awkward looks from the other parents. Divorce with kids was hard, no matter how amicable two people could be.

"I'm sorry," I said. "But you won't return my calls. You won't answer the door."

"Did you bring one with you?"

"One what?"

She huffed. "A subpoena."

So Pamela Corso knew her way around the court. Of course she did. I could have pretended. Made more small talk and tried to ease into it. But she'd been direct with me so far. I would do the same. I reached into my bag and pulled out a sealed envelope. I'd gotten Judge Niedermayer to sign the thing the day before yesterday. I handed it to her.

"Can we talk?" I asked.

"I'm not your friend."

"I'm not looking for one. But you were Megan's. You already talked to the police."

"Don't tell me you're just trying to get to the truth. You're on Reed's side."

I paused. I had something else in mind to say. I decided against it. "Yes," I said. "I'm advocating for Reed. But it doesn't mean I'm against Megan. It doesn't mean I think what happened to her was right or deserved or that she isn't entitled to justice. And I'm not looking to put you on the spot or do anything you feel is a betrayal. I just want to talk to you. Find out more about Megan. From what I understand, you were closer to her than just about anybody in those last few months."

Pamela ran a hand through her hair. "Does it matter what I want? Because I really don't want to be involved beyond what I told the cops." She waved her subpoena in the air. "But you're not gonna give me a choice, are you?"

"No," I said. "But we don't have to do this here."

She looked around. Most of the other parents had already left the lot. We were relatively isolated.

"Just get in," she said. "I don't want to talk out in the open."

I came around to the passenger side of her van. She unlocked it. I climbed in. Pamela turned the ignition but left the vehicle in park. She turned down her radio. So we would do this here. I pulled a pad of paper and pen out of my bag.

"Ask your questions," she said, staring out at the soccer fields.

"I just want to understand how things were with Megan in those last few weeks. From what I'm hearing, you and she had a falling out. I've seen a series of text exchanges from Megan's phone. She'd started to ghost you."

I had a copy of some of those texts. Most of them involved Pamela trying to get Megan to call her or to meet her for lunch. Text after text went unanswered in the two weeks prior to Megan's murder.

"I told all of this to the police. I knew Megan was involved with Reed. It had been going on for a while. At first, I kept my mouth shut. He was married. She knew he was married. And they have a kid. I don't know Dahlia Karl very well. I mean, I've seen her around. It's a small town. She only lives about two miles away. She always kind of came off as snobbish. Acting like she was better than everybody. But she's British. Maybe it's just a cultural thing. Anyway, my point is. Megan always knew Reed was married. I told her from the beginning she was making a mistake."

"Did she tell you right away? That they were seeing each other?"

Pamela shook her head. "No, But I knew she was seeing somebody. And I knew it was getting serious because she started canceling plans with me. With all of her friends. It was probably three or four months into it when she finally 'fessed up who she was seeing."

"How did you react?"

"I tried not to at first. Look, Megan had a string of loser boyfriends. She was one of those people who just always gravitated toward guys who were bad for her. With Reed, she was just lost."

"What do you mean?"

"She fell hard. God. She was so in love with him. Waiting for him to call. Watching her phone. Going nuts from just the simplest text from him."

"What do you mean nuts?"

"Like a high school kid. Hanging on every word he said. And from what I saw, he seemed just as into her. But it was a mess. Doomed from the start. Nobody would say anything to her. She was so damn happy. But we were all worried. Finally, after it became pretty clear this wasn't just some short-lived fling, I spoke up."

"When was this?" I asked.

Pamela kept her eyes on the ball fields. "Maybe two months before she died. Three. It had been going on for a while. Almost a year. I tried to stage an intervention of sorts. I told Megan he was never going to leave his wife. We all knew that. And did she really want to be the woman who broke up a family even if he did? I've been on the other end of that. That's why everybody thought I was the best person to confront her. That's what happened with Gregg and me. He started sleeping with one of his business partners. He left me for her. And now here I am, going home alone after a soccer game while he takes Ash out for ice cream. It's awful. Ashlynn didn't deserve this. Neither did I. And no matter what kind of person Dahlia is, she and her daughter don't deserve this either."

"No. They don't. How did Megan take it?"

Pamela finally turned to face me. "You said you saw her texts. That's how she took it. She didn't want to hear it. She killed the messenger. Me. We got into a huge fight. She said she and Reed weren't the same as Gregg and Charlene. It was bullshit. A rationalization. I told her no matter what she told herself, she was the bad guy in this because she had the power to walk away."

"So did Reed, though," I said.

"Sure. Only they never do. It's always the women who have to do the hard stuff. Clean up the messes. Take care of everybody."

"You have a point," I said. "Pamela, you told the police you began to have concerns about Megan's mental state. What specifically?"

"She would drive by his house. That was happening before she and I had our argument. I was with her a couple of times. She'd go down Reed's street just to see if his car was in the driveway. That made me really angry. And she started getting ... I don't know. It was like she was an addict where Reed was concerned. She couldn't get enough of him. Even though she knew he was bad for her. I'd never seen her like how she got."

"What do you mean?"

"She was self-medicating. Drinking more than normal. Crying all the time. If he didn't call her, if she hadn't heard from him in a few hours, she'd start texting him like crazy. If you've seen Megan's phone, does that mean you've seen Reed's?"

"Yes," I admitted.

"Well, then you know. And Megan would call and call and call. Text bomb. You saw all that, right?"

"I did." And I had. In the weeks leading up to her death, Megan had a habit of texting Reed up to twenty times a day. It was one piece of evidence in Reed's favor if I could use it in front of the jury.

"It wasn't healthy. I was worried. In our group of friends, we were starting to talk about whether maybe Megan needed some kind of rehab or professional help."

"She was seeing a therapist already," I said. "Were you aware of that?"

"She mentioned it a couple of times. But I don't think whoever it was was doing her any good. Or I don't know. Maybe Megan wasn't telling them the truth about what she was doing. How Reed was affecting her."

"When was the last time you spoke to Megan?" I asked.

"I went over to see her. It was three or four days before they found her. God. You know, that's the thing that keeps me up at night. One of them. I went there that day to check on her because I was sick of her ghosting me. I went into her house because she wouldn't answer the door even though I knew she was home. I knew where she kept her spare key. I found her in the backyard. She was just sobbing. A total wreck. She told me Reed broke up with her. I was so relieved. I was sad because she took it so hard. But I was relieved. I told her that. Then, I just held her, you know? Let her have a good, ugly cry. After a while, I picked her up off the floor, helped her wash her face, and we went for a walk around the block."

"You were a good friend," I said.

Pamela let out a sob. She quickly recovered. "I should have done something."

"What could you do?"

"I should have insisted she come stay with me for a while. So I could keep an eye on her. If I'd done that, she wouldn't have been home when Reed showed up a few days later."

"Pamela, were you aware that Megan had contacted Dahlia Karl? Would it surprise you to know Dahlia was afraid of Megan?"

"I don't know. No. Megan didn't tell me she'd talked to Dahlia or anything. I just know she felt lost without Reed."

"She wasn't acting like herself, was she?" I asked. It was a risky question. I didn't want to be accused of coaching Pamela Corso if I put her on the stand. But she'd already used words that could call attention to Megan Lewis's mental state in those final days. In her statement to the police, she described an argument she got into with Pamela where Megan got angry enough to break a dish. But I decided not to press her about the details of her statement now. Now, I just wanted to try to establish a rapport with her.

"She was just ... I don't know. I hadn't seen her like that before. No. But if you're trying to get me to say she was evil or something."

"I am absolutely not."

Pamela started to cry. "She was my friend. She was in love with that asshole. He made her crazy. He broke her. Do you understand what I'm saying? He used her. Then he broke her. She was a mess. Out of her mind. And that wasn't even enough. What he did ..."

"I'm sorry," I said. "I really don't want to upset you. I have to ask you something else though. In the time Megan was dating Reed, did you ever see bruises on her? Did she ever confide in you that he'd gotten physical with her?"

"No," Pamela whispered. "I never saw anything like that. But how would I know? People can be bruised in places you don't see. Some men are good about that."

There was something ominous in her tone. Did she mean Gregg? Had he hurt Pamela in ways other than infidelity? Pamela didn't elaborate and I knew I'd long past worn out my welcome.

"Again, I'm sorry," I said. "I won't bother you anymore today."

"Are you going to make me testify?" she asked. "Will you really do that?"

I held the door open as I hopped down from the passenger seat. "Yes," I said. "You'll have to tell your story, Pamela."

"It might not help Reed," she said. "I don't want it to."

"I understand that. You just have to tell the truth."

She let out a bitter laugh. "Just," she repeated. "I think I'd like you to go now."

I gave her a grim smile. Then I left Pamela Corso alone, hating myself a little that it wouldn't be for long.

Chapter 10

To SAY that Tori was beautiful seemed inadequate. She was. But it was more than that. She walked down the aisle toward my brother with a quiet strength and determination that moved everyone in the room to tears. One day, not long ago, just taking a single step, then another had brought her agony I could not fathom. Today, though, she clung to her simple bouquet of white roses with one hand. With the other, she held on to little Sean. He stared up at his mother, smiling. In his free hand, he held on to his favorite blanket, one end of it trailing on the ground, the other end was the head of a stuffed elephant. He'd loved it so much its trunk was hopelessly bent.

Matty's eyes filled with tears as his soon-to-be wife and son came down that aisle to take his hand. My brother Joe, serving as his best man, kept a hand on Matty's back. I wondered if he might have fallen over if not for the support Joe gave him. Matty had been a mess of emotions all morning.

I caught Eric's eye as he sat in the front row next to Jeanie and Miranda. Things had been uneasy between us for the last couple of weeks. He had not been back to the office since the day I told him I would take Reed Karl's case to trial if it came to it. As each day went on that Rafe Johnson failed to reach out, trial seemed inevitable.

I tried to focus on my job. My one job. I'd agreed to let Reed tell his story. To explain why he did what he did so that someday, his daughter might be able to know it.

But today wasn't about any of that. Today was about the triumph of Tori's spirit and my brother's willingness to let someone else claim his heart. It was easy to believe Tori and Sean had saved him. Matty struggled with his Leary demons far more than the rest of us at times. A few years ago, I feared he would end his life at the bottom of a bottle. I still feared that. But now I felt confident Matty knew what he was fighting for.

I don't remember their vows. I watched them take them through my own tear-filled eyes. Joe put his arm around me. He hadn't cried yet. He might not. But I could feel his emotions bubbling up in him, too. Weddings were hard. They reminded him of what he had lost in the last two years. Again, though, today was not about that.

A cheer went up as the minister declared Matty and Tori husband and wife. Sean squealed as Matty tossed him up and perched him on his shoulder. Sean favored his mother with his blond hair and wide-set eyes. But that day, I saw the beginnings of a change in him too. He had my brother's solid build. The slight tilt to his head when he was annoyed or inquisitive. He was a Leary through and through.

As we all marched down the aisle, Eric rose. He silently took my hand. I looked up at him. He would be by my side today. But I couldn't pretend things were okay.

We made our way to the reception hall across the street. Eric looped an arm around me, steadying me on the uneven sidewalk as I wore my three-inch heels.

"You look amazing," he whispered.

"Tori's doing," I said. I kicked out my leg, flaring my royal blue skirt. I wore it with an off-white silk blouse. "She boycotted bridesmaids' dresses."

My sister Vangie had gone with a sheath dress in the same royal blue. Her date met her at the end of the sidewalk.

"How's that going?" Eric muttered under his breath. Vangie had rekindled a romance with Deputy Jeff Steuben. We weren't sure how we felt about it. Steuben was clearly more enamored with Vangie than she was with him at the moment.

"Oh," I said. "He'll get his heart broken."

"Damn," Eric said. "He's a good dude. She could do worse."

"I don't know. Maybe they'll surprise us."

Jessa brought up the rear as a junior bridesmaid. She looked stunning in her own blue dress. It had a swing skirt that fit her just above the knees. She had another growth spurt this past summer. At fourteen, she topped five ten and would likely get even taller. Her long hair flowed behind her.

The modest-sized reception hall had been transformed with twinkling white lights and linen tablecloths. I put my bouquet on the head table. Eric would sit at one of the round tables just in front of it. He claimed his seat by placing his jacket over a chair. Then he held another chair out for Jeanie. She'd brought a date of her own. Mel Simmons, the retired fire chief. He and Eric excused themselves and headed up to the bar.

Joe took the seat beside me. Emma was at another table with a group of guests her own age, including her latest boyfriend, a sous chef at a new restaurant in Ann Arbor. His name was Byron and he was ten years older than Emma.

"How's that going?" I asked Joe, parroting what Eric had asked about Vangie.

Joe sighed. "I don't know. He's nice. He says all the right things. He's got a house of his own. He makes good money."

"But …?"

"But … he's also already got an ex-wife and a stepkid he's still involved with."

"Well, one way to look at it. He's a stand-up guy?"

"Emma's not ready for it. She's still trying to figure out what she wants to be when she grows up."

I nodded. "True. But she's doing really well, Joe. She's been a godsend to me at the office. She's headed in a good direction."

He raised a brow. "You really think it's a good idea her going to law school?"

"If she wants it badly enough, yes. I think she might."

Eric and Mel Simmons were at the other end of the room, sipping their drinks. Joe got quiet. Then he turned to me.

"Do you think she's okay?"

"Who? Emma? Joe, she's great!"

He looked so serious. Emma leaned in close to the boyfriend. He had an arm around her. He said something that made her blush.

"I feel like I'm losing her. I feel like I missed everything."

I smiled and rubbed my brother's arm. "You're a dad whose baby girl is growing up. She's okay, Joe. She's making good choices in her life. Try not to worry so much."

He laughed. "Coming from you, that's rich."

I nudged him. "Shut up."

"The thing is, Cass. I'm not sure you are."

"Are what?"

"Making good choices."

One of the wait staff came by and put champagne in front of us. I picked mine up and took a swig. I wished for something stronger. I supposed the champagne was intended for a toast as soon as Matty and Tori came back inside after the photographer was done with them.

"Eric's really upset with you," he said.

"What's he told you?"

Joe shook his head. "No. No way. I'm not a spy."

"You brought it up. And it kinda feels like he maybe asked you to."

"Right. And if he had, how do you think that would have gone? You're my sister."

"Fine. Fair point. Eric's issue with me is professional. It's not personal. And we'll get through it."

"Cass, Eric's waiting on you. Haven't you figured that out yet?"

I put my champagne down. "What are you talking about?"

"Are you really that dense? Come on. The guy is the poster child for long-suffering boyfriends."

I felt my temper rising. "Not here, Joe."

"I think here's perfect. It's a wedding. It's exactly the kind of event where people could use some good personal reflection."

"Really? We're sitting here at the head table. Waiting for our brother and his new wife. You'll be giving a toast in a few minutes. You're laying into me now?"

"I'm not laying into you. I'm just saying. Eric's been different these last few weeks since you got involved in Reed Karl's case."

"You know I can't talk about that."

"I'm not asking you to divulge client confidence. You're fully aware of what I'm asking you."

"You're not asking me anything. It seems to me you're gearing up for a lecture."

"Fine," he said. "Maybe I am. Look, you can marry Eric Wray. You can not marry Eric Wray. I just think at some point you might want to clue him in to what your plans are. Because he's got them."

I took another glass of champagne when the waiter went by. "He does not. We've talked about it. At length. Not that it's any of your business. Besides, a few months ago, you were the one talking about the Leary marriage curse. You flat out told our baby brother to run the opposite direction from the altar. Now you're telling me it's time for me to shit or get off the pot?"

He laughed. "Like you said. Fair point. I'm just telling you what I see. And what I see is a guy who's at a crossroads. You may be fine with some kind of Oprah and Steadman arrangement, but Eric's not. Not forever."

"Oprah and Steadman? Who even are you?"

"You're deflecting."

"I'm not. Or maybe I am. I just don't get why you have a sudden interest in my future with Eric."

Joe's expression hardened. I felt a twinge of guilt at the harshness of my tone. He wasn't wrong. Maybe I was deflecting.

"I just see what I see."

"Okay. But we're good, okay?"

I felt hands on my shoulders. I looked up. Matty smiled down at me, then put his arms around me, squeezing me. "You two look too serious."

I kissed my brother's cheek. "That's Joe's fault. I'm a delight."

Matty took his seat beside me. Tori was at another table, beginning to make her rounds.

"The ceremony was beautiful," I said.

"She's the one who's beautiful. Tori did it all. I just showed up in a tux."

Joe cleared his throat. "You barely did that. Baby brother couldn't figure out how to tighten his own cummerbund."

"Cummerbunds are stupid." Matty and I said it in unison. Then we laughed at each other.

"I was just telling Cass what we were talking about this morning."

"Wait ... this was the topic of discussion?"

"Oh, you mean Eric? Yeah. Everything okay over there, sis?"

I let out an exasperated sigh. "Stop. Both of you. Just stop."

"He's really bothered you're involved in Megan Lewis's murder case. Was the money really all that good?" Matty asked.

"It's not about the money," I said. "I mean, yes. The money is very good. It's the most I've ever made on a case. For me, it's more about the family. Reed Karl has a little girl about Jessa's age. She's dealing with a lot. I don't know. I guess I relate to her."

"I think Jessa knows her," Matty said. "They're maybe in the same grade?"

"I guess that's right. She hasn't mentioned it. Anyway, I'm just trying to make sure the man has a chance to get his story out. He's entitled to a defense."

Joe and Matty looked at each other with an expression that clearly transmitted, "Whatever you say!"

Before I could bitch at either one of them again, the D.J. cranked up a slow song. It felt like a good opportunity to extract myself from the conversation. Or maybe an even better opportunity to prove them both wrong.

I left the table and weaved my way through the crowd. I stopped to give Tori a quick hug. She had found a seat at one of the tables near some of her high school friends. She couldn't stay on her feet for very long. The day had taxed her already, but you wouldn't know it from the radiant smile on her face.

I found Eric talking to one of Matty's coworkers. They stood in the shadow of a potted fern.

"Mind if I cut in?" I joked.

Eric smiled, put his mostly empty glass of bourbon on the nearest table, then looped his arms around me.

"Come on," I said. "I like this song."

He gave me an odd tilt to his head, but smiled and followed me out to the dance floor. A few other couples had come out as well. Soon, the D.J. would announce Tori and my brother again and the wedding party would dance. Joe would be my partner.

"I love you, you know," I said, staring up at Eric. He smiled.

"I know."

"There's a rumor going around that you're pretty mad at me."

He held me out away from him, frowning. "Says who?" Though I didn't have to answer. He tracked my line of sight over to my brothers, still huddled together at the head table.

"Ah," Eric said. "Are we going to have the same argument again? Can we skip it? At least for tonight."

"No argument. Not ever. I just ... are we okay?"

He held me closer. "Cass ..."

"I mean it. Are we okay? Is this case the deal-breaker for you?"

"Have I ever said anything like that?"

"No. Not to me. But ..."

He swung me around so we were on the edge of the dance floor. "Stop."

"Eric ..."

"No. Stop. I really don't want to talk about Reed Karl tonight of all nights. And certainly not in the middle of a slow song at your brother's wedding."

"I'm not talking about Reed Karl. Well, I'm not only talking about Reed Karl. I just want to know where your head's at when it comes to us."

"My head?"

"Yes."

"*My* head. Woman, you drive me nuts."

I pulled out of his arms. The nearest exit out to the parking lot was to my right. I headed for it. With a great sigh, Eric followed me. Thank God.

I turned. "I don't mean to," I said. "Drive you nuts."

"I know."

"But this?" I gestured toward the hall. More couples filled the dance floor. My niece Jessa had my nephew, Sean, in her arms. He laughed as she twirled him around.

"Do you want that?" I said, pointing to Jessa and Sean.

"What?"

"Kids. Because ... those are my kids. Sean. Jessa. Even Emma. I can't do more than that. It's not in me, Eric. I've spent my entire life taking care of them all. Vangie. Matty. Even Joe, though he'll never admit it. Since I was fourteen years old. Even before that. Just like ... Clara Karl. Those people in there mean everything to me. I don't regret it. But the ship on all that sailed for me a long time ago. I'm not ..."

"Cass," he said, softly.

"And I'm almost forty-three. You're forty-six. We're not young. We're not old, but we're not young. Hell, in a couple of years, Emma will probably have kids of her own and then it'll be like I'm a grandmother. Her own mother isn't in the picture. And Katy's just ..."

"Cass!" he shouted, grabbing me gently. "Stop. Just stop it. Who said anything about having kids?"

I froze, my mouth hanging open mid-sentence.

"I'm not in this because I want to be a dad, Cass. I was married to Wendy for a long time. And for a long time, it was good. If having kids was in the cards for me, I could have done it twenty years ago. The world is full of kids who need help. I get it. Clara Karl is one of them. I could argue about whether helping her father is really helping her. But you're right. Those kids in the other room need help. I love them too." He pointed toward Jessa and Sean. Jessa was spinning Sean around. He squealed with laughter.

"Come on," he said. "You're starting to spin yourself. You're actually starting to make me dizzy."

"I'm sorry," I said quietly. "I'm just ... I'm very used to doing things on my own terms."

"You said it. You've spent your whole life worrying about other people. Taking care of everyone else. Well, you don't have to take care of me. All I'm asking is that you let me do that for you. Let me take care of you once in a while. That'll keep me more than busy."

He had a twinkle of mischief in his eye. God. It was one of the things that drew me to him in the beginning.

"I love you," I told him again.

"I love you too," he whispered. Behind him, the D.J. called Matty and Tori to the center of the floor. In another few seconds, I would hear my cue.

Eric pulled me to him. He kissed the top of my head. "Quit worrying so much. I promise. If and when the time comes that I'm not okay, you won't have to hear it from your brothers."

"Promise?" I asked.

"Absolutely. Come on. It's a wedding. It's Matty and Tori's day. Let's not make it about anything else."

He felt so strong as he held me against him. He always did. It should be so easy to just let him take care of me the way he wanted. Sometimes it was. But for me, the hard part was always admitting when I needed the help.

A cheer went up as the new Mr. and Mrs. Leary took the center of the floor. Later, Tori would throw her bouquet. Emma would catch it. Joe would frown as Byron, the new boyfriend, came to her side. There was trouble brewing there. I could feel it. But Eric was right. Tonight wasn't about anything else as Tori and Matty twirled the dance floor as husband and wife.

Chapter 11

In two weeks, Reed Karl would go on trial for the rest of his life. I stood outside Rafe Johnson's office door, my hand still on the knob. There would be no plea deal. I had laid out what I could. Megan Lewis had become increasingly unstable. Reed felt the safety of his family was at risk. All those things could be true, but from Rafe's perspective, none of it explained how he could beat a woman to death in her sleep.

He had a point. As I walked away from the closed door and out to the parking lot, I sent a text to Jeanie.

No deal. Why did you let me take this case again?

She sent me a rolling eyes emoji. Then an actual response.

What now?

I'm heading out to talk to Dahlia again. I'll grab Emma on the way. Then I have to break the news to Reed. He's heading to trial.

Jeanie responded with a thumbs up.

When I swung by the office, Emma was already waiting. She wore a blue suit I'd given her when she graduated from college. With her hair pulled back and her fresh face, she reminded me a lot of my mother. It was uncanny, really. She slid into the passenger seat.

"Thanks for waiting for me," she said. "It was a no go with the prosecutor?"

"He likes his chances in front of a jury," I said. "I was hoping I could talk him into voluntary manslaughter."

"But even with that, the Karls are going to face bankruptcy, don't you think? Jeanie took a call from a lawyer representing Megan Lewis's family. Will you be involved in defending the wrongful death action?"

I shook my head. "No chance. No way. I've given Dahlia the names of a couple of civil attorneys I trust."

"Geez, their best bet there would be a settlement, don't you think?"

"Probably. But nothing will happen until after the criminal trial is over. If Reed's convicted of first degree ..."

"If," Emma said.

"You doubt me?"

"No," she said. "This has never felt like a first degree case to me. Second degree makes more sense. This was a crime of passion if ever there was one. I just wish ..."

Her voice trailed off.

"You wish what?"

"I wish I knew what happened that morning. What escalated it like that? The coroner's report is pretty specific that Megan was probably asleep when the first blow hit her."

A few minutes later, I pulled into Dahlia Karl's driveway and headed up the walk. I knocked once.

"Does she know you're coming?" Emma asked.

"No. I told her I might stop by after I talked to Johnson. But I didn't give her a time."

No answer. Emma stepped off the porch. She peered into the small square windows in the garage door.

"Just one car in there," she said. "A black Porsche."

"That's Reed's car," I said. "Dahlia doesn't drive it. She must not be home."

I took my phone out and sent a quick text to Dahlia. I saw three cursors blink for a moment, but got no response.

"I'll call her later, I guess," I said.

"Emma?"

The voice came from the side of the house. Emma turned. Her face lit up into a huge smile.

"Elyse?" Then Emma threw her arms wide as a young girl, roughly Jessa's age, came running down the driveway.

"My goodness!" Emma said. "What happened? You look like ... you're all ... dang it, kiddo. You make me feel old."

Emma had her arm around Elyse Baker as she turned her toward me. "Cass, this is Elyse. Kim and Dean Baker's little girl. Er ... I mean lovely young lady. Former squirt."

She was lovely. She had Kim's eyes and a tall, athletic frame.

"Nice to meet you," Elyse said. She extended a hand to shake mine.

"We were looking for Mrs. Karl," Emma explained.

Elyse looked back at the house. "She's not here. She didn't tell my mom where she was going. Clara's over at my place. She was actually right behind me. She wanted to grab a change of clothes. She's gonna spend the night."

I couldn't hide my frown. The Bakers didn't know where Dahlia was, which meant Clara was more or less on her own.

"Is she doing okay?" Emma asked, reading my expression.

Elyse shrugged. "She's Clara. She's always okay. I don't know. She doesn't like to talk about anything."

"I can understand that," Emma said. "It's good that you're her friend, though. You're a good one, Elyse."

Elyse gave Emma a thin-lipped smile. "Thanks. Is her dad going to stay in prison, do you think?"

"Don't worry about that," Emma said. "My Aunt Cass is going to do what she can for him."

The garage door opened and Clara came out holding a plastic grocery bag stuffed with clothes. She looked startled when she saw Emma and me in the driveway with Elyse.

"What happened?" she asked. "Is something wrong?"

"No," I quickly reassured her. Clara looked tired. Dark circles shaded her eyes. She had the weight of the world on her young shoulders. I hated the thought of it. Where the hell was her mother?

"I was just stopping by to see if I could catch your mom," I said. "It's boring stuff. Nothing to worry about."

Clara didn't seem convinced. "I can go with you," she said. "Help you find her."

"No," I said. "You and Elyse should just do whatever you had planned. You're going to stay with the Bakers tonight?"

Clara nodded. "Good," I said. "Why don't you let us drive you back over there?"

"No need," Clara said. "We just cut through the backyard. We're stopping at another friend's house on the way."

I was glad to hear it. It sounded normal. It sounded ... fourteen. Elyse went over to Clara. Clara turned and punched the code into the garage door. She hung her grocery bag of clothes over her arm.

"I can send my mom a text," Clara said. "Tell her you stopped by."

"I've already texted her," I said. "No worries. Just go have fun. And be careful."

"We're always careful," Elyse said, rolling her eyes. That made me laugh. It was such a teenage girl expression she gave me. She whispered something to Clara. Clara faked a smile and tossed me a wave. Then the two girls disappeared around the house.

I waited until I knew they were far out of earshot. "That's weird, right? That Kim doesn't seem to know where Dahlia is. And yet Clara's running around the neighborhood and spending the night with them?"

"Yeah. Though it makes me happy that Clara's with the Bakers right now. She's doing kid stuff. She *should* be doing kid stuff."

"I agree," I said. I checked my phone, hoping Dahlia had returned my text. She hadn't.

As we were about to leave, I looked next door. Dahlia's neighbor lived in a huge brick ranch. There was a half an acre between the properties, but I heard someone talking in the backyard.

"Come on," I said to Emma. "This has been on my list, too."

We walked around Dahlia's house and made our way to the back porch of the next-door neighbor. We were just in time to see Elyse and Clara opening the back gate between the properties and heading down the trail cut into the woods. Clara waved back one more time.

"See ya, Mr. Thompson," she called out.

"Stay out of trouble, kiddos!" The neighbor, a white-haired gentleman with deeply tanned skin, waved back at the girls. He wore a pair of navy-blue pants and a yellow golf shirt. Early November and it had been warm enough to golf today.

"Hello," I called out. "I'm sorry to bother you, but do you mind if I ask you a couple of questions?"

"You from the township?" he asked. He walked to the edge of a covered kidney-shaped pool. Emma and I waited while he unlatched the gate and let us in.

"No," I said. "My name is Cass Leary. I'm Reed Karl's attorney."

The man's white eyebrows went sky high. "Oh, I know who you are. I thought you looked familiar. My name's Thompson. Sawyer Thompson."

"Good to meet you, Mr. Thompson," I said. "This is my assistant, Emma."

Thompson shook both of our hands. As he did, a dark-haired woman came out the back door, no doubt curious about the voices she heard.

"Lettie," Sawyer said. "This is Reed's lawyer."

"Oh!" Lettie Thompson called out. "My heavens. Can I get you two something to drink? I've got some fresh iced tea."

"No, thank you," I said. "Unless you'd like something, Emma."

Emma put a hand up and shook her head no.

"Come on in," Sawyer said. "We can have a seat in the sunroom like civilized folks."

I let Sawyer and Lettie Thompson lead us into a screened porch overlooking the pool. Emma and I sat side by side on a long Rutan couch. Sawyer and Lettie took matching chairs opposite us.

"So," Sawyer said. "You're helping Dahlia out?"

"Well, I'm representing Reed."

"His trial is coming up," Lettie said. "We've been so worried about Dahlia. That poor thing. Sawyer's been going over there doing some work around the house. Tilling the garden. Running the mower. I mean, it's no trouble. He likes riding around on his John Deere. Keeps him busy and out of my hair."

Lettie laughed at her own joke. Sawyer patted her on the knee.

"These ladies didn't come out here to hear about my lawn care."

"No," I said. "Though it's good to hear you're looking out for Dahlia. I'm sure it's a great relief to her."

"How long have you lived next door to the Karls?" Emma asked.

"Oh, we were here long before they moved in," Sawyer said. "We built this house in '79. Right after we got married. It was one of the last new ones built in this neighborhood. The Karls' house was built a few years earlier than that. Rich and Tammy Gorley lived there. Sweet couple. They had seven kids. Maybe you knew some of 'em."

"I did," I said. "I believe I went to school with Jenny Gorley."

"They're all scattered to the four winds," Lettie said. "They were such great neighbors. They used to host the block parties back in the day. Oh, those were some fun times. But Rich hurt his back. The kids all moved out. Tammy didn't see the need to live in a house that had stairs and all those bedrooms anymore. So they moved down to Palm Beach into a condo. Boy, it was sad to see them go. Rich always said he should have built a ranch like we did."

"The Gorleys sold to the Karls?" I asked.

"Oh no," Sawyer said. "Then the Marshalls moved in. Brad and Laura. They weren't very friendly."

Emma shot me a look. We could be here a while.

"Sawyer, stop," Lettie said. "I can't imagine these women are here to listen to the oral history of Eden's Edge."

"No," I said. "Not exactly."

"The Karls moved in twenty years ago now," Sawyer said. "Just the two of them. The kids came later."

"How well do you know Dahlia and Reed?" I asked.

"Reed's a good guy. Always lending a hand. Every spring he'd help me get the pool opened up. I'd return the favor."

Lettie's face went dark. I could guess why. Dahlia and Karl filled their pool in not long after their son Ian drowned in it.

"Do you mind if I ask you some, perhaps, uncomfortable questions?" I said. "Were you aware of any difficulties the Karls were having? In their marriage, I mean."

Lettie and Sawyer clasped hands. "He was gone an awful lot," Lettie said. "I worried about Dahlia. That woman just went through hell after Ian died. Blamed herself. And look, accidents happen. It could have happened to any one of us. Don't think I don't fret every time our grandkids are over. But she was just so sad all the time. Even before that. Before the kids, she was just the bubbliest person you'd ever want to meet. And so cultured. I always found her accent kind of exotic, you know?"

"She's English, Lettie," Sawyer said with a sigh.

"Anyway," Lettie said. "Dahlia had struggles with her pregnancies. Both of them. After the babies came, she just cried a lot. Wouldn't come out of the house. I went over there countless times. Bringing her baked goods. Offering to watch Clara after Ian came. You know. Just to get her out of her mother's hair. Dahlia just shooed me away most of the time. And like we said, Reed was gone a lot for his job."

"I had a talk with him once," Sawyer said. "Told him we were worried about Dahlia."

"How long ago was that?" Emma asked.

"Maybe a year, year and a half ago," Sawyer answered. This would have put this talk around the time Reed started things up with Megan.

"What did he say?" I asked.

Sawyer shrugged. "He really blew me off. Kinda politely told me to mind my own business. Which I could respect. But Dahlia wasn't coming out of the house ever as far as we could see. Then we'd see poor Clara outside doing all the things her mother used to keep up. That's really when I started offering to mow their lawn. But Clara was out there weeding the garden. Taking out the trash. Pulling the cans back in. Getting the mail. Last Christmas she was out there putting out Dahlia's Christmas decorations all by herself. That girl's been pretty much raising herself for years."

That was the exact impression I had, too.

"Look," I said. "I'm sure you're aware of some of the more salacious details in Reed's case. It's been in the news."

"He was carrying on with that Megan Lewis," Lettie confirmed. "Yes. That's what we heard."

"Did you ever talk to Reed about that in particular?"

"Oh no," Sawyer answered. "That wouldn't have been any of our business."

"Did you ever see her here? Megan Lewis? Here at their house?"

"No. I don't think so."

"Sawyer, that's not true," Lettie reprimanded him. "You aren't protecting Reed by keeping your mouth shut."

"So you did see Megan Lewis here?" Emma asked.

"I saw somebody driving by a few times. And a couple of times knocking on the door when Dahlia wasn't home. I saw Reed talking to her on the porch," Sawyer said, sighing. "And a few times walking down the sidewalk like she was exercising. I don't know who it was. I couldn't recognize her. Just that she was blonde. And I knew it wasn't Dahlia. This woman was skinnier. Blonde. And she didn't dress like Dahlia. She was sloppier. Sweat pants and leggings and things like that."

"We don't judge," Lettie said. "But we know or recognize pretty much everybody who lives in Eden's Edge. It was just a little odd seeing somebody from Pine Circle doing their walking over in our neighborhood."

Pine Circle was the next neighborhood over, the one where Megan Lewis lived.

"How do you know this woman was from Pine Circle?"

"One of the other neighbors told me," Lettie said. "I know it sounds like I'm a busybody. But everybody just looks out for everybody else in here. When we see somebody new, it gets noticed."

"I see," I said. "Do you have any idea when it was that you might have seen Reed with Megan Lewis here at the house?"

"Last summer," Sawyer said. "And only a couple of times."

"Okay," I said. "But did you ever see Reed let her in the house?"

Sawyer and Lettie exchanged a look.

"Not *let* her in. But there was this one time," Sawyer said. "And that's the only time I really got into it with Reed. It was real late one evening. Reed and Dahlia weren't home. They went out to dinner or something. Clara was over at her little friend's house. We get a kick out of watching those girls together. Peas in a pod. Well, our little Yorkies started barking their heads off. Both me and Lettie heard it. We knew nobody was supposed to be over there. I went to the back door. I saw that woman running out of

Reed's house. Out the back slider. I went to get my shotgun but she was gone by the time I got back. Have no idea what she was up to."

"Megan Lewis," I said. "You're sure you saw Megan Lewis coming out of Reed's house when Reed and Dahlia weren't home?"

"Sure, I'm sure," Sawyer said.

"Did you ever tell the police this?" Emma asked.

"I never talked to the police," Sawyer said.

"They never came here," I said, knowing full well there were no interviews with either Thompson in the formal report on Megan's murder or when Reed supposedly reported a break-in.

"You're sure it was Megan Lewis?" Emma repeated my question.

"I'm sure it was the woman I saw Reed talking to on the porch and the woman I saw walking and driving by," Sawyer said. He pulled his phone out of his back pocket.

"You don't have to take my word for it," he said. "When was that, Lettie? Do you remember? It was the weekend we had Kyle over. When Josie had to have the pins put into her arm. Kyle and Josie are our grandkids. Josie broke her arm falling off a swing set."

"That would have been back in May. Um ... the weekend of May 29th. Yeah. It was Memorial Day Weekend."

Sawyer scrolled through something. Then he turned the phone to me. He'd opened up the app for his doorbell cameras. Sweat formed between my shoulder blades. A moment later, Sawyer played a grainy video for me. My mind raced. May 29th. A week before Megan Lewis's murder.

Sure enough, in the video, I saw a blonde woman run out Reed's back door. She wore a maroon sweatshirt with yellow lettering on the back. The inside of the hood was gold.

"Central Michigan," Emma said. She pulled her own phone out, typed something in, and showed it to me. It was Megan Lewis's Facebook profile. I'd seen it before. The police had searched for it as well. Megan Lewis was wearing her maroon and gold CMU sweatshirt in her profile picture. It was old and well worn. In the comments under the picture, one of her friends pointed out that she needed a new one. Megan had responded that it was her favorite and she'd had it since college. The right forearm had bleach stains on it.

I looked at the image from Sawyer Thompson's security camera. Megan's face was in profile, her blonde hair spilling out from under the hood. She was running. Her right arm was slightly raised. The same bleach stains marred the right sleeve of her sweatshirt.

May 29th. Dahlia's words echoed through me. This was the night they found Ian's stuffed animals cut up and hanging from her ceiling fan.

"Do you think you could send me a copy of that?" I asked. I quickly jotted down my cell phone number. Sawyer pressed another button. Two seconds later, I got a text alert. The video came through.

"You never talked to the police?" Emma asked.

"No, honey," Lettie answered. "Sawyer went and talked to Reed about what we saw. Did you show him this video?"

"I don't remember. I might not have. But we had some words. I told Reed I didn't much care what he did in his private life. It wasn't my business. But whatever was going on, he better get a handle on it. I think he said he was gonna file a police report. I don't know if he did. But nobody ever talked to us about it."

My heart thumped. The Thompsons should have been questioned. Reed told Detective Patel he was concerned for his family's safety after Megan broke in. Sawyer Thompson had proof! And Patel never bothered to canvass Reed's neighbors. My cross-examination of Patel began to take shape in my mind.

"Thank you," I said. "I know this is a difficult subject, but you both have been very helpful."

"Just telling the truth," Sawyer said. "There's nothing hard about that."

"You'd be surprised," I said. As I was talking, Emma pulled two sheets of paper out of her briefcase. A smile crept across my face. She was a step ahead of me. She scribbled furiously on the blank forms she'd brought out. Then she handed them to me. I'd have to file originals for these to be valid. But the information Emma wrote would tell the Thompsons what they needed to know.

"I may need to call on you," I said. "You understand Reed Karl's trial starts in just a couple of weeks."

"To testify?" Lettie said, barely able to contain the excitement in her voice. "Oh ... I've never seen a trial before. You want us to be witnesses?"

"Maybe," I said.

"What would we say?" Sawyer said.

"The truth," I said. "Nothing is easier than telling the truth."

"I guess we can do that," Sawyer said. "Doesn't mean I think Reed's not guilty. You better know that going in."

"I understand," I said. "And I respect it."

I shook both Sawyer and Lettie Thompson's hands. I pocketed my cell phone. I would upload Sawyer's video as soon as I got back to the office.

It was something. Maybe not everything. But Sawyer and Lettie Thompson had just opened another door for Reed Karl. And that could make all the difference.

Chapter 12

"NIEDERMAYER's never going to let it in."

I stood in front of the whiteboard in the conference room. Jeanie sat at the end of the long table. Emma sat criss-crossed on the floor, sifting through the mounds of exhibits we knew Rafe Johnson would try to admit.

On the big screen next to the whiteboard, the grainy image of Megan Lewis leaving the Karl home on the night of May 29th played on a loop.

"She might," I said. "It goes to Reed's state of mind. If he believed Lewis was a threat to him and his family. I mean, here she is, coming out of his house when nobody else was home."

"You'll have to put Dahlia on the stand," Emma said. "You sure she'll hold up?"

"Is there any proof Dahlia or Reed ever saw this footage? I mean, did the Thompsons tell them?" Jeanie asked.

"Sawyer Thompson talked to Reed about it. He doesn't remember if he showed him the tape. I don't think he did. Reed would have mentioned it. He would have told the police to talk to them," Emma said.

"Well," Jeanie said. "There's a big wide hole for you to blow into Rodney Patel's testimony."

"Regardless of any of that," I said. "Ian Karl's toy collection was hanging from nooses inside the house that night. With their throats slit. Dahlia tried to tell the police. She can testify to all of that. She'll have to."

"She'll break down," Emma said. "Rafe will come at her hard on cross."

"I don't necessarily think that's a bad thing," I said. "Also, Rafe's not stupid. Dahlia Karl is a victim in this too. He knows the jury will see that. She's lost a lot. Her husband. Her financial security. And he betrayed her before all of that. She's going to get up there and say that the witness box is the last place she wants to be. My bigger concern is the can of worms it could open up about Ian's accident. That's what Reed's worried about."

"You really think Johnson would hammer her about that?" Jeanie asked. "That would be pretty callous of him. Her kid is dead. Her husband cheated on her and is on trial for murder."

"I just know it's what Reed's worried about," I said. "I am too. But it may not be enough to keep her away from the jury."

"You'll have to call the Thompsons too," Jeanie said. "At least to authenticate that footage. You think Rafe's going to put up a fight with that? They're not on any witness list. They were never interviewed by the police."

"That's a plus on our column, not his," I said. "Even Eric thinks that was an oversight."

"You asked him?" Jeanie said. "He's willing to give you an opinion on this?"

"He doesn't blindly think all detectives are in the right. And he wants to make sure Megan Lewis's homicide investigation was handled properly too. He has issues with it. He just isn't willing to work on the case directly."

"Well," Jeanie said. "I miss him around here."

The room fell silent for a moment. I found a smile. "I miss him too. And he'll be back. After this trial is over, he'll be back."

"Until the next case he morally opposes," Jeanie said, half under her breath. "Cass, you need an investigator. You don't have to worry about pissing off."

"Are you suggesting we fire Eric outright?"

"What? No. God, no. I'm just saying. This is ... sticky. You know?"

"Yes. But I still believe in my soul we're doing the right thing. And we're doing it for Dahlia and Clara. Remember that. We're giving Reed his constitutionally guaranteed legal defense. That's it."

"Boy, I wish Rafe Johnson would see reason and plead this sucker down," Emma said. "Though ... I can't say I'm disappointed I'm going to get to help you at trial, Aunt Cass. I've been looking forward to seeing you in action. It's half the reason I wanted to work here this year."

"Oh, she's brilliant, honey," Jeanie said. "You won't be disappointed. I think this case is a big fat turkey. I haven't been shy about telling you that. But I've seen Cass pull things out of her ass that can turn the whole thing upside down."

"Well, that's a lovely compliment." I laughed. "I'm going to need all hands on deck. You're right, Emma. Dahlia is going to be tricky if I put her on the stand. I'm going to need you to wrangle her. Sit with her. Make sure she's in as good a place mentally as she can be. You'll be my Johnny-on-the-spot once we get into the courtroom. And it'll start with voir dire. I need your eyes and ears. Your impressions of the potential jurors. Their reactions. Anything that pops out at you. Tori has a really good sixth sense about that stuff. She's not gonna be there this time. But I trust your judgment of people just as much."

Emma beamed. "I can do all that."

"And I know I can count on you to hold the fort down here," I said to Jeanie.

I took a step back from the whiteboard. I drew two columns. One titled "Things For Us" the other "Things That'll Kill Us."

The things that would kill us was a far longer list. Reed's confession topped it.

"You know," Emma said. "If he'd have just stayed quiet, I honestly think you'd have a real shot at an acquittal. There's no physical evidence at the crime scene. Sure, there are some hairs and fingerprints. But the police can't pinpoint when those were left. There's no secret that Megan and Reed were having an affair and that most of the time, they had their liaisons at her house, not his."

"He has no alibi," Jeanie said, pointing to the "Things That Will Kill Us" column. "And he's the only person with a real motive. Nothing was taken from Megan's house. There was no forced entry. Even without his confession, he'd have been arrested."

"We aren't trying for an acquittal," I said. "Don't lose sight of that. That's not what this case is about. It's about trying to keep Reed from earning himself a life sentence without parole. That's it."

"And it's about paying for our office addition!" Miranda yelled from downstairs. "Mrs. Karl's check just cleared."

"God love her," Jeanie muttered.

"What about Reed?" Emma asked. "Have you decided whether you're going to call him to testify?"

I stared at the whiteboard. The "Things For Us" column was woefully short. That didn't mean there weren't powerful pieces of evidence there.

"It was the agreement we made when he hired me. He wants me to get him through Rafe's cross-examination. But Reed isn't the only person who can testify about Megan's mental decline. In fact, his testimony on that would probably hurt him more than help him. She's dead. She died violently. I have other witnesses without any personal biases who will do a better job explaining who Megan was in those last few weeks. What she was capable of."

Jeanie got up and stood beside me. She folded her arms in front of her and stared at the lists I'd written. She scowled. I knew that look. Jeanie Mills's wheels were turning. Hard. She picked up the dry erase marker and poised it over the "Things That Will Kill Us" column.

Emma walked over to us. She stood on my other side.

"This won't be easy," Jeanie said. She took the pen and circled Reed's confession.

"I know," I said. "It's going to be impossible."

"It's not too late to back out," she said.

"Except it is."

Jeanie stood back. She looked at me, then wrote five words in block letters at the bottom of the "Kill Us" column.

When she stepped back, she put her arm around me. She'd written. "They're going to hate you."

I took a breath. I put my arm around Emma so the three of us stood linked, staring at the whiteboard words in black and white.

"I know," I finally said. "Believe me. I know."

Chapter 13

JUDGE GRETA NIEDERMAYER RAN A SMOOTH, efficient courtroom. By the lunch break on the first day of trial, we had our jury of twelve plus two alternates. Four women, eight men. It was a good mix. Each seemed attentive, if not exactly eager to be there.

Reed Karl sat beside me in an expensive suit that fit him well. Freshly shaven, his hair hung a bit longer than I liked. He was a handsome man, with those bright-green eyes and rugged complexion. It would be easy to see why someone like Megan Lewis might have been initially attracted to him. He looked confident. Competent. Rich. I wasn't sure that impression would help him with the jury.

Emma sat directly behind me. She had taken studious notes on every juror. Later, I would pick her brain on what she'd observed. For now, Rafe Johnson stood at the lectern, ready to address the jury.

"Ladies and gentlemen," he started. "This is a simple case, but that doesn't mean your job will be easy. But I thank you for the time and attention you are about to give it. The next few days may be some of the most uncomfortable you'll have to endure. I am sorry for that. But it's necessary. It's critical. Because Megan Lewis no longer has a voice. It was taken from her. Beaten out of her in the most brutal fashion.

"I want to warn you of that right up front. There are things you need to know. Things you must see as this trial progresses. I wish there were a way I could spare you the photographs. The graphic testimony. Because Megan Lewis doesn't deserve to be remembered for her very last moments on Earth. She deserves to be remembered for how she lived her life. How she chose to serve the people of this community. How she took an oath to protect all of you. To protect me. In the end, there was no one there to protect her. In fact, the person she had grown to love, who had promised to protect *her*, ended up being the one who took her life.

"Megan Lewis wasn't a perfect person. I'll admit that to you right up front as well. She had flaws. She made bad choices. She loved the wrong person. But none of us are perfect. None of us have lived lives free from bad choices. Still, nothing she did can justify what happened to her. What was done to her. How she died.

"I will tell you that Megan Lewis's murder is one of the most savage acts of violence I have ever seen. She wasn't just killed. She was destroyed, ladies and gentlemen. She was obliterated. Not only was her voice taken away that night, but so was her face. Her face. Let that sink in. She was violated. I can only describe what happened to her as obscene. It's the stuff of horror movies. And it was done to her by someone who promised to love her. Who she loved in return.

"I told you this case was simple. It is. It's simple because there is no mystery here. No question as to who the perpetrator of this heinous act was. The killer is Reed Karl. And you don't even have to take my word for it. You will be able to hear his own words. His confession. He spoke at length for over an hour, detailing his intentions, and his actions. Reed Karl has admitted to the brutal killing of Megan Lewis."

Johnson paused. He looked over at Reed, shaking his head. Reed had the presence of mind not to meet his gaze. He looked down. He trembled. All color drained from his face. For a moment, I thought he might be sick. But he recovered. Slowly, he raised his head and stared at some point on the wall.

"The evidence will show that Reed Karl and only Reed Karl made a decision to end Megan Lewis's life. She had become an inconvenience to him. A threat to the lie he'd built. His marriage. His reputation. He'd taken from her everything she had to give. Her heart. Her love. Her body. He made promises to her. Strung her along thinking they would have a future together. Week after week. Month after month. He made her believe he would leave his wife for her. That he would marry her. Maybe start a new family with her. She believed him. She trusted him. Even as everyone around her warned her she was making a mistake. Her love for Reed was too strong. Her trust in him, absolute. Little by little, he stripped away her dignity. Her self-respect. Made her question her judgment. Her reality. She hung on. Held out hope that someday, Reed would make good on all of his promises.

"Then, one terrible night, Reed Karl entered Megan's house while she slept. While she *slept!* He didn't call ahead. He didn't ring the doorbell. He gave her no warning that he would come. So Megan Lewis, peaceful, in the sanctity of her own home, not having any reason to think she was in danger ... slept. Reed Karl entered her bedroom, stood over her. Maybe even watched her without her knowing. And then he picked up a blunt object and bludgeoned her to death. He beat her so brutally, so terribly, you will hear how the police couldn't even use her dental records to identify her.

"Members of the jury, when the time comes, you'll be instructed by the judge about your burden of proof. You may already think you know it. Reasonable doubt. Reasonable. Not any doubt. Reasonable doubt. But the thing that makes this case simple, is Reed Karl's own words. His confession. There is no doubt that Reed Karl planned and committed this horrifying act. This unspeakable crime. This desecration. And for that, I am confident when all the evidence comes in, you will be able to deliver a just verdict. The only verdict appropriate in this matter. You will find him guilty beyond a reasonable doubt for the first degree murder of Megan Lewis. I thank you in advance for your time and attention. And I apologize in advance for what I know this case could do to you. What it's already done to those of us who have had to see what was done to Megan Lewis. Thank you. I know you'll execute your duty with the utmost care."

Rafe shook his head as he walked back to his table. He seemed genuinely shaken. I'd never known him for over-the-top theatrics. He took a breath and ran a hand over his face. Most of the jury kept their gazes straight on Reed. He sat with his hands folded on the table, staring forward. He then turned only slightly, imploring me with his eyes. I gave him a subtle smile of encouragement, then rose to face the jury. A single thought filled my brain. Unbidden. Unwanted. And yet ...

What am I doing?

I took my time, giving the jury a moment to breathe. A moment for me to breathe. I felt their expectant eyes. To their credit, every member of the jury seemed earnest. I saw no hard stares or hateful expressions that would lead me to believe they had closed their minds. That might come later. I knew Rafe would start out with his big guns as soon as I finished my remarks. The best I could do was try to give them something to hold in their minds as they listened to the damning evidence that was about to come out.

"Megan Lewis didn't deserve what happened to her," I said. "There's no disputing that. To suggest otherwise would be a disservice to her, and to you. But the story that my colleague Mr. Johnson has told you isn't the whole story."

I paused. I chose to stand directly behind the lectern, my hands resting on top of it. I wanted the jury to focus on me. Not Reed. Not Rafe Johnson. Not the judge.

"This is the story of a family. A family that was broken by tragedy. Betrayal, yes. But also deep loss. What would you do to protect your family? What could drive a person to do something unspeakable in defense of his family? His wife. His daughter. Those are the questions that drive this case. The ones we can't turn away from even when the prosecution tries to convince you to. Keep that single question in your mind. What would you do to protect your family?

"Reed Karl would be the first to admit he is a deeply flawed man. One who has made terrible mistakes. Unforgivable mistakes. He's hurt people. My God. He's hurt people. But this case isn't as simple as Rafe Johnson wants you to believe.

"First degree murder. That is the charge the state is looking to convict Mr. Karl of. Mr. Johnson is right. You'll be instructed on the definition of that charge. But you'll be told that first degree murder requires planning. It requires premeditation. Mr. Johnson will have to prove that Reed Karl went to Megan Lewis's home with the intention of killing her.

"I submit to you that is simply not the case."

I took a sip of the water I'd brought with me up to the lectern. My hands were steady.

"Megan Lewis is not to blame for what ultimately happened to her. Violence. The taking of a human life should never be the answer. But it's important for you to understand what happened between Megan Lewis and Reed Karl in the days and weeks leading up to that terrible night in June of this year.

"Reed Karl did love Megan Lewis. He is guilty of infidelity. He is guilty of damaging his family, probably forever. But he is not guilty of premeditated murder.

"I told you ... I agreed with Mr. Johnson that the taking of a life should never be the answer. And it shouldn't. But there are factors that can mitigate the taking of a life. Some are straightforward. We are each of us permitted to take a life if we act in self-defense. Or if we act in defense of someone else.

"Ladies and gentlemen, I believe the evidence will show that Reed Karl had reason to believe that Megan Lewis was a danger to his family. Physical danger. Physical harm. Not theoretical. Not psychological. Not a threat to his marriage. The evidence will show that Reed Karl had already confessed his infidelities to his wife. She knew. He was not acting to silence Megan Lewis. And he did not go to Megan Lewis's house with the intention of killing her. There was no plan. No premeditation.

And thus the state will fail in its attempt to prove the elements of first degree murder."

I took a beat, realizing I was in danger of losing them already. As much as I wanted to argue legal elements, it would go right over their heads.

"What could drive someone to hurt someone else in the way Megan Lewis was hurt? What could they have been thinking? There has to be a reason. You have to ask yourself, who could be capable of taking a life like that? What would make someone do it? What would make a person feel that they had no other choice?

"Is there anything that could make a killing like that justified in the eyes of the law? In the eyes of another human being? The answer to that question is yes. It has to be yes. If you believed you had no other choice. If you believed you were protecting someone else. The state's evidence in this case is not everything Mr. Johnson wants to make it out to be. It is not as cut and dry or simple as he has told you. Brutal. Yes. Disturbing. Yes. Heartbreaking. Of course. But it is not simple. This is not a case of premeditated murder. It may not even be a case of murder at all. What I ask of you. What the law demands of you. At every turn, is there a reason, a justification for what happened? Is the story Mr. Johnson wants to tell the whole story? Or is something else going on?

"Justice demands that you look harder than just the surface. That you listen to the evidence. All of the evidence. If you can do that, I'm confident you'll see that the state cannot meet its burden of proof. They cannot prove beyond a reasonable doubt that the defendant, Reed Karl, is guilty of premeditated murder. Thank you."

I walked back to my table. Reed sat just as he had when I stood up, with his hands folded in front of him. This time, he chanced a look toward the jury.

"Mr. Johnson," Judge Niedermayer called out. "Are you ready to call your first witness?"

"I am, Your Honor. The state calls Elena Lange to the stand."

I straightened my jacket as I took my seat. Elena Lange strode confidently from the back of the courtroom. I knew I would spend the rest of this trial trying to overcome what the jury would see and hear over the next hour.

Chapter 14

ELENA LANGE WAS a crime scene analyst from the Michigan State Police. I knew Rafe thought she would make a good witness. But it almost didn't matter. The power of her testimony came as Johnson admitted the crime scene photographs one by one.

Shock and horror registered on the jurors' faces. Reed went rigid beside me. I'd warned him to keep breathing. Behind us, Megan Lewis's family—those who had decided to stay in the courtroom—wept. Megan's mother had passed away some years ago after a lengthy battle with cancer. Her father, I'd been told, was in a Memory Care unit in Chelsea. Two of Megan's maternal aunts were in the courtroom. Megan's paternal uncle remained. Frank "Flip" Lewis had been a fire chief for Jackson County. I knew he'd seen plenty of dead bodies, injured, burned and broken people. But as Johnson showed the slides of Megan's remains, Flip broke down and had to excuse himself.

"Ms. Lange," Johnson said. "Is this an accurate representation of the scene at 415 Lilac Court when you arrived?"

"It is," Lange said.

"Can you describe what actions you took that day?"

"As I testified earlier, I was called out to the scene by Detective Rodney Patel of the Woodbridge County Sheriff's Department. Detective Patel had taken control of the scene. My department was asked to conduct the crime scene investigation which first involved documenting the scene, taking photographs, then methodically collecting evidence."

"Can you describe what that method entails?"

Ms. Lange went through the most dry part of her testimony. She outlined what are known as the "Seven S's" of crime scene investigation. Secure the Scene. Separate. Scan. See. Sketch. Search. Secure the Evidence.

I knew Lange's testimony would be one of the strongest pillars of Rafe Johnson's case. Lange was objective. Thorough. Formidable. Any real hope I had of chipping away at the elements of the crime would come later. But the crime scene itself was a horror we could not change.

"What physical evidence were you able to recover from the scene?" Johnson asked.

"Well, of course, the victim's remains. Ms. Lewis's injuries were extensive. There was blood spatter on the back wall, part of her headboard and also spray on the walls to the left and right of the victim's bed. We found massive amounts of blood on the bed and the headboard."

Johnson went through the photographic evidence of every important item Ms. Lange collected.

"What were the significant findings you made at the scene itself?" Johnson asked.

"Working in conjunction with Detective Patel, we were able to establish that there appeared to have been no forced entry. No windows were broken. No locks on the doors broken. The victim's utility door leading out from the garage was closed but not locked. Same with the back door heading from the garage and into the victim's mudroom or laundry room. The front door to the victim's home remained locked as did her back sliding door off the kitchen. The house is a ranch that sits on a slab. Those three entries are the only ones with the exception of the windows. The garage door itself was also locked."

"Do you have a theory as to how the assailant entered the home that night?"

"I do," she said. "Based on the fact that both the rear sliding door and the front door were locked, it is my best guess that Ms. Lewis's attacker entered from that service door off the garage and then through the side door into the kitchen."

"Why do you assume that?"

"The locks on the front door and back door both engage from inside the home. And as I testified before, the locks on the service and garage door leading into the home were unlocked when I arrived and to my knowledge unlocked when Detective Patel and Deputy Tony Fields, the responding officer, arrived. As such, logic, the physical evidence, and common sense dictates that was the point of entry for Ms. Lewis's killer."

"All right. Detective, what else did your analysis of the crime scene reveal in terms of physical evidence at the scene?"

"Well, the majority of the blood and hair fibers we collected belonged to the victim. We did find both fingerprints and hair samples that belonged to someone other than the victim."

"Were you able to establish who those samples belonged to?"

"Yes, sir," Lange said.

Lange went through the science of DNA mapping with regard to the blood and hair fibers.

"And your conclusions?" Johnson asked. I looked over at the jury. So far, Johnson hadn't lost them. It was easy to do during this portion of the crime scene analysis.

"We identified two strands of short, dark hair as belonging to the defendant, Reed Karl. There was also a distribution of hair found in the living room of the victim's home. Those were long, blonde hairs and were later identified as belonging to the victim's aunt."

"Three people? You only found hair fibers for three people, including the victim herself?"

"That's right. I should add that the victim's home, with the exception of where the assault took place in the bedroom, was relatively clean. There were vacuuming marks in the living room, the spare bedrooms, even the victim's bedroom. The bathrooms appeared to have been recently cleaned as well. In fact, the smell of disinfectant was still prominent in the home."

"I see."

Johnson stood at the lectern with his arms crossed. "What about the blood?" he asked.

"The blood collected at the scene belonged only to the victim, Megan Lewis."

"And the fingerprints?"

"Most of the prints recovered again belonged to the victim, Megan Lewis. There was a partial palm print lifted from a kitchen counter. That was matched to the defendant, Reed Karl."

"So if I'm understanding correctly, you found Reed Karl's fingerprints in the home."

"That's right."

"What about a murder weapon? Did you find one?"

"No."

"You said you found blood on the walls and the victim's bed. Looking at the photo that's been marked Exhibit Twelve. Can you tell me what it is?"

"It's a photograph of the victim's nightstand at her bedside."

"For the record, can you tell me what's on it?"

"There is a lamp with a gold metal base. A phone charger. A box of tissues. A bottle of foot balm."

"Were those items examined as part of your investigation?"

"Yes. The entire room was examined for signs of physical evidence. Fingerprints. Footprints. Blood. Hair. DNA."

"Did you find any physical evidence on the nightstand itself? Any blood or anything like you've described?"

"No. It was clean."

"The lamp was clean?"

"That's correct."

"As in no blood?"

"Correct."

"Can you identify what's in Exhibit Ten?"

"It's a photograph of the victim's bedside table after we moved the lamp."

"Is there anything significant about that?"

"Yes. There was a pattern of dust around the lamp which would indicate it had not been recently moved."

"No indication that it or anything else in the room could have been used as the murder weapon?"

"Objection," I said. "Counsel is leading the witness. Also asked and answered."

Rafe put up a hand as if he were surrendering the point. "Thank you." He scowled. He looked down at his notes. Something seemed off about him. I couldn't quite put my finger on it, but he almost seemed unsure of himself. I couldn't read his mind. But I wondered if he was thinking this all seemed too easy for him.

"Thank you," he said again. "I don't have any further questions at this time for this witness."

Even Judge Niedermayer looked a little stunned by that. I wasn't. I could sense Johnson's strategy. He didn't want to bog the jury down this early. His big guns were coming in the testimony of the medical examiner, and then Reed's own confession.

"All right, then," the judge said. "Ms. Leary, your witness."

"Thank you." I stepped up to the lectern. I'd never had the opportunity to cross-examine Elena Lange before. She was new to this part of Michigan, but had almost fifteen years under her belt as a crime scene investigator.

"Ms. Lange," I began. "I don't want to belabor too much of your testimony on direct. But I do have a few things I'd like for you to clarify. Starting with the fingerprint evidence you described. So I'm clear. You're saying you discovered a partial print in the kitchen of the victim's home, is that correct?"

"Yes. A palm print. It was discovered on the edge of the sink."

"The edge of the sink. All right. And isn't it true you cannot determine how long that print was actually there?"

"Not exactly, no. There is no scientific way to determine the age of a latent print. Generally, we look at other evidence, including how long ago the surface might have been cleaned. As I testified on direct, the home itself was relatively clean and still had the smell of disinfectant in the air. Especially in the kitchen and bathrooms. Based on that, I would assume that print was relatively recent."

"But you don't know whether that print was left on the night Megan Lewis died, do you?"

"I can't say that, no."

"It could have been left the day before. Or the week before. Possibly even the month before?"

"That's theoretically true, yes. Though unlikely for the reasons I've already stated."

"Okay. Thank you for that. Let's move on to what you discovered in Ms. Lewis's bedroom. You testified the blood found in and around the victim's body all belonged to the victim, isn't that right?"

"That's correct, yes."

I had to be careful. Every instinct in me wanted to follow up with that. There was no physical evidence placing Reed Karl in that house on the night Megan Lewis was killed. And yet he admitted to being there. Not for the first time, I wished I had a time machine. I wished I could have kept Karl from saying anything to the police without having a lawyer present.

"You found no fingerprints belonging to Mr. Karl in the victim's bedroom."

"That's correct."

"No hair fibers belonging to Mr. Karl were found in the bedroom."

"That's correct."

"You have theorized that the assailant entered the victim's home through the garage service door. Did you find any fingerprints on those doors?"

"None that could be identified. We found some partial prints, but they were too degraded to be useful."

"I see."

I walked around the lectern. From the corner of my eye, I could see Reed. He kept his eyes on Ms. Lange. Then he picked up his pen and jotted something down on the piece of paper I left for him.

"If I'm understanding correctly," I said. "The physical evidence that you were able to collect essentially provided you with a theory as to how Ms. Lewis's assailant entered the home. And, of course, the manner in which Ms. Lewis died. But that's pretty much it, isn't it?"

"I'm not sure I take your meaning."

"Well, I mean ... you don't know how long the assailant was in the home that day. You don't know what transpired between Ms. Lewis and her attacker. Isn't that right?"

"Objection." Rafe Johnson stood up. "Your Honor, Ms. Leary appears to be trying to make a closing argument, not conduct proper cross."

"Ms. Leary?" Judge Niedermayer said.

"Your Honor, I believe it is fully within my rights to define the scope of this witness's investigation and her conclusions."

"Overruled."

I turned back to Ms. Lange. "Do you need me to repeat the question?"

"No," Ms. Lange said. "And the answer is no. The results of my investigation would not permit me to draw conclusions about the length of time the defendant was inside Ms. Lewis's home. And I do not know what transpired between them prior to the fatal blow to her head."

"Okay. Thank you. And you don't ... you didn't recover a murder weapon, isn't that right?"

"That's correct. And I'll defer to the medical examiner's report in terms of theories on what was used to bludgeon the victim to death."

"Thank you," I said. "I have no further questions."

"Any redirect, Mr. Johnson?" the judge said.

"Just a few questions," Rafe said as he traded spots with me at the lectern.

"Ms. Lange, you didn't observe any so-called defensive wounds on the victim, did you?"

"Objection," I said. "Now counsel is asking questions that are beyond the scope of this witness's expertise."

"I'll allow it," the judge said. "The detective can make that clarification."

"The victim's hands didn't appear to be bruised," Ms. Lange said. "But of course, I have to defer to the coroner on that. The victim's hands were bagged and fingernail scrapings were taken."

"All right," Rafe said. "But let's turn your attention to the room itself. Were there any signs of a struggle?"

"No."

"No furniture overturned?"

"No."

"No lamps broken?"

"No."

"How about the status of the bedding itself? Can you describe it?"

"Well, there was a significant amount of blood. But if you're talking about the sheets, the blankets? Ms. Lewis's bed and bedding was found in the condition in which you see it in those photographs. She was lying in bed, on her back, her arms bent and above her head. The blankets were drawn up just over her breasts."

"She wasn't tangled in the bedsheets?"

"No."

"Her feet were fully on the bed?"

"Yes."

"She didn't try to or didn't appear to have the chance to even get up?"

"Objection," I said. "I'll use Mr. Johnson's own objection. He's making a closing argument, not asking questions within the scope of cross or this expert's expertise."

"Never mind her expertise," Johnson said. "Ms. Lange was in the room. She saw the condition of the victim and the room as it was after Ms. Lewis's murder. I'm only asking for her firsthand observations."

"Sustained in part," the judge said. "I believe those questions are within the scope of her observations. However, you're outside the scope of cross. Let's move on."

"We don't need to, Your Honor. Thank you. I have no more questions for this witness."

With that, Elena Lange left the witness box. Rafe stayed at the lectern.

"The state calls Dr. Amelia Trainor to the stand."

Amelia Trainor, Woodbridge County's Medical Examiner, rose from the back of the courtroom and made her way up to the box.

Chapter 15

Not long ago, a sloppy, cruel true crime blogger described Amelia Trainor, ME as Doctor Vampire after her testimony in another murder trial. The name came from her bloodless complexion and somewhat cold delivery as she answered questions about some rather horrific subject matter. Alabaster white with fair hair she wore tied and slicked back, Amelia looked ageless. She could have passed for thirty, or seventy. I knew the truth was almost smack dab in the middle. If Dr. Trainor took the moniker personally, she never showed it. For the most part, she refused all requests for media interviews, preferring to issue press releases from her office.

Rafe Johnson took her through the meat of her testimony. She delivered it in her cool, methodical way. Explaining the nuts and bolts of an autopsy, starting with her arrival at the crime scene.

"You personally oversaw the removal of Megan Lewis's body from her home?"

"I did," Dr. Trainor answered.

"Why was that necessary?"

"For a variety of reasons. Among others, I can ensure that the body is removed according to standard protocols. I am also there to ensure any medications or illicit substances are cataloged."

"So it's fair to say your investigation, or rather, your post mortem, involves more than just the autopsy."

"That is correct. I view the position of the body. How it was found. And as I said, the presence of any prescription medication, over-the-counter medication, illicit substances."

"Just to be clear, were there any illicit drugs found at the crime scene?"

"No. There was a wine glass in the bathroom containing about a teaspoon of red wine in the bottom of it. But we did not find any illegal substances, no."

"Okay. Dr. Trainor, can you describe the position of the body, how it was found?"

"Certainly. The victim was found in a supine position, that is, lying on her back on top of her bed. Her arms were slightly bent above her head. Her feet were pointed toward the foot of the bed with her right leg slightly bent at the knee. Call it a figure four position."

"I see," Johnson said. "Was there anything remarkable about the way she was found?"

"If I may refer to the exhibits," Dr. Trainor said. Rafe obliged her and pulled up state Exhibits Fourteen through Twenty-eight. These were the crime scene photographs taken of Megan as she lay on the bed. A few of them were extreme close-up shots of Megan's head injuries. A few members of the jury still winced as they saw them, but the remainder kept stoic expressions.

"I would say the victim's injuries were of course readily apparent upon visual inspection."

"Dr. Trainor, could you describe the victim's injuries and cause of death?"

"Of course. The victim suffered from multiple blows to the head from a blunt object. She had a broken left clavicle and contusions to the chest and both breasts. Nearly all of her front teeth were knocked out or broken. Some were found in her throat."

Dr. Trainor paused to take a sip of water. Cool as she was, Amelia Trainor understood the theater of this moment. Rafe queued up the X-ray images taken of Megan Lewis's skull. The doctor used a laser pointer to highlight Megan's forehead region.

"The anterior surface of the frontal bone, what you might call the forehead, was in pieces. This blow alone was not survivable in my opinion. It caused a massive brain bleed. And here, the glabella, between the eyebrows and above the nose, as well as the mandible, the jaw bone, and nearly all the victim's nasal bones were fractured. Several pieces of these bones were actually pushed into the victim's brain."

"I see," Rafe said. "Were you able to determine how many blows the victim might have received?"

"I couldn't give you an exact amount, no. But it was certainly multiple blows. The fractures to the bones I described, the frontal bone, the glabella and left orbital bones, teeth and mandible, along with the broken clavicle and contusions to the breasts. These were multiple blows delivered with great force.

There was blood spatter on the wall, behind the bed, and even on the ceiling."

"Were you able to determine an exact cause of death?"

"Well, as I said, the blows to the frontal lobe were not survivable. The exact cause of death was a massive brain bleed due to the significant blunt force trauma to her head ... her face."

"Do you have an estimated time of death?"

"Due to the body temperature and lividity, I would estimate Ms. Lewis expired roughly six to eight hours prior to the discovery of her body at eleven a.m. by the responding officer."

"I see. Doctor, were you able to determine how long it would have taken Ms. Lewis to die?"

"Within minutes of the first blow."

"The first blow," Johnson said. "Were you able to determine how many times Ms. Lewis was struck while she lay in bed?"

"Her injuries were consistent with being struck at least three distinct times to the head. But as I said, I cannot tell you how many total times she was struck."

"She was beaten repeatedly?"

"Yes."

"You're saying Ms. Lewis could have been struck five or six times?"

"Again, can't say exactly how many times the victim was struck. But it was multiple times with significant force. At least three distinct blows to the head, at least two distinct blows to the chest and shoulder region."

"Someone stood over her and beat her to a pulp," Johnson said.

"Objection," I said. "Asked and answered. Counsel is making speeches now."

"Sustained," Niedermayer said.

"Doctor, were you able to determine what weapon was used to strike Megan Lewis?"

"It was a blunt object," she said. "Based on certain features of her wounds, I believe it was an object with rounded edges, not sharp. It might have been a baseball bat. It might have been a lead pipe. Something heavy enough to shatter bones in one blow. But as I understand it, no weapon was found at the scene. And I was not able to find any residue in Ms. Lewis's wounds."

"What kind of residue?"

"Wood splinters, metal shavings. Whatever was used, I found no part of that weapon embedded in Ms. Lewis's wounds."

"Could it have been a lamp or a candlestick holder or something with a squared base?"

"Not based on what I observed of the injuries. That type of object that you described, with corners or squared edges, would have left very distinct marks. We don't have that in this case."

"So you are confident that the murder weapon was cylindrical and couldn't have had squared edges."

"Yes," Dr. Trainor said. "I actually wrote a paper on this subject some years ago and performed lab work. I presented my findings to a national medical examiner's conference and it has been widely accepted by my peers."

"Dr. Trainor, do you have a theory on whether Megan Lewis was conscious during any part of this brutal assault?"

"I can't say for sure regarding the initial blow."

"I'm not asking for certainty. I'm asking if you were able to formulate a theory."

"Yes."

"And what is that theory?"

"Based on the positioning of the body, supine, with her hands above her, my educated guess is that Ms. Lewis was either still asleep or caught off guard when the first blow came down. It would have incapacitated her. She likely would have been rendered unconscious fairly quickly after that. But there were no signs that she tried to move or get up."

"She didn't move. She didn't try to get up. Likely because she couldn't, is that your testimony?"

"It is."

"What about defensive wounds? Can you describe for the jury what those are, typically?"

"In cases where victims were involved in a violent struggle, there are any number of wounds that would fall under the category of defensive in nature."

"Such as?"

"Well, you might have skin under the fingernails where a victim tries to scratch at their attacker. Or bruising to the forearms and hands as one tries to shield themselves from a blow. Broken fingers aren't uncommon if a victim attempts to strike their assailant with a closed fist."

"Did you find any injuries to the victim that might have been characterized as defensive wounds?"

"No."

"Did you find skin under Ms. Lewis's fingernails?"

"No."

"Did she have any broken fingernails?"

"No."

"No bruising to her hands or forearms?"

"No."

"So it's your theory, based on an extensive examination of the victim's wounds, that she did not fight back?"

"I found no wounds on the victim that would be consistent with her taking a defensive posture, no."

"She quite literally didn't know what hit her, is that right?"

"Well, I can't say that. I cannot say for sure whether Ms. Trainor was awake before the first blow was struck. I can't say for sure whether she was rendered immediately and completely unconscious after the first blow was struck. As I said, she was most certainly incapacitated after that first blow. But that's not the same as concluding she didn't know what hit her, as you phrased it."

"Thank you," Johnson said. He paused for a moment, as if he were about to open a new line of questioning. Then he shook his head. "I have no further questions."

"Ms. Leary?"

Reed had started to fall apart beside me. He kept his mouth hidden behind one hand, but his eyes filled with tears. He squeezed them shut.

"Thank you," I said. This was tough. Megan Lewis's wounds were her wounds. There was no factual dispute about how she died. It was brutal. Heinous. Awful. I also knew Amelia Trainor was unflappable on the stand. She could not be rattled.

"Dr. Trainor, to be clear, you cannot offer any definitive conclusions as to what transpired in the moments before Ms. Lewis was struck, can you?"

"Other than the positioning of her body, no. As I indicated in my direct testimony, Ms. Lewis appeared to be in a relaxed, natural sleeping position."

"But that doesn't mean she was asleep?"

"It does not, no."

"You performed a toxicology exam as part of your autopsy, did you not?"

"That's correct. That is standard."

"Of course. So were you then able to conclude what drugs Ms. Lewis had in her system at the time of her death?"

"I was. Yes."

"And what were they?"

"Ms. Lewis had a blood alcohol level of .09 percent at the time a blood sample was taken after her death."

"Point oh nine percent," I said. "So she was likely legally intoxicated at the time of her death?"

"It's hard to say. Although the body ceases metabolizing alcohol after death, there are a variety of chemical processes going on that can impact that post-mortem blood alcohol level."

"Let me ask it another way. From your findings, would you say Ms. Lewis was sober when she died?"

"No. I don't believe she was sober."

"What about prescription drugs?" I advanced the slides and pulled up a photograph of the interior of Megan Lewis's medicine cabinet. "Can you identify what she was taking?"

"Her toxicology report indicated the presence of levothyroxine, a thyroid medication, as well as estrogen and progestin at therapeutic levels consistent with a prescription birth control pill. There was also isocarboxazid and buspirone in her system. Both at therapeutic levels."

"What is isocarboxazid used to treat?" I asked.

"It is an antidepressant. Not one of the more common ones. Typically it's used when other antidepressants don't prove effective."

"And what about buspirone?" I asked.

"It's another type of antidepressant."

"Did you have occasion to consult with Ms. Lewis's primary care physician during your investigation?"

"Yes. That's standard practice."

"What was Ms. Lewis's diagnosis?"

"She was being treated for depression and had been recently diagnosed with bipolar II."

"I see. Are there any contraindications for taking buspirone along with isocarboxazid?"

"There are many. Dozens. The one we worry most about would be hypertension, high blood pressure, also what's called serotonin syndrome. That can lead to too high levels of serotonin in one's system. Things like increased anxiety, confusion, disorientation, and agitation are all possible."

"So those two drugs are generally not prescribed together?"

"No."

"No," I said. "Let me clarify so as not to waste your or the jury's time. Is alcohol contraindicated when taking either of those antidepressants found in Ms. Lewis's system?"

"It is, yes."

"In other words, a person who is on buspirone or isocarboxazid, alone or together, probably shouldn't consume alcohol, is that right?"

"It is not advised, no."

"What could happen?"

"Well, the side effects of either drug could be exacerbated."

"And what are the major side effects?"

"As with any antidepressant, we would always worry about suicidal ideations, hallucinations, disruptions in sleep, judgment, that sort of thing."

"Thank you," I said. "I have no further questions."

"Any recross, Mr. Johnson?"

Rafe rose. "No, your Honor, the state is ready to move on."

Judge Niedermayer looked at the wall clock. "Who do you have next, Mr. Johnson?"

"We'd like to call Detective Patel."

Niedermayer frowned. The jury was starting to get restless. "Okay. It's already almost four o'clock. We'll adjourn until the morning. Tell Detective Patel he's first up."

Ms. Lange's testimony and the entry of the crime scene photographs was bad. Dr. Trainor's chilling description of Megan Lewis's injuries was devastating. But tomorrow morning, when Rodney Patel made his way to the witness box, the jury would hear Reed Karl speak in his own words. The results could be catastrophic and there was very little I could do to stop it.

Every reservation, every naysayer who told me I was a fool to take this case ... by the end of tomorrow's testimony, they might all be proven right.

Chapter 16

RODNEY PATEL HAD BEEN INVESTIGATING homicides and testifying about them long enough to know how to walk a jury through it without overwhelming them. He spent an hour on the stand and I got off a couple of hits. There was some sponginess about how quickly Megan Lewis's house had been secured. A log book wasn't started until after Patel got there and an hour after her body was discovered. These were things I could touch on in closing, but none of it would matter.

None of it.

The only thing that mattered would begin an hour into Detective Patel's testimony on the morning of that second day of trial.

"Detective Patel," Johnson said. "How many times did you interview the defendant?"

"Twice," Patel said. "The first was more of an informal interview. As I testified earlier, one of Detective Lewis's friends identified Reed Karl as the man she'd been having a romantic relationship with for some time. So naturally, he was someone we needed to speak to fairly early on."

"And how did that interview go?"

"I went to Mr. Karl's place of business. I had hoped to talk to him alone. I was sensitive to the fact that Mr. Karl was a married man. Mr. Karl was cooperative at first. He took me to an empty break room in his office space. I informed him that Megan Lewis was deceased."

"How did he take that?"

"He was upset. Ashen-faced. I asked him if he could account for his whereabouts for the preceding twenty-four hours."

"Did he?"

"He told me he had returned home from his office at approximately six p.m. the evening before. Stayed home. Had dinner with his wife and daughter and went to bed at approximately ten p.m. that evening. He said he returned to his office at nine a.m. that morning."

"What time was it when you spoke to him?"

"This was roughly four p.m. on the afternoon of June 6th."

"What else did he tell you in that interview?"

"I asked him about the nature of his relationship with Detective Lewis. Mr. Karl indicated that their relationship had ended approximately two weeks prior. He claimed he hadn't seen her in several days but admitted that she took the break-up hard and had continued to text and call him. Mr. Karl insisted he hadn't been responding back to her. I asked him if he would be willing to let me search his phone and take a DNA sample. For a moment, I believed he would cooperate. He said yes. But a minute or two later, he changed his mind and said that he'd better talk to a lawyer. At that point, I ended the interview and asked him to stay available. I informed him that I would be securing a warrant for both his cell phone and a blood and DNA sample. He said he understood and that was the end of the interview."

"Did you have occasion to speak to Mr. Karl again?"

"Yes. Two days later, Mr. Karl voluntarily came to my office and indicated he had something to tell me."

"He came voluntarily. Can you elaborate on that?"

"It's just what I said. Mr. Karl remained a person of interest due to his relationship with the victim. I had interviewed several other friends and family members of Detective Lewis. Their story was consistent in that Ms. Lewis had been distraught in the days after Mr. Karl ended their relationship. I had secured the warrants for Mr. Karl's cell phone and computers and was getting ready to execute them. Mr. Karl simply showed up asking for me on June 8th. So I took him to an interview room and told him I intended to record the interview."

"What did he say?"

"He said he understood and wanted to proceed. I began recording at 1:41 p.m. on June 8th."

"Your Honor, at this time I'd like to move for entry of Exhibit Forty-seven and ask if we may play it for the jury. Authentication has previously been stipulated to."

"Ms. Leary?"

"No objections," I said. The tape would be played in its entirety.

My earlier motion to suppress it had been denied, as I knew it would be.

A moment later, the large flat screen monitor mounted to the right of Judge Niedermayer and facing the jury sparked to life. It was an overhead shot of Reed Karl sitting to the left of the screen at a table. He had a glass of water in front of him. Rodney Patel sat to the right of the screen with a pen and paper in front of him. Johnson pressed play and I watched the video I had seen dozens of times before. The jury was seeing it for the first time and sat at rapt attention.

"Mr. Karl," Detective Patel said on screen. "I want to make a few things clear. Did I ask you to come here today?"

"No, sir," Reed said, his voice breaking at first.

"You've come voluntarily."

"Yes, sir."

"Mr. Karl, you understand you are free to leave at any time?"

"I understand that."

"Out in the hallway, you told me you had something you wanted to tell me. Once again, you approached me. We haven't spoken in two days, is that correct?"

"That's correct. I just need to get this out."

"Okay. What is it you'd like to tell me? You understand and agreed to me recording this conversation."

"Yes. Yes. I understand."

"All right. So what do you want to talk about?"

"Megan," Karl said. It was hard to hear him. He whispered the word.

"Reed," Patel said. "I'm going to need you to speak up."

"Megan," Reed said, almost shouting it. "I came here to tell you what happened. What I did."

"What did you do?"

Reed hung his head. His right foot bounced up and down. He kept his hands flat on the table. Then he looked up at Rodney Patel.

"I killed Megan."

"You killed Megan? What happened, Reed?"

"I killed her. God, I didn't mean to. I didn't mean for it to get like this. I'm so sorry. So so sorry. That's what I need you to understand. I didn't want to hurt her. I didn't. I didn't. But I didn't have a choice."

Rodney Patel went completely still. "Reed, I'm going to need you to walk me through this. I'm going to need you to tell me exactly what happened."

"What is there to tell? You know what happened. Megan's dead. I killed her. So do whatever you need to do. Arrest me. Lock me up. I don't care anymore. I only care that my family is okay. That they're safe."

"Why wouldn't they be safe?"

Reed shook his head. "I killed her. I'm confessing. That's why I'm here. I'll sign whatever I'm supposed to sign. I just want this to be over. I killed Megan Lewis."

"How?"

"What do you mean how? What does it matter? I don't want to go into details. I killed her. You know I killed her. You knew it when you came to see me."

"No, Reed. I didn't. I still don't. I'm going to need you to tell me. That's how this has to work. And it also has to work like this. You have the right to remain silent. Anything you say can and will be used against you in a court of law. You have the right to talk to a lawyer and have that lawyer present with you while you are being questioned. If you can't afford one, one will be appointed to you before we proceed with questioning. If you want. You can decide to exercise these rights at any time and not answer any more questions. Do you understand those rights as I've explained them to you?"

"Yes. I know my rights. I don't want a lawyer. I don't deserve one. I'm guilty. I killed Megan. I loved her, but I killed her."

"Okay. Okay, Reed. So let's just take a step back. I want to help you. I really do. Do you believe me?"

Reed shrugged.

"Well, I do. So let's start at the beginning. Tell me what you did on June 5th and into June 6th. Take me through your day."

"I went to work. I already told you that."

"You did. But you also told me you came home around six. And you told me you stayed home, ate dinner with your family, then went to bed. Now you're telling me that's not true?"

"I left again," Reed said. "I went back to Megan's and I killed her."

"What time was this?"

"It was late. Dahlia and Clara were already asleep. They'd been asleep. I went over to Megan's in the middle of the night and I killed her. I came back home and I pretended like nothing had happened."

"Tell me what happened when you went over to Megan's that night. Did you talk to her?"

"What?"

"Did you talk to Megan?"

"What are you asking me? What possible difference could that make? I'm telling you I killed her. You want to know if we had a conversation?"

"Well, actually ... yes ..."

"I need this to be over. Do whatever you have to do. Put cuffs on me. Book me. Let's just get on with this."

"Reed, you keep saying do whatever I have to do. Well, this is what I have to do. I have to know exactly what happened at Megan Lewis's house on the early morning of June 6th. Do you understand?"

"I can't breathe."

"Take a sip of your water. We can take our time. I'm not going anywhere. We can talk. It's going to be okay."

"Okay? How is it ever going to be okay? She's dead. Megan's dead and I killed her. That's all you need to know. I had no choice. She gave me no choice. You don't understand what she's done."

"So tell me. Make me understand."

"Megan's not who people think she was. She wasn't who I thought she was. She changed. She got ... she was dangerous. She did things. I had no choice."

Something changed in Rodney Patel. His posture shifted. He leaned in, bringing himself closer to Reed. Reed had his head down, his nose almost pressed against the table.

"You had no choice. Tell me how you had no choice, Reed. Tell me how you decided your only choice was to beat that woman to death!"

Reed's head snapped up. He moved backward, putting distance between himself and Detective Patel.

"I didn't ... you can't ... She was dangerous. I had to keep everybody safe."

"Who? Who were you keeping safe, Reed?"

"You won't believe me. You won't understand. It doesn't matter now anyway. I'm here to face up to what I did. I'm not asking for sympathy or your understanding."

"Really? It seems to me you've asked me about three times to understand you. So help me, because I'm having a really rough time understanding how you could do what you did."

"Do you have a family?"

"Yes. I have a wife. I have two sons."

"Then you should be able to relate."

"Relate? You think I can relate? No. No, Reed. I can't relate."

Patel took a photograph out from behind the pad of paper he held. He slid it across the table and put it in front of Reed.

"Here's your chance, Reed. Explain it so I can understand."

Reed picked up the photograph. It was grainy from this angle, but I knew what it was. It was one of the more gruesome close-ups of Megan Lewis's battered face.

Reed choked out a sob. "God. Oh Megan. I'm so sorry. I'm so so sorry."

"Tell me what you did, Reed," Patel said. "It's right here. You and me. There's only now. Tell me what you did."

"I hit her. I must have ... Oh God. I hit her. I didn't want to hurt her. I didn't. I didn't. I just didn't have a choice. I didn't know any other way. She'd gone crazy. She was trying to scare my wife. She came into my home. I told her it was over but she just kept calling. Kept texting. It's in my phone. You said you wanted to search my phone. So do it. You'll see. She just wouldn't leave us alone. She came into my home!"

"When?"

"A few days ago. Last week. She left a warning. She cut up my son's toys. She wasn't herself. I tried to talk to her. I tried to get through to her but Megan just wouldn't listen. So I finally had no choice. I went over to Megan's house. She was sleeping. Right there in her bed. And I hit her until I knew she wouldn't ever wake up. Until I knew she couldn't hurt any of us ever again."

"How many times did you hit her?"

"I don't know. A few. I wasn't counting."

"What did you hit her with?"

"What difference does that make? Don't make me do this anymore. I can't do this anymore. I told you what you want.

What you need. It was me. I hit her. I killed her. I wish I could have made a different choice. But this is on me. I can't live with it anymore. I don't care what happens to me. I deserve everything. All of it. I brought this into our lives. It was my mistake. All mine. I went over to Megan's and I hit her."

"How many times, Reed? What did you hit her with?"

"Just ... she keeps a big lamp next to her bed. I picked it up. I just picked it up and I hit her."

"With a lamp? Come on, Reed. Tell me the truth."

"I am. I don't know. I don't know. I can't ... it all happened so fast. I don't know."

"You don't know what you did?"

"No one would listen to me. Dahlia was scared for her life! I was scared for her life. You don't get it. What we've been through. What Dahlia's been through. We lost our son. Our baby boy. Megan knew that. She used it. She broke into my house. She went into Ian's room. She took his things. She cut them up. She hung them up where Dahlia would find them."

Reed took out his phone. He pulled something up and showed it to Patel. I knew they were the shots Reed took of Ian Karl's stuffed animals, cut up and strung up on the ceiling fan.

"What is this?" Patel asked.

"It's what Megan did. I filed a police report the day after but you guys wouldn't do anything. Megan's a cop too. I know how this works."

"I'll look into it," Patel said. "But I need you to walk me through every step of what happened at Megan's house that early morning. Did you talk to her? Was she sleeping?"

"You don't want to listen. You want to sweep it all under the carpet. Just like when I tried to tell the cops she broke into our home. But that was the end of it, not the beginning. She's been harassing my wife for weeks. She left a note on the door threatening to hurt Dahlia."

"Where? What note?"

"I took it. I tore it down before Dahlia could see it."

"Do you have it? Did you take a picture of it?"

Reed shook his head. "No. I ripped it up. I didn't want anyone to see it."

"Sure," Patel said.

"You don't believe me."

"I'm trying, Reed. So help me. Tell me what happened at Megan's house. Tell me what you did. Was she asleep when you got there?"

"Yes. I don't know. She was lying there. Just lying there like in that picture. Please. I don't want to look at it anymore. We didn't talk. It's horrible. It's all so horrible. I'm sorry. God. I'm sorry. I know you probably don't believe me. I know how hollow that sounds. But I am. I'm sorry to everyone. To Dahlia. To my daughter. Of course to Megan. I just didn't know what else to do. I snapped, okay. I just snapped. Dahlia's fragile. She's been through so much. I knew this was going to break her. She was terrified. And Megan knew it. She just wouldn't take no for an answer. I'm an asshole. I know that. Worse. I cheated on my wife and then I dumped Megan. I led her on. I'm weak. I'm everything you think I am and worse. But I just didn't think I had another choice. I couldn't make Megan leave us alone. So I went over there. And I ended it. I ended it. I hit her until I knew she wouldn't wake up again. That's all. That's all of it. Now I think I'm going to be sick."

Then he was. Patel got a garbage can in front of Reed just in time for him to vomit into it. The interview ended just after that. Patel stood up and pressed a button on the camera, sending the video to black.

"Thank you, Detective," Johnson said. He paused. The jury, all twelve members, looked stunned. Wrecked.

Beside me, Reed buried his face in his hands. He kept whispering, "I'm sorry. I'm sorry. I'm so sorry." I put a hand on him in an effort to quiet him.

"Detective," Rafe said. "I'd like to focus on something you asked Mr. Karl about. This business of the murder weapon. In his taped interview, Mr. Karl said he used the bedside lamp to hit Ms. Lewis, correct?"

"That is what he said, yes."

"You're obviously aware of the crime scene analysis conducted by the Michigan State Police in this case. It's part of your report."

"Of course."

"And you're familiar with the coroner's report on Ms. Lewis's injuries and cause of death."

"Yes."

"What do you make of what Mr. Karl said about the lamp then?"

"Well, obviously, his version of events is inconsistent with the physical evidence in this case. There was no blood or human tissue found on that lamp. It was clean. Additionally, when the lamp was moved, there was no dust under it. You could see a distinct circular pattern where the lamp had been sitting which would indicate it had not been recently moved. We do not believe that lamp or any other item in Ms. Lewis's home was used as a murder weapon. Dr. Trainor's conclusions were compelling as well. Most likely, a cylindrical object like a bat or a lead pipe was used in this case."

"Why is that significant?"

"Well, it would indicate that Mr. Karl was not being truthful in part during his confession. He said he used the lamp to strike Ms. Lewis but we don't believe he did. The evidence indicates that Mr. Karl most likely entered the home with the weapon and took it with him when he left."

"Did you ever find this weapon?"

"We did not."

"I have no further questions," Johnson said.

I walked up to the lectern. I asked those few questions, pointing out the minor sloppiness of his securing of the crime scene.

"Detective," I said. "Did you ever speak to Megan Lewis's doctors?"

"Her primary care physician, yes. I received a list of medications she had been prescribed at the time of her death."

"Did you ever speak to Megan Lewis's therapist? Her psychologist?"

"No."

"So you didn't find it necessary to determine why she was taking psychotropic medication, did you?"

"No."

"And you never interviewed Reed Karl's neighbors, did you?"

"No."

"Didn't find it necessary to verify any of the claims Mr. Karl made about Ms. Lewis trespassing on his property?"

"No."

"So you didn't think what Mr. Karl showed you on his phone that day was significant?"

"No."

"Detective, you're aware Mr. Karl attempted to file a police report involving what he suspected was a break-in of his home on the night of May 29th?"

"Yes."

"What is your understanding of what happened?"

"My understanding is consistent with what you saw in his taped confession. He claimed Ms. Lewis had broken into his home and destroyed some toys."

"He called the Sheriff's Department on May 30th, didn't he?"

"Yes."

"Was a deputy sent out?"

"Yes. Deputy Genevieve Janson responded to the call and interviewed Mr. Karl. It's my understanding that Mrs. Karl refused to come to the door. A report was made but Mr. Karl never pursued charges as I understand it."

"Are you aware of whether Deputy Janson ever interviewed Ms. Lewis about these claims?"

"She talked to her, yes."

"But no formal charges were filed?"

"Deputy Janson didn't find the report credible. Mrs. Karl was unable to provide a statement. Ms. Lewis denied any involvement or being anywhere near the Karl premises on the night in question. So the matter didn't go further. Additionally, Ms. Lewis was murdered a few nights later. She wasn't in a position to answer any other questions."

"So the Karls' concerns weren't taken seriously, isn't that right?"

"I would not say that, no. But there was no real evidence that Megan Lewis had anything to do with this incident with the toys. And as I said, it was rendered moot after Megan Lewis was bludgeoned to death."

"It's your opinion still today that Megan Lewis was not harassing the Karl family?"

"I can't say that."

"There were some rather disturbing things found on Megan's computer though, are you aware of that?"

"I've seen the digital forensics reports, yes."

"You've seen more than the report. You've seen the photographs Ms. Lewis had on her computer, haven't you?"

"Of course."

"Megan Lewis had pictures of Dahlia Karl asleep in her bed on her laptop, isn't that true?"

"There were photographs of Mrs. Karl on Ms. Lewis's laptop. Yes."

"And yet you've still decided that Megan Lewis wasn't posing any kind of threat to the Karls?"

"I haven't decided any such thing. My investigation was into the murder of Megan Lewis. Mr. Karl confessed to killing her. Regardless of their past history, I am satisfied that Mr. Karl went to Ms. Lewis's home with the intention of killing her in the early morning of June 6th. And he succeeded in doing that, while Ms. Lewis slept in her bed. His motive for doing so is immaterial from my point of view."

Patel glared at me. In his eyes, I was trying to justify the actions of a cold-blooded killer. I waited. Took a breath. Johnson would call the phone forensics experts. Possibly a few of Megan's friends or family members. But I knew as far as he was concerned, he'd hit a home run. Of course he would. Anyone would in his position. Reed Karl confessed to the brutal killing of a sleeping woman. He'd admitted to being a monster.

As I looked at that jury that November afternoon, I knew they had every reason to think he really was a monster.

Chapter 17

Judge Niedermayer dismissed the jury for the day just after three that afternoon. It would give me time to collect my client and have a conversation before he was taken back to the county jail. While I handled a few procedural motions, Emma arranged for Reed to be brought back to the law library down the hall from the courtroom.

When I joined them, Reed sat with his head buried in his hands.

"It's over, isn't it?" he asked.

I wanted to tell him no. I wanted to give him the hope and optimism clients needed to have at this stage. But Reed Karl wasn't like any other client and this wasn't like any other murder trial.

"I told you at the beginning of this, these first two days would be the hardest."

"They've made up their minds," he said. "I can see it. Those jurors. The way they look at me. Their faces when they watched that tape. Cass, they have to understand. They need to know why all this happened."

"And I'll have a chance to present your defense. You will have a chance to explain. What happened at the house? We've laid some of the groundwork. Tomorrow, the jury will get to see all the texts Megan sent you. When the digital forensics detective gets up there, I'll be able to show them the photographs found on her computer."

"Will it matter?"

Emma sat in the corner watching Reed. She was careful not to change the expression on her face. I knew what she was thinking. I was thinking it too.

"We can't know," I finally said. "But when we started this, you told me you just wanted the opportunity to get your side of it out. I can promise you that you will. The jury will hear the facts. And then they'll make their decision."

"I can tell them," Reed said. "I can tell them I had no choice. I did what I had to do. I had no choice."

He repeated it like a mantra. Reed began rocking back and forth in his chair. He seemed on the verge of a breakdown.

"I mean, they heard that," he said, looking at me. "It's like I told Detective Patel. I had no choice. Megan was going to do something terrible. She'd already done something terrible."

"Reed," I said. I knew where this might go, but I had to broach the subject again.

"Reed, we have to talk about Dahlia. You have to reconsider letting me put her on the stand."

He furiously shook his head. "This is a nonstarter, Cass. I told you. Dahlia's been through enough. She can't handle this. I don't want her anywhere near it."

"I think she's stronger than you think she is. She's been through a lot. Yes. But don't forget, she's the one who came to me, asking me to represent you. She's fighting for you. And it might not even be the worst thing if she breaks down on the stand."

His eyes went wide. "You can't say that. How can you say that? I told you. Dahlia's too fragile. It's not a breakdown on the stand I'm worried about. She's all Clara has. You don't know what it's like when Dahlia goes to her darkest places. Sometimes ... I don't know if I'm going to be able to pull her out. She's lost everything. And this is all my fault. The least I can do is take responsibility and protect her the way I should have."

"You have. But have you considered the fact that maybe she'd like a chance to fight for you? She still loves you, Reed."

"No. I do not want her on the stand. I don't even want her in that courtroom."

"She has to be," I said. "We've kept her away during the more gruesome parts of it, but the jury is watching. You're right about that. If they're going to be made to understand why you did what you did, they have to see Dahlia."

"No!"

I sat back, frustrated. How could I get through to him?

"Reed, you asked me if this was over. I don't believe it is. But the last two days of testimony are killing you. Right now, all anybody knows is that Megan Lewis had her head bashed in while she was probably sound asleep. They don't see her as a threat. They see her as a victim. Because she is. Dahlia can shed a different light on all of this. And to be honest, having you testify will be a mistake."

He reared back as if my last words struck him like a blow to the face. "No. You promised me. The whole reason I agreed to fight this at all was so I could be the one to tell the story. It has to be me."

"And I'm telling you, if you take the stand, this won't end well for you. Not if you act like you did in that interview. Reed, you lied in that interview. You told them you hit her with a lamp. That's not true. Do you see what the prosecution is trying to do? If they convince the jury that you walked into that house with the murder weapon, then they make premeditation. It's over."

"I didn't. I'm sorry. I didn't mean for this to happen. I didn't intend to hurt Megan. I just wanted to protect my family. That's all. I don't know what happened. It's like I told you. I went on autopilot. I panicked. I just ... I didn't know what I was doing. If you let me explain."

"You don't seem to understand. This is the problem. If you lied in the interview, why should the jury believe you aren't lying on the stand? Reed. The murder weapon. You have to have an answer for it. You will be cross-examined about it. It will be fair game."

"I don't know. I told you. I just don't know. It's all a blur."

"I don't believe you. If *I* don't believe you, what do you think the jury is going to think?"

"I'm not lying. I'm not. I just couldn't think straight. Not then. I was thinking of Ian. I was thinking of Dahlia. I said I was sorry," he cried. "And I am. They need to know that. I wish this hadn't happened. All of it. I wish I'd never met

Megan. I wish I'd had the strength to say no. To leave her alone. To ... to honor my wife the way she deserves. So I can do that now. I failed her. I didn't protect her. But I can do it now."

Emma looked at him. "What do you mean you didn't protect her? How else could you have protected Dahlia?"

"I'm trying. My God. I'm trying," he said. Reed was on the verge of a full-fledged panic attack. Is this how it was the night he decided to go over to Megan Lewis's house? Had he been so out of his mind?

I went back and forth. The only way the jury could see this side of him was if I agreed to put him on the stand. He wasn't wrong. It was the deal we made the day I agreed to represent him. Let him testify. And yet, every legal instinct in me told me opening him up to Rafe Johnson's blistering cross-examination would be the biggest mistake.

"What if she's stronger than you think she is?" I said to him. "What if the thing Dahlia needs more than anything is to have a voice in this? Let's be real. You are going to spend a significant amount of time in jail for this. I'm doing everything I can to try to minimize it. To make sure it's not the rest of your life. But Dahlia is the one who has to pick up the pieces without you in the meantime. She has to start seeing herself as capable of it. Of being strong. Of being able to handle her life without you. You think you're protecting her by insulating her from the trial. I'm not so sure."

"You don't know Dahlia like I do," he said. "She's been through hell. Even before all of this. Losing Ian broke her. She should have died back then. She wanted to. But she got through it for Clara. Not for me."

"Right," I said. "And it's Clara holding her together now. I've seen it, Reed. She's fourteen going on forty. She needs her mother back. She needs you too. But she needs Dahlia. So let her stop being a victim and start being an advocate. Let her tell her story. Her fears. What Megan did to her. That's the only way there's any hope the jury will understand what you did."

"They'll never understand." His voice boomed. "They can never understand. And I won't do it. I'll fire you right now. I'll tell the judge I just want to represent myself. I'll go up there and tell them everything. How I went to that house because my wife was terrified. Because Megan tortured her for weeks without me knowing about it. Then when I did know about it, she wouldn't stop. She escalated. You didn't see her. You don't know. Dahlia was going to kill herself. She was going down that road again. Megan knew just how to twist the knife. Those stuffed animals? She kept them because they were Ian's. Megan took Ian's things and left that gruesome display. And that's my fault. Because I confided in her. I was weak and I told Megan how vulnerable Dahlia was. I thought if she understood, she wouldn't pressure me as much as she was to leave her. I just needed more time. There was no talking to her. Megan got incensed. And she broke into my home! She did those awful things. So I ended it. I made it so she couldn't hurt Dahlia ever again. I made sure she couldn't ever come near my family again!"

The walls seemed to vibrate with Reed's rage. He collapsed, sinking his head onto his arms, and sobbed.

"Okay," I said. "That's enough for today. We're not accomplishing anything here. But I heard you. We both have a lot to think about. For your part, you need to rest as much as you can. I need you fresh in the morning. I believe Rafe's going to rest his case after he calls the digital forensics experts. I don't think I'll have to make a final decision about who I'm putting on the stand first until at least the day after tomorrow."

Emma was up. She opened the door and beckoned the deputy to come back in. Reed rose to his feet. His head still slumped, his shoulders stooped, he waited for the deputies to come and take him back to holding. He said nothing more. He seemed mentally spent. So was I.

Emma and I drove in silence back to the office. It was after five by the time we got there. I'd told Miranda to close everything down after lunch. I wanted the building empty when I got back.

Emma stayed. She followed me up to the conference room where I'd laid out most of the trial materials. Stacks of papers and boxes of all our copies of the trial exhibits were laid out all over the table and along one wall.

I went to the mini fridge in the corner and pulled out two small bottles of wine. I tossed one to Emma.

"Thanks," she said, unscrewing the cap. She took a seat at one end of the table. I downed my bottle of wine in three huge gulps. It barely made a dent.

"You staying here tonight?" she asked.

"Probably. I need to think. To clear my head."

"You can't put him on the stand," she said. "You know that, right?"

"Yeah."

"He doesn't come off as sympathetic. He just comes off as angry. And you're right. That crap about the lamp is going to do exactly what Johnson thinks it's going to do. It makes Reed a liar in the eyes of the jury."

"Yeah."

I went over to the bookshelves. I didn't keep up my subscriptions to the bound volumes of the Michigan statutes anymore, but they still looked pretty. I ran my hands along the maroon and gold binding.

"It has to be Dahlia," I said.

"What you said, it made sense, Aunt Cass. If everyone keeps telling Dahlia … if they keep treating her like she's fragile. How can she ever be anything else?"

"She can't," I said.

"I just can't get over it. I can't wrap my head around it. How does Reed Karl end up thinking the only solution to his problem is bashing Megan Lewis's head in? That's what the jury is going to wonder too. They already are."

"I can prove she was there in the house, I think," I said. "I can use the camera footage from the neighbor. I can introduce the pictures of the toys she hung from the ceiling. When you put it into the context of Ian Karl's death, it raises questions about state of mind."

"And you have the psychologist. The side effects of Megan's medication."

Yes. I did. I picked up one of the file folders on the desk. It contained the crime scene photos. I flipped it open and pulled out one of the photos of Megan Lewis's body. The jury had seen this one today. I knew it was burned into their brains.

Emma tilted her head so she could see which photo I pulled. She sighed. "And none of that will weigh as heavily as that picture."

176

I sat down. Reed's desperate pleas still rang in my ears. If he lost his temper like that on the stand. If he let the jury see that type of rage, he would be convicted of first degree murder and dammit if I didn't think he might deserve it.

"He hated her," Emma said. "In those last few seconds, he hated her. There's no other way to view it, Aunt Cass."

Those last few seconds. Reed's rage. His stinging words at the courthouse.

Something shifted in me. A question. A word. I picked up another file. This one contained a copy of the transcript of Reed Karl's confession. I flipped through it. Reed had lost his temper in that interview room too.

Only ...

"Emma," I said. "This photograph. The one of Megan. It's the same one Detective Patel showed Reed when he was interrogated. When he came to offer up his confession."

"Right," she said. "It's really the worst of them. And that stupid business with the lamp. Why did he say it?"

"He's never going to tell us."

"I just don't get it," Emma said. "He admits to killing her. But he lies about what he used. Why?"

"Well, Rafe's going to argue it's the key to premeditation. That he walked into that house with a baseball bat with the intention of killing Megan. Then he took it with him and hid it or destroyed it when he left."

"But why lie?"

"If I were Rafe, I'm going to say it's more evidence of Reed's calculation. If he just picks up the first thing he can get his hands on, it's easier to argue he acted in the heat of the moment."

"Then it's not first degree murder," Emma said.

"Exactly."

"It bothers me that he's not telling *us* the truth though," she said.

"It bothers me too."

"Do you believe him that he just blacked out? The stress of it?"

I stared at the photographs. I looked at the transcript again. I went to the laptop at the end of the table. I fired it up and pulled up the video file of Reed's interview. It took a moment, but I queued up the portion where Reed broke down.

"There," I said.

"What?"

Patel was talking. He leaned far over and almost in Reed's face.

"You had no choice. Tell me how you had no choice, Reed. Tell me how you decided your only choice was to beat that woman to death!"

Reed had his head almost on the table. But at Patel's words, his head snapped up. There was an odd expression on his face. If I had to name it, it looked like shock. I rewound and replayed that portion. Again and again, as Patel shouted that he beat that woman to death, Reed reared back and up. I let the video play. Reed began to shout.

"I didn't ... you can't ... She was dangerous. I had to keep everybody safe."

"Who? Who were you keeping safe, Reed?"

"You won't believe me. You won't understand. It doesn't matter now anyway. I'm here to face up to what I did. I'm not asking for sympathy or your understanding."

"Really? It seems to me you've asked me about three times to understand you. So help me, because I'm having a really rough time understanding how you could do what you did."

"Do you have a family?"

"Yes. I have a wife. I have two sons."

"Then you should be able to relate."

"Relate? You think I can relate? No. No, Reed. I can't relate."

It was at this point Patel pulled out a photograph. It was the one sitting on the table next to me now. Megan Lewis's battered face. Unrecognizable. Blood everywhere. He laid it in front of Reed Karl.

"Here's your chance, Reed. Explain it so I can understand."

Reed collapsed. He let out an animalistic cry.

"God. Oh Megan. I'm so sorry. I'm so so sorry."

"Tell me what you did, Reed," Patel said. *"It's right here. You and me. There's only now. Tell me what you did."*

"I hit her. I must have ... Oh God. I hit her. I didn't want to hurt her. I didn't. I didn't. I just didn't have a choice. I didn't know any other way ..."

"Aunt Cass?" Emma said. "What's the problem?"

The air in my lungs burned. My knees felt weak. I sank into the nearest chair. I looked at Emma. She didn't see what I saw. It didn't dawn on her like it did me. Not yet.

I replayed that portion of the interview one more time. I'd been looking at this thing so hard, it's like I never saw it. The big picture. The one critical error Rodney Patel made when he interviewed Reed. I knew it. It was right there. The biggest lie Reed had told. I also knew there was one person who would be able to see through it too. Only I couldn't tell him.

But as I replayed that video for the third time that night, I knew in my soul that Reed Karl had never been in Megan Lewis's bedroom that night.

Chapter 18

"The state calls Detective Ronald Corning to the stand."

Ron Corning had served as one of a two-man digital forensics team for the county for a number of years. He was still young, in his mid-thirties. He climbed into the witness box and let the clerk swear him in.

Reed fidgeted beside me. He'd asked me one question this morning and I hadn't been able to give him an answer.

"Will you put me on the stand first?"

We knew Corning was likely Rafe's last witness. Judge Niedermayer had some other hearings scheduled this afternoon so in all likelihood, I wouldn't begin to present my case in chief until tomorrow morning. We had a lifetime to decide what to do. Only I'd already made up my mind.

I never answered Reed's question.

Rafe went through Corning's qualifications. He allowed Corning to explain how he became involved in the Megan

Lewis murder case. Then he steered the questioning to the real reason Ron Corning was here.

"Detective," Rafe said. "What was your role in the investigation of the murder of Megan Lewis?"

"I was called upon to analyze Detective Lewis's cell phone, personal computer, and tablet. I was also given the defendant's cell phone and computer."

Corning explained the technicalities of performing those types of forensics examinations. Rafe kept a rigid posture, then leaned forward on the lectern.

"Detective, I'd like to focus your attention on Megan Lewis's cell phone. Were you able to retrieve her text messages?"

"Yes."

Earlier, Rafe had moved for entry of a string of messages sent from Megan Lewis's phone to Reed. He had produced screenshots of most of those messages though Corning would be allowed to read them into the record.

"All right. Was Ms. Lewis communicating with the defendant by cell phone?"

"She was. I would say in the three to four months leading up to her death, Mr. Karl was the most frequent text contact Detective Lewis had."

"I see. How far back did the text exchanges go?"

"Detective Lewis received a text message from Reed Karl's phone on March 17th last year. They began a text exchange where they communicated several times a day every day over the course of the next fourteen months."

"How would you describe the character of those exchanges?"

"Objection," I said. "It's not up to this witness to interpret the character of those text exchanges. The transcript has been admitted as an exhibit. They speak for themselves."

Rafe looked frustrated, but I could tell he knew I'd made my point.

"Sustained, Mr. Johnson."

"All right," Rafe said. "Let's focus on a particular grouping of exchanges. Can you read the texts starting on March 25th of this year?"

"I can," Corning said.

Megan

"I'm sorry."

"You don't have to be sorry."

"I love you."

"I love you too."

"This isn't working. I can't wait around forever. I can't put my life on hold."

"I've never asked you to."

"I don't want to be some home wrecker. I hate that you put me in that position."

"I can't deal with this right now."

"You never can. You never could. You just took my heart and ripped it in two. You have everything. I have nothing. I have you.

Only I don't even have you. God. Reed. I can't eat. I can't sleep. I wait for you to call me. My heart leaps out of my chest when I hear your car in the driveway and my garage door opens. I'm losing my mind over it. I'm making mistakes I shouldn't make at work."

"I'll call you later."

"Fuck you!"

"Just stop."

"You say you love me then you blow me off. You don't love Dahlia. You said it. She makes you miserable. You think you're protecting her. But I think you're being even more cruel to her than you are to me."

"Enough. Please stop texting me here. I'll send you another phone number."

"If you don't tell her, I will."

"If you don't tell her, I will," Rafe said.

"That's the last text from that day, the 25th of March," Corning said.

"Did Mr. Karl text her back?"

"No," Corning said. "There are a series of texts from March 26th over the next few weeks. Detective Lewis texts him pretty much once a day for the next two and a half months. For the most part, he stops responding."

"For the most part? Does he respond at all?"

"He does. There is a text on May 25th. Megan Lewis, as you'll see from the transcripts, keeps imploring Mr. Karl to call her. She asks him to meet her on various occasions. On May 25th she texted him that she meant what she said."

"Can you read that exchange into the record?"

Megan

"I meant what I said, Reed."

"Stay away from us, Megan. It's over."

"All right, what else of significance did you learn from the text exchanges after May 26th?"

"May 26th was the last incoming text I found on Megan Lewis's phone from the cell phone registered to Reed Karl. When we searched Mr. Karl's phone, it appears he put a block in place."

"You're saying Reed blocked Megan Lewis's number?"

"Yes."

"Okay." Rafe stood a few feet away from the lectern, rubbing his chin. "Did she make any other calls or texts related to Reed Karl that you were able to find?"

"Yes. There is an outgoing call from Megan Lewis's phone to Dahlia Karl's phone on June 2nd at 1:45 p.m. It went unanswered."

"She tried to call Dahlia Karl four days before her murder?"

"A call was made from her phone to Dahlia Karl's phone, yes."

"After she threatened to tell Dahlia Karl about the affair she was having with her husband?"

"Yes. But as I said, that call went unanswered."

"She didn't get through."

"Objection," I said. "Once again, the transcript has been entered into the record. To the extent counsel is asking this witness to make his own personal interpretations about the meaning of any of these calls or texts, it's beyond the scope of his expertise and impermissible."

"I'll move on," Rafe said. "Detective Corning, were you able to trace the movement of both the defendant and victim's cell phones on June 5th and 6th of this year?"

"Yes. That was a significant window of time in light of what happened to Ms. Lewis."

"Of course. So what can you tell me about the movement of those two phones?"

"Ms. Lewis's phone pinged towers closest to the public safety building in Taney County. It remained at that location from 7:58 that morning until 4:12 p.m. at which point it traveled in a trajectory consistent with Ms. Lewis's route from the Taney County Sheriff's Department to her home on Lilac Court in Delphi."

"She went to work, then she went home. At least, that's what happened to her phone?"

"That was the phone's movement, yes. And it remained at her home location until it was retrieved as evidence in the early afternoon of June 6th."

"All right. What about Mr. Karl's phone during that same time frame?"

"Mr. Karl's phone moved from its home location at 7:13 a.m. It followed a trajectory consistent with a travel route to 1539 MacGregor Road in Brooklyn, Michigan."

"What's at the MacGregor Road location, if you know?"

"It's Mr. Karl's place of business."

"Okay. Then what happened?"

"Well, again, confining my analysis to the movement of the phone, at 5:37 p.m., there is movement along the same route going in the other direction. Until the phone pinged the tower at Paisley Farm. That's near Eden's Edge. The location closest to Mr. Karl's home. At which point, the phone remained stationary until 8:15 the next morning."

"Got it. I want to be clear. What does that tell you about Mr. Karl's movements?"

"Nothing."

"What do you mean?"

"I mean, I can only tell you about the movement of the cell phone. Not Mr. Karl."

"So if he left the house after say, 8:00 pm on the night of June 5th, he didn't take his cell phone with him. That's what you're saying?"

"That's what I'm saying."

"Okay. But what about a pattern? Were you able to discern a pattern of movement for Mr. Karl's cell phone?"

"Yes."

"Can you describe that pattern?"

"During the week, Monday through Friday, Mr. Karl's phone was generally found to travel the same trajectory. Leaving the tower area nearest his home between eight and eight thirty in the morning, arriving at the MacGregor Road, Brooklyn location and remaining there until roughly five to five thirty in the evening."

"Every day?"

"Most days."

"Where did the phone move on the other days?"

"Well, again, in most cases, it hits the tower in Brooklyn by nine in the morning. But there are a handful of days during the month where it travels northeast to the Detroit metro area during the standard workday. There are also a series of days where it travels during the regular workday to the tower closest to Ms. Lewis's home."

"A series of days. Is there a pattern there?"

"Yes. From June of last year up until April of this year, about every fifth day, the phone hits the tower near Ms. Lewis's and remains there from approximately noon to two p.m."

"He's meeting her at her home during his workday?"

"Once again," I said. "Detective Corning can testify about what his digital forensic analysis showed. Not the behavior of the defendant or the victim."

"Sustained."

"Okay. Fine. So back to the pattern of Mr. Karl leaving his house, or rather, his phone leaving the house and traveling along the path to his office. How consistent a pattern are we talking?"

"Very consistent. Monday through Friday. A roughly nine-to-five workday."

"To work, to home. Until he starts communicating with Megan Lewis. Then every fifth day, he's over at ... or the phone is over in the area of Megan Lewis's home."

"Yes."

"Do you know what is significant about every fifth day?"

"I know that on those days, Ms. Lewis's phone doesn't leave the range of her home tower."

"Her days off," Rafe said.

"Presumably."

"All right. So how long did you track this pattern of Reed Karl taking his phone with him as he drove to work then back?"

"Months. As far back as I was asked to analyze."

"He doesn't leave his phone behind when he leaves the house?"

"I can't answer that."

"Let me put it this way; based on the pattern of movement you found, would it surprise you if Mr. Karl left his house without taking his phone with him?"

"It would not be within his normal pattern of behavior, no."

"If he leaves the house, he takes his phone with him," Rafe said.

"Objection, asked and answered."

"Sustained."

Rafe put his hands up in capitulation. "It's all right. Thank you, Detective. I have no further questions."

"Ms. Leary?" Judge Niedermayer said.

I rose to my feet, shocked at how much Rafe had left out of Corning's report. It was an opening he knew I had to exploit.

Chapter 19

I FELT my fury rising as I walked up to the lectern. I glared at Rafe Johnson. He avoided my gaze. I took a breath. Angry as I was, it wouldn't come off well with the jury.

"Detective Corning," I started. "I just want to make a few things clear before we delve into the parts of your report Mr. Johnson conveniently forgot to ask you about." So much for my plan to contain my rage.

"Objection!" Rafe was fuming. I could almost feel the heat coming off of him behind me. I refused to even turn to look at him.

"Counselor," Judge Niedermayer said. "Let's do better."

I took another breath. "Detective Corning, regarding your analysis of Reed Karl's cell phone ... all you can do is track where the phone was within a specific range at a specific time, isn't that right?"

"That's correct. We can triangulate its location based on which cell towers it pings."

"You know where the cell tower's precise location is, not the phone's. Correct?"

"That's correct."

"Anything else ... even the conclusion that Mr. Karl's phone was at home or at his office ... that's an inference based on where the tower is, not the phone."

"Correct."

"You can't even be certain that Reed Karl was in possession of his phone during any of these readings you took, isn't that right?"

"I'm not sure what you mean."

"Oh, I think you are. But to be clear. Let's take what you said about this pattern of movement during the last year. It's a pattern of movement regarding the phone. You can't say for sure whether Reed Karl was the one carrying the phone."

"Well, no."

"Okay. I'm just trying to make sure we all understand the parameters of your analysis."

"Yes. I'm tracking the movement of the cell phone. That's all."

"Thank you. Now I'm curious. You testified about text exchanges between the defendant and Ms. Lewis. But that's not the only data you were asked to analyze, right?"

"That was one aspect of my analysis, yes."

"But you also were able to pull the camera rolls of both of those phones, right? Mr. Karl's and Ms. Lewis's."

"Of course."

"Great. But Mr. Johnson didn't ask you about those photographs at all, did he?"

"No."

"Right. So now I'd like to. Let's talk about Mr. Karl's cell phone first. I'd like to direct your attention to what's been marked as Defense Exhibits Seven through Thirteen. Can you tell me what those are?"

Corning cleared his throat. "Yes. Those are photographs retrieved from Reed Karl's camera roll on his phone."

"And are you able to determine when those photographs were taken?"

"They're time stamped and geotagged. Yes."

"Geotagged?"

"The location where they were taken is part of the metadata we can look at."

"All right. When were they taken and where were they taken?"

"All seven photographs were taken within three minutes of each other on May 29th of this year."

"May 29th. So a little more than a week before Megan Lewis's death."

"That's correct."

"Your Honor," I said. "I'd like to move for admission of Defense Exhibits Seven through Thirteen."

"Objection, Your Honor, relevance."

"Are you kidding?" I said. "Your Honor, these photographs were referred to in Reed Karl's interview with Detective Patel. The interview the jury was allowed to hear in its entirety. Mr. Karl showed Detective Patel these photographs during that interview. Never mind the fact that they are critically relevant to the defense being put forth in this case. Mr. Johnson opened the door about as wide as it gets."

"I have to agree, Mr. Johnson. They're admitted. You may proceed, Ms. Leary."

"Thank you." I went to my laptop and brought the first photograph up on the screen. It was a wide shot of Reed and Dahlia's bedroom. The toys were hanging from the ceiling fan with makeshift nooses.

"What are we looking at, Detective?" I said. "If you could describe it for the transcript."

"These appear to be photos of the defendant's bedroom as I understand it. There are toys hanging from ropes on a ceiling fan."

I advanced the photos, zeroing in on perhaps the most disturbing one, the teddy bear with its throat cut, its head lolling to the side. One of the female jurors behind me gasped.

"Once again, you found these on Reed Karl's phone?"

"That's correct."

I advanced the next photograph and had Corning describe it. It was a stuffed elephant, also with its throat slit. The one after that was a plastic dinosaur hanging upside down.

"All right," I said. "Let's move on. You also searched Megan Lewis's laptop and tablet, isn't that right?"

"That's correct."

"Incident to that analysis, you retrieved Megan Lewis's search history on her laptop, didn't you?"

"Yes."

"How far back did you go?"

"Several months. She didn't actually use her laptop very much. It appeared she preferred to use her tablet and phone. That's where the majority of her weekly screen time came from."

"Thanks," I said. "But I didn't ask you that. I want to talk about the search history you did find on the laptop. Specifically, what was the nature of her search history on June 2nd of this year?"

Corning straightened his tie. If I was pissing him off, he didn't show it. "There were a series of internet searches involving what levels of arsenic were fatal to a human being."

"A human being. Not just a human being. Specifically, what did she search for?"

"She made inquiries about the fatal dosage or concentration of arsenic in a one-hundred-and-twenty-pound female."

"Got it. Thank you. And how about this one? You searched her documents on that laptop too, didn't you?"

"Yes."

"Detective, what was the last saved document you retrieved off Megan Lewis's laptop?"

"Objection," Rafe said. "Your Honor, I'd like a sidebar."

Niedermayer waved us forward. "Go," she said to Rafe.

"Once again, Ms. Leary is headed toward irrelevant, highly prejudicial material."

"Once again," I said. "The letter Corning found was specifically referred to by Reed Karl in his police interview. He saw it. He said the contents of it were partly responsible for the actions he said he took. Frankly, it was irresponsible of Rafe not to get into this stuff on direct. But he certainly can't try to ignore it now."

"Your Honor, there's no evidence this document was ever seen by anybody other than Megan Lewis."

"There absolutely is. Reed Karl referenced it in his confession."

"He referenced a letter that he admits nobody ever saw but him. There's no evidence these things are connected."

I sighed. "The jury can make an inference. This didn't exist in a vacuum."

"Rafe, she's right," Niedermayer said. "And you know you're wasting everyone's time with this. The defendant's confession interview has already been admitted into evidence. If anything else comes up with this witness or any others that was directly referred to in that interview, you're stuck with it. Are we clear?"

"Yes," Rafe said. We went back to our positions.

"All right," I said to Corning. "I was asking you about the last document you retrieved off of Megan Lewis's computer. Let me refer you to Defense Exhibit Fourteen marked for identification. Can you tell me what it is?"

"It appears to be a copy of the letter I retrieved and saved in Ms. Lewis's document file."

"When was that letter created?"

"It was created at 3:18 a.m. on May 14th. Authored by Megan Lewis. Or at least, it was authored during her account login."

"Okay. I move for the entry of the letter."

Rafe stood granite-jawed behind me, but didn't raise another objection.

"Detective Corning," I said. "Will you please read the letter into the record?"

Corning brought the paper closer to his face. In a clear voice, he read it. "Dahlia. You lose. Reed doesn't love you. You know it. You're hanging on to something that doesn't exist anymore. I know what you're trying to do. You think you can keep him tied to you. All you have to do is threaten to kill yourself. We both know you're never going to do it. But maybe you should. Maybe you should do everybody a favor and leave the planet. We all know you're a terrible mother. And we know why. You aren't a good person. I know the game you're playing. I'm on to you. You'd better be careful. Very careful. Megan."

"May 14th," I said. "Megan Lewis wrote this letter roughly three weeks before her death?"

"It appears so, yes."

"She didn't just write it though. You know that it was printed as well, isn't that right?"

"It was printed, yes. A hard copy was also found among the papers on Ms. Lewis's desk."

The jury had already heard Reed's confession where he described finding the letter taped to the front door and what he'd done with it. I would underscore it in my closing argument.

"Detective Corning. I'd like to direct your attention to three photographs that have been marked as Defense Exhibits Eighteen through Twenty-one. Can you tell me what they are?"

"They are photographs retrieved from Megan Lewis's hard drive."

"What do they depict?"

"They are shots of the same woman, asleep in what appears to be her bed."

"Who is the woman in those pictures, Detective Corning?"

"I didn't know at the time, it later came to my attention that these photographs are of Dahlia Karl."

After further authentication, I moved for admission of the three photographs. I then displayed them on the overhead screen for the jury to see. I studied their reactions. They seemed disturbed, as they should be.

"When were these photographs taken?" I asked.

"I can't answer that. But they were dated May 27th of this year. That's when they were uploaded to the hard drive."

I scrolled through the pictures. One was taken from the foot of Dahlia's bed. The other two were close-ups of her face.

"Uploaded from where?" I asked.

"I can't say. We didn't find these photographs on Ms. Lewis's phone. Not in her camera roll or in any of her recently deleted pictures."

"Detective, did you have occasion to review Megan Lewis's social media profiles in the course of your investigation?"

"Yes. She was on Facebook, but she wasn't very active there. She hadn't posted in several months prior to her murder."

"Okay, I'd like to show you what's been marked as Exhibit Twenty-three. Do you recognize it?"

"Yes. That's Megan Lewis's Facebook profile picture. We found the same picture in her camera roll."

I moved to admit the picture then showed it on the screen for the jury. "Detective, can you verbally describe what we're looking at here?"

"Ms. Lewis is standing in front of what looks like a hibiscus bush."

"What is she wearing?"

"Uh. She's got on a sweatshirt. A hoodie. Central Michigan University."

"Is there anything distinctive about it?"

"What do you mean?"

"Would you describe it as a new sweatshirt, old?"

"I wouldn't know. It looks to be fairly well worn. Oh, but there are bleach stains on the right arm."

"Thank you. One last thing," I said. "Back to what I asked you at the beginning. On the evening of June 5th, you indicated that Reed Karl's cell phone pinged the tower closest to his home, right?"

"That's correct."

"And remained there, for the next, what, fourteen hours, give or take?"

"That's correct. The phone did. As you were so careful to have me point out, I track the phone, not the user."

"Got it. But you also testified at length about this pattern of movement. Right? You said over the course of days, weeks, months, the pattern of movement of that phone was predictable. Almost, immutable. Isn't that right?"

"There was a clear pattern."

"You indicated the pattern was that Reed took his phone with him wherever he went. That was your inference."

"That you objected to. Yes. That was my inference."

"And yet, on June 5th into the early morning hours of June 6th, the phone stayed home."

"In the evening and through the night, it pinged the tower closest to Mr. Karl's home. Yes."

"Thank you," I said. "I have no further questions for this witness."

"Mr. Johnson?" The judge said.

Johnson sprang up. "Just want to touch on what you just said. Reed Karl's phone moved around quite a bit day to day, didn't it?"

"I don't know what you mean by quite a bit. There was a pattern of movement. That's all I'm saying. And honestly, within that day to day, it was pretty stationary."

"Home to work. Work to home. Then home to work to Megan Lewis's house then back to work."

"Roughly. Yes."

"So if Mr. Karl left his home without his phone, that would be outside of the normal pattern of movement you analyzed?"

"Yes. I've said that. Yes."

"And probably deliberate."

"Objection," I said. "I could pretty much run down the list, Your Honor. Asked and answered. Counsel is leading. Counsel is making speeches. He's asking this witness to speculate outside the scope of his expertise."

Niedermayer raised her hand in submission. "I've got it all. Sustained. Please move on, Mr. Johnson."

Rafe pursed his lips. "All right. I have no further questions for this witness."

"Call your next one," Niedermayer said.

Rafe leaned over this table and whispered something to his paralegal. He shook his head then handed Rafe a piece of paper. Rafe scowled as he read it. Then he nodded. He turned and went back to the lectern.

"At this time, the prosecution rests."

Beside me, Reed shuddered. It was late in the schedule Judge Niedermayer set for the day. She slipped her reading glasses on.

"All right. We'll reconvene first thing in the morning where Ms. Leary can call her first witness for the defense. Everybody satisfied with that?"

"Yes, Your Honor," I said. Rafe repeated my words. Niedermayer banged her gavel and dismissed the jury. I stayed on my feet. Reed was like a live wire to my left. We would have a precious few moments to talk before he was taken back to his cell today. I knew what he would demand. And I knew the fight I had in front of me.

Chapter 20

TODAY, the deputies cleared space for us in the law library at the end of the hall. As we walked out of the courthouse, the last person I expected to see rose on wobbly legs from a bench along the wall.

"Dahlia," Reed choked out the word. We had waited a few minutes after the rest of the courtroom cleared. The deputies had done a decent job making sure the members of the local media had gone down in the elevator. But there was one straggling young reporter walking out of the women's restroom across the hall. She immediately saw an opportunity and pulled out her cell phone.

"Mrs. Karl, do you believe your husband is innocent?"

Dahlia's jaw dropped. Her already pale complexion went almost translucent. There was something wrong with her. I hadn't seen her in a couple of weeks but she looked as if she'd dropped twenty pounds. Her skin had a gray pallor to it.

"Leave her alone," Reed shouted. "It's okay, honey. I'm okay. Everything's going to be okay. I love you."

Every word he said was captured on the young reporter's cell phone as she kept recording. I motioned to one of the deputies. He gave a casual glance over his shoulder but otherwise did nothing to intervene.

Rolling my eyes, I opened the jury room adjacent to Judge Niedermayer's courtroom. "Wait in here," I said to Dahlia. "Reed, come with me. Now!"

Dahlia was in tears. She did as I asked her. I glared at the reporter. She couldn't be more than twenty-five, maybe younger. I'll give her credit for realizing I meant business. Her shoulders slumped and she climbed onto the same elevator her local colleagues had just ridden down.

Reed was agitated. He paced at one end of the room after I shut the door, giving us as much privacy as we were going to get. I could depend on the deputies to at least keep anyone from coming into this room for the next few minutes.

"You have to make sure she's okay," Reed said.

"Dahlia isn't my client, you are."

"She's my wife! She's the whole reason for any of this."

"You need to sit down and calm down. Things are about to get much harder."

"No," he said, gripping the back of the chair in front of him. "I think things are finally about to get really simple. Just put me on the stand tomorrow. Let me tell my story. Let me tell them what I did and why I did it. After that, I don't care what happens."

"Really? Are you really sure about that?"

"You've done everything you said you would do, Cass. The jury got to see what Megan did when she broke into my house. Now I can explain what it means. They have to know those were Ian's things. She did it to torment Dahlia specifically. To punish me because I couldn't be what she wanted me to be. That's all my fault too. So let me take responsibility for it."

"Sit down," I said. I took a seat on one side of the table. He stood at the end of it.

"I feel good. I finally feel like I can take control of my life again. I don't care what Rafe Johnson asks me. I'm not afraid of him anymore."

"Sit. Down," I said with more force. Reed's face went slack. But he did what I asked.

"They're going to see," he said. "When I tell them how it was, they're going to see. My story will be out there. Clara might hate me for the rest of her life, but at least she'll have a chance to know."

I met Reed's eyes. Time seemed to slow down and the room came sharply into focus. Things that mattered. Things that didn't. Things I could control. Things I couldn't.

"I'm not putting you on the stand, Reed," I said, my voice sounding lower than usual.

"She drove me to it," he said. "I know I can't blame Megan. Of course I can't. And if I had it to do over again, I see now I could have made a different choice. But ..."

"You are not taking the stand in your own defense. I will not allow it. I cannot allow it."

"You have to. That was the deal."

"No. The deal was, I present the best defense I can for you

within the bounds of my duty. Putting you on the stand is outside the bounds of my duty."

"What are you talking about?"

"You know what I'm talking about. You've been lying to everyone since the very beginning, Reed. God. I'd like to take a baseball bat to you right about now. I told you when I agreed to represent you that you'd better not lie to me. But you have been. Every single conversation we've ever had has been a lie. I must have been out of my mind taking this case. Do you have any idea what this whole thing has cost me?"

His face didn't change. His eyes searched my face. There was no denial there. No indignant declaration. He just looked at me.

I took a breath. I knew I should never ask. We don't. Defense attorneys walk a fine line. Some people think we're the scum of the earth for it. But I knew, I've always known, I am fighting on the right side of the justice system. Even when my clients are guilty. I believe in the Constitution. I believe in Due Process. I believe in my unique role in defending it. I am necessary. I am a warrior for the system as much as any prosecutor, judge, or law enforcement officer.

"No more lies, Reed. Not to me. I can't put you on the stand because I cannot suborn perjury."

He started to shake his head.

"Because you didn't kill Megan Lewis. You weren't in her house that night. You told me one thing that was true. You told me you were protecting someone. You were. You still are. But I can't."

"You don't know anything," he said.

"Reed, you didn't kill Megan. And I can prove it."

A muscle jumped in his jaw. He folded his hands in front of him. There was just the tiniest flicker of his eyes. I knew the truth. He knew it too.

"You weren't in her house that night," I said. "You want everyone to believe it was a slip of the tongue when you told the police what you hit Megan with. It wasn't a lamp. The trauma of the moment didn't short-circuit your memory. You didn't black out. You weren't just distraught and out of your mind when you made that confession. You were lying."

"Cass, don't …"

He was right. I should stop. The best thing for me professionally was to stop asking the question. Don't go down this road. Pretend I could remain ignorant. Plausible deniability. Only I couldn't. Because there was something more important at stake.

"You think you're protecting Dahlia, but you're not. She needs help, Reed. Real help. I can see to it that she gets it."

"Stop it."

"I believe it all. Maybe the jury will too. Megan *did* become unhinged. She threatened your family. She was taking very powerful psychotropic medication and she was mixing it with alcohol. That's going to come out. I'll make sure of it. But the only way I'm going to put you on the stand is if you retract your confession and tell the truth."

"No."

"She snapped. I believe that. I can even believe in her mind … in the reality she constructed … Dahlia thought she was protecting herself or you or your family. She saw Megan as a threat because she was a threat. But you can't take the fall for her. You know you can't."

All color drained from his face. He started to tremble. For a moment, it looked like he'd be sick the way he was in Rodney Patel's interview room.

"You didn't kill Megan. But Dahlia did. That's what happened, isn't it? You've been very specific about the things you've said. You were protecting Dahlia. I believe in your mind, that's what you're doing. But you aren't. It's a lie. Dahlia killed Megan and you're trying to take the fall for it."

Something seemed to break inside of him. His shoulders dropped. Beads of sweat rolled down his face. It was as if his body was no longer physically capable of holding the lie.

"You cannot go down for Dahlia," I said. "It's killing you, Reed."

"Yes," he said. "I can. I can because none of this would have happened if I hadn't brought Megan into our lives. So it is my fault. I did this. And now I have a chance to make it right."

"How is this right? Reed. My God. It isn't just about Dahlia at this point. It never was. It's about Clara. You have a duty to protect her too."

"I am! I'm making sure she can be with her mother."

"Her mother isn't who she should be with!" I yelled. "Dahlia is sick, Reed. Very sick. She killed Megan. You know it. Look at me. You know it. You've known it all along."

I charged him. Real rage took hold of me. I grabbed Reed by the shoulders. "Reed, the truth. No more lies. This isn't about you. It's about Clara. That's who you need to be thinking about. She's not safe."

"No," he said. "Dahlia would never hurt Clara."

"She hurt Ian," I said. It was a low blow. Part of me hated myself for saying it. "I'm not saying she meant to. Accidents happen. But Ian died on Dahlia's watch. She didn't keep him safe. And she can't keep Clara safe either. Killing Megan didn't keep anyone safe. It's your job to protect Clara, not Dahlia. Don't you see that? You can start right now by telling me the truth once and for all. It was Dahlia. She killed Megan that night. Not you. Say it. For Clara's sake. Say it!"

He went rigid. I felt something snap inside of me.

"Say it," I said, the words tasting bitter in my mouth. "It's just us now. Say it. Admit it. Dahlia killed Megan."

"I don't ... I can't ..."

"Say it!" I shouted. There was still a chance. I could still walk out of this room and not hear his next words. But I didn't.

"Yes!" he shouted back. "Yes. Goddammit. Yes. But I left her no choice."

He dropped his chin to his chest. He took a great, heaving sigh. It was almost as if I could hear something breaking inside of him. Like a yoke he'd been trying to carry.

"She didn't know what she was doing," he whispered. "Dahlia wanted to protect herself. And Clara. Against what I brought into our family. It's not her fault."

"She beat that woman to death."

"You can't prove that. Nobody can prove that. I made it so they can't. I made it so Clara and Dahlia can have a life. They can have the peace they deserve."

"Reed, Dahlia killed Megan. Think about that."

"They can't prove it!" he shouted.

"No. Not yet. But if you force me into it, I will. I'll prove it."

"No," he said. He lifted his head. If something broke inside of him a moment ago, something else reformed at that moment. A realization. A new plan. "You can't do anything. When you walk out of this room, you can't even tell anyone. This conversation is protected by attorney-client privilege. I'm not about to commit a crime. I'm not about to hurt somebody. You are ethically bound to keep this secret forever. Just like I will."

My blood roared in my ears. I wanted to argue the point. He knew I couldn't. He was right that I was now trapped in this forever. I couldn't tell Rafe Johnson or the judge. I couldn't go to Rodney Patel. That was the price I would have to pay for asking the question. I knew it. But I asked anyway.

"Let me talk to Dahlia," I said. "Reed. It doesn't have to be jail for her. She needs real mental health help. We can get that for her."

"What, at some state hospital? No, thank you. She won't survive it."

"They will send you to prison for the rest of your life."

"No," he said. "You're winning. You're making the jury see how everything happened."

"It's a lie!"

"It's not a lie. Megan tormented my family. She was a threat. I was terrified of what she was going to do. So you make sure the jury understands that. I can tell them."

"No, Reed, no. You can't. You've got the law right. You've got my ethical duties right. I can't tell anyone about this conversation. I can't even tell Dahlia. But I will not put you on the stand when I know you're going to lie."

He squeezed his eyes shut. "You have to. You have to do what I say."

"I most certainly do not. Has it occurred to you that Clara might be in more danger with you going to jail?"

His eyes snapped open. "Clara needs her mother. Dahlia needs Clara."

"You're right about that last part. But what kind of mother do you think Dahlia can really be to her now? She's barely functioning. She's sick. She's mentally ill and what you're doing is denying her the ability to get help. She snapped once. What makes you think she won't snap again?"

"She won't. I know her."

"Really? Did you know she was capable of bashing Megan's face in?"

He winced.

"No. You didn't. And that was Rodney Patel's great mistake in that interview. The reason you said the wrong thing about the murder weapon. Because you didn't know how Megan was killed. You didn't know if she was shot or strangled or suffocated or stabbed. Not until Patel said it, then showed you that crime scene photograph. That's when you snapped and said what you said. It's right there. If you get on the stand and tell the truth now, I think the jury will believe you. I think there's a real chance of an acquittal."

"I won't do it," he said. "I made my choice. I chose Dahlia."

"And I want you to choose Clara."

"I'm sorry you can't see things the way I do. But this is the only way, Cass. My way. What happened to Megan was my fault, even if I wasn't the one who killed her that night."

There it was. He'd said it. There could be no room for error. No misunderstanding. No equivocation. I felt like I had just allowed myself to be shackled to him. We were headed for a cliff and I would have no choice but to head over it with him now.

"You're my lawyer," he said. "Please, Cass. Put me on the stand. Let me finish this."

"I will not. I will withdraw from the case, first."

"Judge Niedermayer isn't going to let you. Not in the middle of trial. And you can't tell her why you want to."

"What do you want me to do?" I said, my tone growing desperate.

"Finish what you started," he said. "Call the witnesses you want to call. But I will not retract my confession. It stands."

"Then let me call Dahlia as a witness."

"No," he said. "She stays out of this. I don't even want her in the courthouse again."

"Reed ..."

"No! You won't put me on the stand. I don't agree with it, but I can abide by it. But you're still my lawyer. You still represent me. And I am telling you, Dahlia stays out of this. I don't even want you talking to her again. Stay away from the house. You talk to me and me alone."

Something rose up inside of me. It was a rage, an anger, a frustration I could barely contain. I leaned in close.

"Or what?" I said.

"Please," he whispered. "I'm sorry for what happened. That's the truth. And I'm sorry that you feel trapped inside of it with me now. But you are. Dahlia isn't going to hurt anyone."

"She already has. How do I know she's not a threat to ..."

"She isn't."

"Reed, has she admitted to you what she did?"

"Stop."

"I need to know."

"No. You don't. I am your client. This is almost over. So let's just finish what we started and you let me worry about my family. Dahlia will get help. I'll make sure of it."

"How are you going to do that from the inside of a jail cell?"

"As soon as that jury reads its verdict ... no ... as soon as they walk out of that courtroom to deliberate, that is no longer your problem."

Things went very still for me again. It was the one thing Reed said today that I could agree with. It would no longer be my problem. But the road from here to there was deadly.

There was a soft knock on the door. "We need to get him back, Leary," one of the deputies said.

"I'm sorry, Cass. I really am."

"So am I."

I left him there. I couldn't stomach looking at him anymore. And yet, there was that small part of me that felt empathy for the position he'd put himself in. In his own twisted, misguided way, he really did think he was protecting his family.

I walked out of the room. I took the stairs, not the elevator. It was an unseasonably warm November day as I took the side door out of the courthouse.

I had an innocent client. What a rare thing, that. Only I couldn't tell anyone. Not the police. Not the judge. God. Not even Miranda or Emma. They weren't lawyers. They weren't bound by the same privilege that I was. I wouldn't even tell Jeanie. I would carry this burden myself.

I took a faltering step. Eric. Of everyone in my life, he was the one I wanted to tell. Only I couldn't. Not now. He didn't work for me. He wasn't on this case anymore. It was just me. Alone.

As I walked down the sidewalk toward the parking lot, two Woodbridge County deputies stood at the light talking to a third deputy wearing a Taney County uniform. He was one of Megan Lewis's colleagues.

I had to get by them to get to the crosswalk. They saw me. The Woodbridge County boys had no expression on their faces. The Taney County one held open disdain. He leaned forward as I walked by and spit on the ground just where I was about to step. Then all three of them turned their backs on me.

Alone, I thought. No. I was worse than alone. To them, I was the enemy. And there was nothing I could do now but let them believe it.

Chapter 21

AFTER AN HOUR of heated oral argument, Judge Niedermayer granted my request to treat my first witness for the defense as hostile. Fuming, Rafe walked back to his table and sat down in his chair so hard, it scooted back a few inches and emitted an echoing squeak throughout the courtroom.

"The defense calls Pamela Corso to the stand," I said.

Pamela was already red-faced and fighting back tears as she took the stand and swore her oath. She lifted her chin in defiance as I stepped up to the lectern.

"Ms. Corso," I started. "Could you please explain how you knew the victim in this case, Megan Lewis?"

The question seemed to shock her. She had been ready to verbally spar. That would come. But for now, I had invited her to talk about something she wanted to.

Pamela reached for the water glass in front of her. She took a sip. Up went that chin again. When she spoke, she spoke loud and straight into the microphone.

"Megan was my best friend. She was the closest thing I had to a sister and I know she felt the same way about me."

"How did you meet?"

"We live in the same neighborhood. We met maybe ten years ago. We became walking partners first then best friends."

"So you were in each other's lives for over a decade?" I asked.

"Yes."

"How often did you talk?"

"As we got to know each other, I'd say pretty much daily. Megan and I, along with a few other women in the neighborhood, became close."

"Would you say you knew Megan Lewis better than most people?"

"I would say we were extremely close."

"You told each other everything?"

"I think so."

"You talked about your relationships? Who you were dating?"

"Of course."

"She was the maid of honor at your wedding, wasn't she?"

"Yes."

"Did she ask you for advice about men she dated?"

"Advice? I guess so. Yes."

"Megan Lewis never married, isn't that right?"

"That's right."

"In the course of your friendship, how many serious dating relationships did Megan Lewis have, if you recall?"

Pamela looked skyward. She murmured to herself and counted on her fingers. "Megan didn't date a lot of people in the time I've known her. She tended to date one person for a long time before moving on. I want to say she had maybe four or five serious boyfriends in the time I've known her."

"I see," I said. "When did you find out about Megan's relationship with Reed Karl?"

"Maybe a year ago. I knew she was involved with somebody, but at first, she wouldn't tell me anything. She said it was too new. But she was happy."

"She was happy," I said. "At what point did you learn that Reed Karl was the man making her so happy?"

"Last winter. Megan and I met for lunch. She told me his name. I didn't know Reed. Megan told me he was married but in the process of divorcing his wife."

"How did you feel about that?"

"I was worried. Really worried. I told Megan it was a mistake. I begged her to get out of it. But Megan was head over heels for Reed. She believed he was going to leave his wife for her. Even though I warned her that would probably never happen."

"How did Megan react when you told her that?"

"What do you mean?"

"Well, was she upset with you?"

Pamela looked down. At first, I thought I'd have to prompt her again. Finally, she took a breath and looked at me. "She was upset."

"She was more than upset, wasn't she? Megan was angry with you?"

"She was angry, yes."

"She didn't want to hear what you had to say, did she?"

"She was my friend. We didn't always agree on things."

"Sure. But it put a strain on your friendship, didn't it?"

Pamela's eyes narrowed. "She didn't like talking about it."

"About Reed. Would you say that's because she knew you didn't approve of her dating a married man?"

"It wasn't for me to approve or disapprove. Megan was a grown woman."

"Sure. But isn't it true she stopped answering your texts? Canceled plans with you? She froze you out for a while, didn't she?"

"I wouldn't say that."

"You understand that Megan's cell phone records, her texts, they've been entered as evidence. We've seen them. We know what she was texting to you. Or rather ... that she wasn't responding to texts you sent."

"She was mad at me, yes."

"Because you voiced your concerns about her dating Reed Karl?"

"Yes."

"She ghosted you for a time, isn't that right?"

"Yes."

"All right," I said. "Had that ever happened before?"

"I don't know what you mean."

"Well, you just indicated that during your friendship, Megan had just a few serious dating relationships. Had you and Megan ever had conflict with each other relating to the men she dated before?"

"I don't remember any, no."

"But Reed was different, wasn't he?"

"He was married," Pamela snapped.

"Right. He was married. Had Megan ever dated a married man before, to your knowledge?"

"No. That wasn't ... Megan wasn't like that."

"Wasn't the type of person who would date a married man."

"No. Not at all."

"Okay. While Megan was dating Reed, did you ever see them together? Did she ever introduce you?"

"She ... once."

"What happened? How did that come about?"

"I don't know."

"You don't know. It was by accident, wasn't it? You told the police you stopped by Megan's house because she hadn't been responding to your texts, isn't that right?"

"That's what I told them, yes."

"So do you remember what happened when you stopped by Megan's house and found her with Reed?"

"I didn't find them together. It wasn't like I walked in on them unannounced. He was just there. I stopped by on my lunch hour one day."

"And Reed Karl was there. If you recall, where was Reed's car parked?"

"What?"

"Was it in the driveway?"

"No."

"You told the police you wouldn't have stopped if you'd seen Reed's car in the driveway, isn't that right?"

"Yeah."

"So where was his car?"

"It was in Megan's garage."

"What did you think about that?"

She let out a great sigh. "This is stupid. I don't know what you want me to say. It was gross, okay? I found the whole thing gross."

"Because he was married."

"Yes."

"Because he and Megan were trying to hide their relationship. By parking his car in her garage."

"Yes."

"Okay. You got in an argument that day with Reed and Megan, didn't you?"

"Yes."

"What happened?"

"I was just angry. I didn't like that they were sneaking around. You don't sneak around if you're planning on leaving your wife. I was just so frustrated that Megan couldn't see that."

"That's what you told her, isn't it?"

"Yes."

"How did she react?"

"What difference does it make? How does any of this make any difference?"

"Your Honor," I said. "Will you please instruct the witness to answer questions put before her?"

"Your Honor." Rafe stepped up. "I'm afraid I have to object. The witness has a point. How is any of this relevant?"

"This witness gave a statement to the police that later led them to interview Reed Karl as a person of interest. The character of their relationship as well as Megan Lewis's behavior leading up to June 6th is absolutely relevant."

"All right, I'll allow it. Briefly," Niedermayer said.

"Ms. Corso, how did Megan Lewis react when you encountered her with Reed Karl at her home?"

"She was livid, okay? So was I. I tried to make her see that he wouldn't be needing to hide his car in her garage and meet with her in the middle of the afternoon when his wife probably thought he was at work if he was planning on leaving her. Megan got angry. She got upset."

"She didn't just get upset, did she? She got violent, didn't she?"

"She didn't get violent. That's ... I know what you're doing. I know what you're trying to make me say."

"I'm only trying to get you to tell the truth. You've already described this incident to the police. Your statement is entered into the record. I'm now asking you to give it in your own words."

"She threw a dish. She got angry and threw a dish."

"She threw it at you?"

"She threw it near me. It broke. She wasn't trying to hurt me. She was just really angry. I think ... she knew, okay? I think deep down she knew I was right. That Reed wasn't acting like somebody who was going to leave their wife for her. That was upsetting. He was jerking her around and I didn't like it. I said as much."

"Did Reed get angry that day?"

"What?"

"Well, you said Megan threw a dish. What was Reed doing during all of this?"

"He was ... I don't know. He was just there. He was just ... trying to calm her down. He asked me to leave."

"All right. Do you recall when this incident occurred?"

"I don't know."

"Would it reflect your recollection to read your statement to the police?"

"No. I don't know. It was in April. Sometime in April."

"Two months before Megan died?"

"Two months before that monster bashed her head in, you mean!" Pamela shouted.

"Your Honor," I started.

"She's your witness," Judge Niedermayer said. "You put her on the stand, Ms. Leary. But Ms. Corso, I would remind you to answer questions as they are asked."

"Let's move on," I said. "Ms. Corso, you also told the police about an incident that occurred while you were driving in a car with Megan Lewis, did you not?"

She didn't answer. Pamela crossed her arms in front of her and stared at the wall.

"All right," I said. "The incident with the smashed plate. That's not the last time you saw Megan, was it?"

"No."

"You communicated again a couple of weeks later, isn't that right?"

"Yes."

"She called you."

"Yes."

"Was it to make amends?"

"It was to ... she called me. She apologized for losing her temper, yes."

"What did she tell you in her apology?"

"Objection," Rafe said. "Counsel is asking for hearsay testimony."

"Your Honor, I am asking for this witness to testify as to her knowledge of Megan Lewis's state of mind in the weeks prior to her death. It's not being offered to prove the truth of the matter Ms. Lewis asserted. Only as a window into how she was feeling during this time frame as she expressed it to her best friend."

Judge Niedermayer tapped her pencil. "Tread carefully. The witness may answer."

"What was the question?" Pamela asked.

"You said Megan Lewis called you and apologized for her behavior when you saw her at her house the previous week. Do you recall what reasoning she gave you for her behavior?"

"She was just upset. That's all. She loved Reed. She said she loved Reed and that it made her crazy sometimes."

"Objection! Your Honor, I would ask that the witness's last statement be stricken from the record. Ms. Leary is absolutely trying to offer this statement as proof of the matter asserted. Her entire defense is based on victim blaming."

"She wasn't crazy!" Pamela shouted. "You asked me what she said. She wasn't crazy!"

Judge Niedermayer banged her gavel. "Enough. The objection is sustained. The jury will disregard that last statement."

"Your Honor," I said. "You overruled an objection regarding this exact statement. With all due respect, how can you strike the answer to a question you just ruled was permissible?"

Greta Niedermayer was a cool cucumber. She eyed me. I had the sense if she could fling that gavel at my head, she would have. At the same time, she knew I was right.

"Move on, Ms. Leary," she said.

I squared my shoulders. "Ms. Corso, you made plans to see Megan after that apology, didn't you?"

"We went out to dinner the next week, yes. I suggested to Megan that we get together for drinks on her next day off."

"All right. So let's focus on that night. Where did you go to dinner?"

"We went to Mickey's bar. We had burgers. We each had two beers. It was a good time."

"Who drove?"

"I did."

"You drove her home?"

"Yes."

"But you didn't drive her directly home, did you?"

Pamela went into that crossed-arm, defensive posture again. "You aren't going to do this. You are not going to force me into saying things against Megan."

"I'm not trying to do anything of the kind. I just want you to tell the jury what happened when you drove Megan home. Once again, you've already made a statement to the police. It's out there."

"I drove her home," she spat.

"But not directly," I said. "You went somewhere else first, didn't you?"

"We didn't go anywhere. We just drove. We talked."

"Didn't Megan Lewis in fact ask you to drive a particular route? One that was nowhere near her own home?"

"We drove around, yes."

"You drove past Reed Karl's house, didn't you?"

"Yes."

"And that wasn't just some coincidence, was it?"

"No, it wasn't a coincidence."

"In fact, you told the police that Megan asked you to go down Reed Karl's street."

"I said I didn't know it was Reed's street until ... until we passed by his house."

"You didn't just pass by his house. She asked to stop in front of it, didn't she?"

"Yes," Pamela spat. "Megan asked me to slow down. She asked me to stop across the street. But it was nothing. She was just ... it was nothing."

"Nothing. Was anyone at home at Reed's house?"

"Yes."

"She was looking for him, wasn't she?"

"She said … she was looking for his car."

"Why?" I asked.

"I don't know. You'd have to ask Megan. Oh wait, I'm sorry. You can't."

"Ms. Corso, why was Megan Lewis looking for Reed Karl's vehicle at his own home?"

"He was supposed to be out of town on business. She just said he was supposed to be out of town on business."

"So let me get this straight. You were asked to drive by Reed Karl's home and stalk whether he was there?"

"Objection! Ms. Leary is making a speech now. It's not for her to characterize this witness's testimony. She can do that during closing arguments."

"Sustained. I agree, Ms. Leary. Ask your questions."

"All right, Ms. Corso, why was Megan checking up on Reed Karl's whereabouts, to your knowledge?"

"I don't know."

"Do you suppose it was because she didn't trust him?"

"I guess so. I don't know."

"But you were angry about that, weren't you?"

"I wasn't happy. But I wasn't angry. I was more worried."

"Worried why?"

"Because … I didn't want to be there. I didn't want any part of it. She wasn't. Megan wasn't acting …"

"Wasn't acting what?"

"Stop it."

"Megan wasn't acting like herself, is that it?"

"No, okay? No. She wasn't acting like herself."

"You're saying it was out of character for her to drive by a boyfriend's home to check on whether they were home?"

"It wasn't like her."

"But you didn't just drive by. I mean, after you both observed that Reed's car wasn't in the driveway. You parked, didn't you? That's what you told the police?"

"Yes. We parked across the street."

"What did you observe at the Karl home?"

"I don't know. I told you I didn't want to be there."

"The lights were on inside?"

"Yes."

"You could see someone in the house, couldn't you?"

"Yes."

"But it wasn't Reed, was it?"

"No."

"Who was it, Pamela?"

"It was his wife, okay? You could see his wife. She was cooking something in the kitchen."

"His wife. You mean Dahlia Karl?"

"Yes. I guess. I didn't know her name. I learned it later. But yes. We could see her in the kitchen."

"Did Megan ask you to leave at that point?"

"No."

"No. In fact, she had you wait for a while, didn't she? She insisted on sitting there and watching Dahlia Karl from the street while she went about her business in her own home, isn't that right?"

"It wasn't … it was just for a few minutes."

"Was it your decision to drive away or Megan's?"

She looked down. Shook her head. "I hate you for this."

"Please answer the question."

"Me, okay? It was me. I was … the whole thing just upset me. I didn't like that we were sitting there spying on this poor woman. It felt wrong. I said so. So I put the car in gear and I drove off."

"How did Megan react?"

"She was angry."

"She wanted you to remain across the street so she could continue to, as you described it, spy on Dahlia Karl?"

"Yes." Pamela was crying now. "She was upset, okay? She was just upset."

"Just upset, Ms. Corso? Were you aware of a letter Megan Lewis wrote to Dahlia Karl?"

"No."

"She didn't tell you about writing one?"

"No."

"Were you aware that Megan Lewis was being treated for depression?"

"I knew she had a therapist."

"Did you know she had been prescribed antidepressants?"

"I can't believe you're asking me this. You are something else, lady. Megan was a person. A human being. She didn't deserve what happened to her. I will not sit here and let you use me to paint her as some kind of psycho. She loved somebody who wasn't good for her. That's all."

Judge Niedermayer banged her gavel again. "Ms. Corso, you will wait until you are asked a question and you will only respond to direct questions."

"Ms. Corso, isn't it true that you expressed concerns about the amount of alcohol Megan Lewis was drinking when you saw her?"

"She was drinking more in those last few weeks. But she wasn't an alcoholic."

"But you were concerned she wasn't acting herself. You told the police that. You told me that, didn't you?"

"Yes. Yes, okay? Megan wasn't in a good place mentally. That doesn't mean she was crazy."

"Ms. Corso, how many times were you asked by Megan Lewis to drive by Reed Karl's home?"

"What?"

"It was more than just that once, wasn't it?"

"It happened a couple of times. The other times, she was the one driving so she really only asked me to drive there once. I was telling the truth."

"A couple of times. You're saying you were in the car when Megan Lewis drove down Reed Karl's street to spy on his house? Is that your testimony?"

"A couple of times. She drove by his house. I didn't say she was spying."

"So it's accurate to say Megan Lewis made a habit out of driving by Reed Karl's house?"

"I wouldn't say habit. I said it was a couple of times."

"How did that make you feel?"

"What do you mean?"

"Did you think it was a good idea? Did you express any opinion to Megan about this behavior?"

"I didn't think it was a good idea, no. I didn't think anything about her seeing Reed Karl was a good idea."

I put a hand up. "Your Honor, I have no further questions of this witness."

Rafe was already on his feet. As I made way for him, he gave Pamela Corso a reassuring nod. "Your Honor, I don't feel the need to subject this witness to any more. I have no questions."

Pamela broke down as the judge dismissed her. She glared at me as she made her way out of the courtroom, her opinions clear. To Pamela Corso and a growing number of people in town, I was the scum of the earth. And I could never tell any of them why they were wrong.

Chapter 22

KIM BAKER SAT in the hallway just outside of Judge Niedermayer's courtroom. She was alone. Emma walked around the corner. As she caught my eye, she shook her head, no.

I sat next to Kim. "Have you talked to her this morning?"

Kim's eyes were bloodshot. She looked like she'd aged ten years since the day I met her.

"She's not coming," she said. "Cass, I tried to talk to her. I tried to tell her how important it was for her to be in the courtroom these final days. She won't get out of bed. She won't eat. I think it would take two deputies to even get her in a car and bring her here if you subpoenaed her. I don't understand it. She could help. I think it would even be cathartic for her to be able to tell her side of the story."

Cathartic. Only Dahlia Karl's testimony would be based on a lie. As much as I couldn't put Reed on the stand to perjure himself, I couldn't do it with Dahlia either.

"What about Clara?" I said.

Kim shook her head. "Clara tries. But this is all just too much to put on a fourteen-year-old girl. She's missing school. A social worker came to the house two days ago about her truancy. Dahlia promised to make sure she goes. But Dahlia doesn't even know what day it is half the time. So, Dean and I talked. We had Clara pack a bag. She's going to stay with us for a couple of days."

"That's a good idea," I said. I felt a small weight lift from my own shoulders. Child protective services might have to be involved at some point anyway. If Clara had a stable place to live with people who cared about her, that could make all the difference.

"Dahlia asked me to be in the courtroom today. Cass, if you want to put me on the stand, I'll do it. I can tell the jury how scared Dahlia was. God. I can't even believe I'm saying it. Like I'm defending what Reed did. It's indefensible."

Her face fell. "Oh, I'm sorry. I didn't mean."

I put a hand up. Two deputies got off the elevator and glared at me. I was getting used to it. Kim saw. She rubbed her forehead.

"Thank you," I said. "I appreciate it. You don't have direct, firsthand knowledge of anything, Kim. You know what Dahlia told you."

"I know what I see with my own eyes," she said.

"It's okay," I said. "It's fine if you want to be in the courtroom. If you think it'll bring Dahlia some comfort."

I needed to get Jeanie involved. Protecting Clara would be my next priority depending how this trial went. For now, I had a singular job.

I had to finish putting on the best defense I could for Reed. Even as I felt the weight of the stares from the deputies at my back. They would never forgive me for championing who they thought was Megan Lewis's killer. If Reed had his way, the truth would never come out. Megan Lewis would never get the justice she deserved.

"They're just about ready for you, Aunt Cass," Emma said. She had poked her head into the courtroom. "The Thompsons are set up down the hall."

I nodded. Thanking Kim Baker again, I walked into the courtroom. Emma was close behind. Rafe was already at his table. A moment later, Reed was brought in. He must have seen Kim Baker in the hallway too. His shoulders slumped.

"Are you ready?" I whispered to him. He didn't answer.

"All rise!" Judge Niedermayer's bailiff had stepped to the side of her bench. I got to my feet. Looking behind me, Sawyer Thompson had just come in and taken a seat against the back wall.

Judge Niedermayer stepped up to the bench and gave me a nod. A moment later, the jury filed in.

"Ms. Leary," the judge said. "You may call your next witness."

"I call Sawyer Thompson to the stand, Your Honor."

Rafe shuffled through some notes on his desk. Thompson began his slow walk up the aisle and up to the witness box.

"Mr. Thompson," I said. "Thank you for being here today. Will you state your full name for the record and tell the jury where you live?"

"My name is Sawyer Thompson. My wife Lettie and I, we live in Eden's Edge, next door to Reed and Dahlia Karl. We're next-door neighbors. We share a fence."

"How long have you known the Karls?"

"Well, since they moved into that house close to twenty years ago."

"How would you describe your relationship with the Karls?"

"We're friendly. They've been good neighbors to us. Keep their yard picked up. They're not loud. They're respectful. We try to be as well. We both live on the end of a cul-de-sac so out there, it's really just the two of us. We're not very close with the other neighbors in a geographical way. So the Karls and us ... we've always looked out for each other."

"I see," I said. "Do you socialize with the Karls outside of just being neighbors?"

"A few times. There have been some block parties over the years. And we talk over the fence when we're both out. Or we did. Obviously, in the last few months that hasn't happened."

"Of course. Mr. Thompson, were you aware of any marital tension between Mr. and Mrs. Karl?"

"I mean, I never heard them arguing. They always seemed fine together. But I'd say seven or eight months ago my wife started having some suspicions."

"What kind of suspicions?"

"Well, Reed just wasn't around as much. Like he used to come home for lunch from work. Like clockwork. We noticed he stopped doing that. And they used to go out, you know. As a couple. Years ago, we'd babysit for them. They'd send Clara over to our place if they went out to dinner. She's older now so she doesn't need a sitter. But Lettie, she always had baby fever. Our grandkids don't live close. So when Dahlia had her little boy, Lettie was just over the moon about it. She'd go over there to get her baby fix."

"Ian," I said. "Ian Karl is who you're talking about?"

"That's right."

"Mr. Thompson. Can you tell me what happened to Ian Karl? Are you familiar with that?"

Sawyer dropped his head. "They lost him. Ian drowned in their pool. I can't tell you all the circumstances. We happened to be out of town that week. We went on a Disney trip with our son and grandkids. But Ian got out from under Dahlia's watch and had an accident in that pool."

"Do you know how old he was?"

"He was little. Four, I think."

"Thank you. How was your relationship with the Karls after that incident?"

"It cooled. Not that there was any problem. Just as you can imagine, Reed and Dahlia kept to themselves more after that. In their grief. Reed had the pool filled in. They were talking about moving out of that house. Dahlia was just having the hardest time. Again. As you can imagine. Lettie started going over there. Preparing meals. Helping look after Clara, their daughter."

"I see. Did Reed ever confide in you during that time?"

"Confide in me? Like his troubles? Not directly, no."

"What do you mean, not directly?"

"Well, it was obvious they were having problems. Like I said. They stopped going out, just the two of them. Dahlia stopped leaving the house. We would go over there and she was just ... she would keep the house completely dark. It was almost like the light was just too much for her. Like it overstimulated her. It was concerning. I asked Reed a couple of times whether she was getting help. Whether they were getting help as a family. Dahlia was just wasting away in those first few years. And look, I'm not saying that justifies what he did. Any of it. But I just know it was a very hard time for all of them."

"Okay. Mr. Thompson, was there ever a time where you became aware of Reed Karl having an affair with the victim in this case?"

Sawyer took a sip of his water. "I didn't want to believe it, but yes. I was aware that Reed was stepping out on Dahlia after a while."

"Do you know when you became aware of it?"

"Not a specific date, no. But by the beginning of the year, for sure. Probably a little earlier. Like I said, Reed's normal patterns changed."

"In what way?"

"He stopped coming home for lunch. He used to do that every single day for years. In fact, it became a point of contention between my wife and me. She brought it up a couple of times. That we should make a point of eating lunch together every day like the Karls did. So when it stopped happening, we both noticed."

"Did you ever ask Reed about it?"

"No, ma'am. I didn't think it was any of my business."

"Okay. Was there anything else that led you to believe Mr. Karl was having an affair?"

"Well ... I mean ... he told me. I asked him about it one day and he told me."

"When was this?"

Sawyer squirmed in his seat. "I don't relish this. Reed told me this in confidence. But here I am, in a court of law, sworn to tell the truth. And you're his lawyer and you put me up here. So I don't see as how I have a choice but to break that confidence now."

"I appreciate that, Mr. Thompson. My question is, when did Reed Karl confess to you that he was having an affair?"

"It was late spring. May, I think. Maybe April. Look, I could see something was going on. The lunch issue. But also ... we kept seeing this car drive by the house. There was a woman behind the wheel. Pretty. Long blonde hair. And she seemed like she was looking real intently at the Karls' house. One time I even went out in the driveway and tried to ask her what her business was."

"When was this, if you recall?"

"I wanna say March, maybe April."

"Do you know who the woman was? Can you identify her?"

"Well, I didn't know her name at the time, no. We'd seen her walking and jogging in the neighborhood. Lettie started noticing. She was ... this girl didn't live in Eden's Edge. She lived over in Pine Circle, the neighborhood west of us. Another neighbor of ours told us that. But when all this went down.

When I saw her picture in the news. I knew immediately who it was."

"Who was it, Mr. Thompson? Who did you see stalking Reed Karl's house?"

"Objection as to characterization," Rafe said.

"Sustained, Ms. Leary," Judge Niedermayer said.

"Who did you see driving or jogging past Reed Karl's house on multiple occasions, Mr. Thompson?"

"It was Megan Lewis. She was easy to recognize from the picture that was all over the internet. Pretty, like I said. Long blonde hair. And I got a real good look at her one of the times. When I went down the driveway and confronted her."

"Did she say anything to you?"

"No, ma'am. She sped off real quick. And anyway, that's about the time I saw Reed out doing some yard work and I went over there and said my piece."

"What do you mean?"

"Well. I mean, Lettie had been trying to go over there to bring meals to Dahlia. We're married. Of course Lettie and I talk about stuff. I told her about seeing that woman driving by the house. And then you've got Dahlia never coming out. And we kept seeing Clara. She's out there mowing the grass. Taking the garbage out. Collecting the mail. And it's not like those aren't things a teenage kid shouldn't be doing to earn their keep around the house. I don't know. It's just we also kept seeing a lot of meals being delivered to the house so we were worried maybe Dahlia wasn't preparing meals for Clara. Clara just sort of had to grow up so fast. So Lettie and I were concerned and I saw

Reed out there in the yard and I went over and asked him if everything was okay."

"What did he say?"

"He was kind of standoffish at first. Then I told him I knew he was seeing somebody. Well, of course I didn't. I was bluffing. But I had a pretty good idea I was right. And Reed just kind of broke down. He told me yes. That he'd strayed in the marriage and he was trying to break it off but that it wasn't going well."

"How was it not going well? Was he specific?"

"Not really. I mean, I mentioned the drive-bys. That really seemed to upset him. Reed was very worried about Dahlia. He kept saying how sorry he was and he didn't know how it got so out of hand. But that the girlfriend wasn't taking the break-up very well and he didn't know what he was going to do. He was talking about maybe they'd have to move away."

"What did you do then?"

"I told him I hoped they didn't move away. I told him I didn't condone adultery. Not by any means. But I also recognized that Reed and Dahlia had more than their share of heartache in their lives. So I knew it wasn't for me to judge."

"Of course. And you're saying you believe this conversation was in April?"

"Or thereabouts. Maybe early May."

"Okay. Did you ever have occasion to talk to Reed again about his affair with Megan Lewis?"

"Yes."

"Can you describe those circumstances?"

"A few weeks later, we were reading in bed, me and Lettie. All of a sudden we see flashing red lights in the window. I went and looked out to see what was going on and there was a sheriff's car in Reed's driveway. They were there for maybe an hour. So the next day, I went over there and asked Reed what was going on."

"What did he say?"

"Well it was pandemonium. I can tell you that. Dahlia was in the background crying. Mind you, this was later the next morning. So maybe twelve hours after we saw the cops out there. And she was still really upset. Reed took me back outside so Dahlia couldn't hear what was going on. He told me there'd been a break-in. He told me he was pretty sure it was the girlfriend. That she'd done some things in the house when they were gone that were pretty disturbing. He showed me pictures on his phone."

"What were the pictures of?"

"Sick stuff. Toys and stuffed animals all cut up, hanging off the ceiling fan in Reed and Dahlia's bedroom."

"Mr. Thompson, I'd like to direct your attention to a few exhibits that have already been entered. Do you recognize those photos?"

"Sure do. Those are the pictures Reed showed me on his phone that morning."

"Do you know what those are? The things hanging from the ceiling fan?"

"I do. That's the sick part. Those were Ian's things. The boy they lost. I know that because Lettie and I gave him that teddy bear for his first birthday. Lettie picked it out."

"Okay. So you're saying Reed told you he believed Megan Lewis was the one who broke into their home and left those things in that condition?"

"That's what he said, yes. I couldn't believe it. That somebody could be that cruel. Bringing their dead kid into it. I mean, that's just absolutely nuts."

"Objection," Rafe said. "Your Honor, this witness is not qualified to speculate about Megan Lewis's mental state. It's unseemly as well as highly irrelevant and prejudicial."

"Sustained," Judge Niedermayer said. "You need to stick to observable facts, Mr. Thompson, not your opinion."

"Oh sure. Sure, Judge. And I'm not trying to speak ill of the dead. I'm really not. If I've come across that way, I sure do apologize."

"Mr. Thompson," I said. "Did the police ever question you or your wife after this incident, this break-in at your neighbor's house?"

"No. They did not."

"Did you or your wife notice anything unusual that night going on next door?"

"Not that night, no. I mean, other than seeing the police car in the driveway."

"So you didn't see or hear anything unusual going on next door?"

"No."

"Were you aware that the Karls were not at home?"

"I didn't know that until later."

"Did you ever at any point become aware of anything unusual that had taken place that night at the Karls' home?"

"Well, yes. I got to thinking. We have doorbell cameras set up at the front and back of our property. I've got a camera that has a full view of our pool. We did that for safety reasons of course. But also there's a pool alarm we like to have when the grandkids come to visit. Actually I had it installed right after poor Ian Karl's accident. That was Lettie's idea. And it was a good one."

"Mr. Thompson, did you review your doorbell camera footage from the night of the Karls' break-in?"

"I did. Yes, ma'am, I sure did."

"Your Honor, I'd like to mark Exhibit Twenty-nine for identification."

"Go ahead," she said.

"Mr. Thompson, can you identify the photograph that's just been marked?"

"I sure can. That's a still image I took from my camera pointing toward our backyard and pool."

I went through and had him mark the next three stills from the same footage, then the thirty-second video itself.

"I'd like to move for admission of Exhibits Twenty-nine through Thirty-one."

"Objection," Rafe said. "Your Honor, I've let this go on long enough. Defense counsel is engaged in victim-blaming here. This whole line of inquiry is highly irrelevant and prejudicial. This alleged break-in to the Karls' home before Megan Lewis's murder has nothing to do with anything."

"Your Honor, Mr. Johnson could not be more wrong and I don't even think he believes what he's saying, quite frankly. My client has been charged with first degree murder. I am entitled to present a defense on all elements of that crime. Mr. Karl's state of mind. The reality of his fear. His intentions. Those are absolutely relevant issues. Mr. Johnson will be free to argue the elements of self-defense in his closing. But I cannot be denied the opportunity to present evidence of them now."

"I'm going to overrule the objection, Mr. Johnson. Ms. Leary is correct, you will have your opportunity to cross-examine this witness. You will also have the opportunity to present rebuttal and closing arguments. You may proceed, Ms. Leary."

I played the video for the jury. It showed a blonde woman running from the Karls' home, then leaving through the gate and out of frame toward the woods. I froze it at one frame. Megan Lewis's face was in profile, but her sweatshirt was clearly visible. I knew from this angle, the jury could see the bleach stains on her right arm.

"Mr. Thompson, do you recognize the woman in that video or in the stills you took of it?"

"Well, it looks like Megan Lewis. The woman I confronted from my driveway a few weeks before."

"When was this video taken?"

"May 29th."

"Did you show this video to the police?"

"No, ma'am. Like I said, they never even came over and asked us questions after the break-in."

"You didn't offer this footage to them?"

"I didn't, no. From what Reed told me, they weren't going to pursue anything. Reed just kind of wanted the whole thing to go away. It was causing real distress for Dahlia and she was already pretty fragile."

"Thank you," I said. "I have no further questions."

"Mr. Johnson?"

Rafe shook his head in incredulity as he stepped up to the lectern.

"You're guessing, isn't that right?"

"I'm sorry?" Sawyer said.

"You can't see the woman's face in this video, can you?"

"No, sir. Just kind of from the side."

"She's a blonde woman, that's all you can really tell, isn't it?"

"I mean ... I guess."

"It could be any blonde woman, couldn't it?"

"I don't know what you mean."

"I mean ... the only reason you think this woman in the video is Megan Lewis is because Reed Karl told you that's who he thinks it was."

"Well, no. Like I said. I saw her driving by his house those couple of times. And it was suspicious then. So who else could it have been in that tape?"

"Anyone," Rafe's voice boomed throughout the courtroom. "It's a blonde person. Hell, if I told you it was Cass Leary herself, you wouldn't be able to tell me otherwise."

"Objection!"

Sawyer looked at me. Then he looked at the still on the screen. "Well, I mean, I guess," he said before the judge could respond. "But that doesn't make a whole lot of logical sense, does it, Mr. Johnson?"

Judge Niedermayer banged her gavel. "Enough."

"I have no further questions, Your Honor," Rafe said, stomping back to his table.

"No redirect," I said.

Shrugging, Sawyer Thompson left the witness box. We adjourned until after lunch. As I gathered my things and turned, I saw Eric sitting in the back row of the courtroom. He was flanked by several of his and Megan Lewis's former colleagues from the Delphi Police Department. Each one of them looked at me with pure fury. Including Eric.

Chapter 23

IF THE ENTIRE law enforcement community were angry with me now, I knew they would be calling for my head on a spike after I called my next witness. I had no choice. Reed had never given me any choice. He looked stoic as I stood and spoke into the lectern microphone.

"The defense calls Dr. Marilyn Levander to the stand."

Marilyn Levander walked up the aisle with an air of confidence. She'd been in plenty of courtrooms in her twenty-five-year career. She immediately explained her last name was pronounced as rhyming with Evander as in Holyfield, not like the purple, fragrant flower. She'd been a PHD clinical psychologist specializing in anxiety, depression, PTSD, and OCD for most of those years. For a decade, she'd worked in a VA hospital treating combat veterans returning from the Middle East.

We went through her foundational testimony over the course of the next half hour. She delivered crisp, direct answers. I then paused, looked at my notes once, then closed my folder.

"Dr. Levander, how did you come to meet Megan Lewis?"

Marilyn Levander straightened her tan suit jacket. She adjusted the microphone, angling it downward. "Ms. Lewis was a patient of mine. She was referred to me through her Employee Assistance Program."

"When was this?"

"I first saw Ms. Lewis three years ago in my office."

"How often did you see her?"

"We moved to telehealth appointments twice a month. Every six months she would come in for a physical appointment and medication management."

"She was a patient of yours. What was the nature of your treatment?"

"That's a fairly broad question. But Ms. Lewis was seeing me for psychotherapy and medication management."

"You aren't her prescribing doctor though, are you?"

"No. Her medication management was coordinated through my office with my partner, Dr. Werner Getz, who is a board certified psychiatrist."

"So Dr. Getz would actually write Ms. Lewis's prescriptions?"

"Yes. And also her primary care physician, Dr. McKenzie Mcall."

"I see. Were you aware of what medications Ms. Lewis was taking?"

"Yes. We take a holistic approach to treatment in my office. I work in conjunction with Dr. Getz."

"Do you have expertise in the therapeutic benefits of certain psychotropic medications?"

"Yes. I also consult with Dr. Getz routinely regarding my patients' reported responses to various medications prescribed by Dr. Getz."

"I just want to be clear on the dynamic. You are the one providing the counseling to your patients. Dr. Getz prescribes the medications?"

"That's true. But again, we work together. Dr. Getz prescribes medication after consulting with me, the patient, reviewing my clinical notes, etc."

"I see. Dr. Levander, did Megan Lewis have a diagnosis? In other words, what were you treating her for?"

"Well, as I said, Ms. Lewis was initially referred to my office on the recommendation of a therapist through her Employer Assistance Program. Ms. Lewis sought out those services. She was experiencing job-related stress. That is not uncommon for people in her line of work."

"Police officers," I said.

"Exactly."

"Again, what was her diagnosis?"

"Ms. Lewis was initially treated for job-related PTSD and generalized anxiety. She was ultimately diagnosed with clinical depression and we were going through the process of a bipolar II diagnosis. We needed further testing on that."

"Okay," I said. "Do you know what medications she was prescribed for those conditions?"

"Yes. Ms. Lewis was first prescribed buspirone to treat her anxiety and depression—7.5 milligrams twice per day. That was gradually increased to 20 milligrams twice per day before it was discontinued."

"By Dr. Getz."

"Yes."

"But you were part of that decision. As you said, you and Dr. Getz work in consultation?"

"Yes. But I don't recommend medication to Dr. Getz. I present him with my observations and diagnosis. He speaks with the patient directly, and a treatment plan is formed."

"Are all your clients prescribed psychotropic medication?"

"Not at all. Sometimes the treatment plan doesn't call for medical intervention. Sometimes it does. It's determined on a case-by-case basis. Sometimes a patient will come to me who is already on medication and we determine it isn't adequately controlling their symptoms. We might decide to change the medication. We might decide to try to wean them off medication. It really depends on the situation."

"Thank you. You said Ms. Lewis was prescribed buspirone initially. Was she being prescribed that same medication at the time of her death?"

"No. About a year ago, a decision was made to wean her off that particular drug and try a course of isocarboxazid."

"Why was that decision made?"

"Ms. Lewis didn't feel the medication was adequately controlling her symptoms."

"And what were those symptoms?"

"She was experiencing increased anxiety. Episodes of panic."

"Panic attacks?"

"Yes."

"Do you know how those attacks manifested?"

"She reported severe chest pain, difficulty breathing, profuse sweating, and mental paralysis. They were becoming more frequent."

"Were you able to determine the cause of those increased panic attacks? In other words, was it only a medication issue or was it environmental?"

"I believe it was both."

"Okay. What environmental factors do you believe contributed to Ms. Lewis's increased anxiety?"

"Well, she had reported stress at work. Concern about her inability to advance. She was passed over for a promotion. Additionally, she was involved in a romantic relationship that was perhaps not as healthy as she wanted it to be."

"Not as healthy as she wanted it to be. Did she tell you who she was seeing?"

"No. She did not give me a name, no."

"Were you aware that the man she was seeing was married?"

"I became aware of that, yes."

"During your treatment of her? She told you?"

"Yes. Eventually."

"Was that the cause of the stress in that relationship?"

"It was certainly one of the stressors, yes."

"One of the stressors. In what way?"

"Ms. Lewis was frustrated that perhaps her relationship with this man had no future. That she would not receive the level of commitment from him that she was hoping for."

"He wasn't going to leave his wife," I said.

"That was a concern and a stressor for her, yes."

"What advice did you give her?"

"My role as a therapist is more to listen rather than to tell my patients what to do. I aim to help them decide what is best for their own lives based on their goals, their needs, their hopes."

"I see. But you indicated that you felt, or Ms. Lewis felt her medication was no longer working to control her symptoms of anxiety and depression?"

"Yes. Her symptoms were increasing."

"So a decision was made, in conjunction with Dr. Getz, to switch her to isocarboxazid?"

"That's correct."

"When was that decision made? When was the switch made?"

"In January of this year. But we don't just switch from one medication to the next. Ms. Lewis was weaned off buspirone over the course of a couple weeks. Then the isocarboxazid was added in an increasing dose over the next six weeks."

"So, to be clear, she should not have been taking both medications at the same time?"

"No. The process was to wean her off one, then add the other."

"That was the prescribed course?"

"Yes."

"Do you know whether Ms. Lewis followed that prescribed course?"

"She said she did, yes."

"She said she did."

I reopened my notebook. "Dr. Levander. Have you had occasion to review the toxicology reports on Megan Lewis after her death?"

"They were provided to me, yes."

"Okay. I'd like to provide you with a copy of them now, if that's all right."

Dr. Levander put on her reading glasses. I handed her a copy of Megan Lewis's labs.

"Can you tell me what medications were found in Ms. Lewis's system when she died?" I asked.

Dr. Levander scowled. Though the results weren't news to her, they were clearly upsetting to her. "Therapeutic levels of buspirone and isocarboxazid were found in her system. She also had a blood alcohol level of .09."

"Buspirone and isocarboxazid. You indicated that those two drugs were not meant to be taken together, is that right?"

"That's correct. They shouldn't be taken together."

"And why is that?"

"It can lead to extreme hypertension. There is also a risk of developing serotonin syndrome."

"What are the symptoms of serotonin syndrome?"

"It's a range. It can cause a host of neuromuscular issues like rigidity, tremors. But also other physical symptoms like, as I said, hypertension, diarrhea, nausea, tachycardia. And there are also psychological symptoms."

"What kind of psychological symptoms?"

"Increased anxiety or depression, agitation, hallucinations, delusions, in rare and extreme cases, psychosis."

"Okay," I said. "And what about alcohol, can that increase the risk of those psychological symptoms?"

"They can. Absolutely."

"So, in other words, you wouldn't recommend using alcohol while taking either buspirone and isocarboxazid, let alone all three together."

"Absolutely not."

"In fact, there's a warning label on the bottles of those medications, isn't there? About not mixing them with alcohol?"

"Yes."

Rafe Johnson remained strangely quiet through all of this. For a moment, I could forget he was even there.

"So I'm clear. Combining buspirone and isocarboxazid plus alcohol leads to the significant risk of developing hypertension and serotonin syndrome as well as things like paranoia, delusions, and obsessive behavior?"

"Yes."

"Thank you. If I can go back for a moment to your therapy sessions with Ms. Lewis. Did you notice increased paranoia or delusions with what she was reporting?"

"Ms. Lewis seemed to be growing increasingly agitated, yes."

I had previously moved for admission of Drs. Levander and Getz's clinical notes. "In fact," I said. "You charted that she was experiencing paranoia as it related to her romantic relationship, didn't you?"

"I did. Yes."

"Tell me about that."

"Ms. Lewis began reporting fears or concerns that she was being spied on. That her boyfriend's wife was breaking into her house and watching her sleep."

"Did you believe her?"

"I believe she believed it, yes."

"Well, that's not the same thing, is it?"

"It's the truth."

"Were there any other things Ms. Lewis indicated she was paranoid about?"

"Well, as I said, mainly she was concerned someone was breaking into her home. That she was being watched. She reported things being moved or taken from her home."

"What kind of things?"

"Oh, she said her glassware in the cupboard was moved. She

said she thought items of clothing disappeared. That sort of thing."

"Did she indicate to you who she thought was doing these things to her?"

"She believed her boyfriend's wife was trying to gaslight her. Trying to make her look crazy. That's what she said. She said she thought the woman was trying to turn her boyfriend against her."

"Dahlia Karl?"

"Yes."

"All right. You believe she believed it. Did it come as a surprise to you that Ms. Lewis was mixing her medication and drinking?"

"Yes."

"If you'd known, you would have advised her against it."

"Absolutely."

"All right. Thank you. I have nothing further."

Rafe walked casually up to the lectern. "Dr. Levander," he started. "You have certain ethical duties to report a patient to the authorities if you believe they are a danger to someone else, don't you?"

"I do, yes. If a patient threatens to harm someone else, I have a duty to contact authorities."

"But you never did that with Ms. Lewis. She never threatened anyone, did she?"

"Not to my knowledge, no."

"And if you had, you would have called the police."

"Yes."

"You treated Megan Lewis ... you spent an hour a week in session with her. For the three years leading up to her murder. And you never found it necessary to report anything she said to you to the police?"

"That's correct. I did not."

"Because she never gave you cause to, isn't that right?"

"That's correct."

"You weren't ever worried she was a danger to herself or anybody else, for three years. After talking to her for at least an hour every single week. Isn't that right?"

"That's correct," she said.

"So all these side effects you described about this combined medication or alcohol, in your experience with your patient, you didn't observe her suffering from those side effects to the point you had to report it."

"Well, as I said. I observed increased anxiety and paranoia relating to her relationship with her boyfriend and work. But did it rise to the level I felt it necessary to report? No."

"Thank you. I have no further questions."

I had one last question. Rafe had opened the door. "Dr. Levander. I'd like to show you something."

I handed her the letter found on Megan's computer. The one Reed reported had been taped to his front door. Dr. Levander read it.

"Have you seen this letter before?" I asked.

"No."

"Will you read it?"

She read it into the record again.

"Dahlia. You lose. Reed doesn't love you. You know it. You're hanging on to something that doesn't exist anymore. I know what you're trying to do. You think you can keep him tied to you. All you have to do is threaten to kill yourself. We both know you're never going to do it. But maybe you should. Maybe you should do everybody a favor and leave the planet. We all know you're a terrible mother. And we know why. You aren't a good person. I know the game you're playing. I'm on to you. You'd better be careful. Very careful. Megan."

"Dr. Levander, if you had seen that letter. If your patient, Megan Lewis, had brought it to your attention. Would that have risen to the level of something you had to report to the police?"

"It's hard to say out of context. And again, I didn't see this letter."

"Objection," Rafe said. "She just testified she never saw it. So counsel is asking for speculation and an unfair hypothetical."

"It's not a hypothetical," I said. "There is testimony that this letter was actually delivered to Mr. Karl. Taped to his front door. It was found on Megan Lewis's computer. She wrote it. It's not a hypothetical."

"I'll allow it," the judge said. "The witness may answer."

"I'll repeat the question. Dr. Levander. If your patient, Megan Lewis, had told you the contents of this letter. If you'd known she wrote it. Would this have risen to the level of a reportable threat?"

"Hindsight is always twenty-twenty," she said. "But this would have greatly concerned me. Especially if I'd known she was mixing her medications, I would have likely erred on the side of caution, and also knowing that Ms. Lewis had access to firearms, yes. I would probably have felt it was my duty to report this to law enforcement."

"Thank you," I said. "I have no further questions."

"All right," Judge Niedermayer said, looking at the clock on the wall. "I'll dismiss the jury and adjourn for the day. We start at eight in the morning. Be prepared with your next witness, Ms. Leary."

She banged her gavel. The courtroom rose to its feet. I felt the angry eyes boring into me from the back of the courtroom.

Chapter 24

I FACED a gauntlet of angry stares as I left the courtroom. The slow walk across the street to the parking lot saw my pulse race as I waited for a shout, and turned back, or worse from the deputies in and out of the building. Eric was nowhere to be found. That was a good thing. I couldn't face him. Couldn't stand in front of him and hear his disappointment in me.

My client was innocent. Reed Karl did not kill Megan Lewis. But I was powerless to say anything.

"Aunt Cass?" Emma ran to catch up with me. I had her doing some filings for a few other cases we had brewing. After that, she was going to sit in on one of Jeanie's hearings in Family Court. I felt like I could barely face her either. Reed's secret burned inside of me. It made me feel sick.

"I'm going to head back home," I said.

"What are you going to do?"

"What do you mean?"

"I mean, you don't have any other witnesses on your slate. Are you going to put Reed on the stand like he's been asking for?"

I smiled. "No."

Emma's face fell. She was shocked at my answer. She quickly recovered and found an encouraging smile. "Well, you'll deliver an amazing closing like you always do. You've done enough."

"Have I?"

Emma crossed the distance between us and put her arms around me. "You've done all anybody can do. You got Reed's story out. That's what he hired you to do."

Reed's story. Reed's lie.

"Have you talked to Kim? She was in the courtroom. I didn't see her when I left."

"She slipped out halfway through Dr. Levander's testimony. She was going to go back home."

"Clara's staying with her."

Emma nodded. "That's a good thing. Kim was asking whether we could maybe arrange for a nurse to come in and check on Dahlia. I thought ..."

I put a hand up. Anger swelled within me, unbidden. "No," I said. "Dahlia Karl isn't our problem. We've done enough for her."

Emma seemed shocked by my words. Maybe they were shocking. But at that moment, I felt no compassion for Dahlia. She was a killer. I knew she was mentally ill. I could even believe she'd done what she'd done out of grief, fury, desperation. But the fact remained, no matter the outcome of this trial, Megan Lewis would not get justice. Despite what every cop in town thought, that mattered to me. Deeply.

"You should get some rest," Emma said. "Get away from all of this for a little while. Come back strong in the morning. Whatever you decide to do in there tomorrow, you've been incredible. And I'm ... I'm proud that you're my aunt."

I felt a half-hearted smile form. I didn't feel incredible. I felt trapped. But one thing was true. I needed to get away from all of this for a while. I only wished it was summer. I wanted to go home, peel off my suit, and slip under the refreshing, gentle waves of Finn Lake. As if they could wash away the sins and secrets it was my job to keep.

"Ms. LEARY, please call your next witness."

Greta Niedermayer showed up the next morning with a fresh haircut. Her new bob framed her face, making her look more youthful. The jury looked expectantly at me. At my side, Reed seemed defeated. Before we walked into court, he'd made one more plea for me to put him on the stand.

"Your Honor," I said. "At this time, the defense rests."

A murmur went through the courtroom. Rafe Johnson had been quickly combing through a notepad. His chin jerked up. His eyes widened in surprise. He quickly recovered and rose to his feet.

"All right," Judge Niedermayer said. If she were shocked at my words, she didn't show it. "Mr. Johnson, do you have any rebuttal witnesses you would like to call?"

Rafe leaned down and whispered something to his paralegal. He was a young kid. Tall. Skinny. Whatever Rafe said to him, he gave no verbal answer back.

"No, Your Honor," Rafe said. "The state doesn't feel rebuttal is necessary. We're ready to move to closing arguments."

"Very well," the judge said. "You may proceed."

Rafe buttoned his suit jacket. He looked crisp and clean sporting a bold red tie with tiny gold dots on it. He glanced at the back of the courtroom. Megan's colleagues from the Taney County Sheriff's Department lined the back wall. The jury sat straighter in their seats. They understood the power in this room was about to shift. They would be eager to seize it and deliberate.

"Ladies and gentlemen," Rafe started. He took no notes. He stood straight with one hand resting on the lectern. "I almost don't know what to say to you. I almost think my words are meaningless to you. Because the one person with the most to say has already said it. Reed Karl has already told you everything you need to know.

"Reed Karl told you what he did. He told you why he did it. His actions were violent, brutal, almost unspeakable. You saw with your own eyes the consequences of his actions. The cold-blooded nature of them. I can't even ..."

Rafe paused. A tremor went through him. I knew him well enough to know this wasn't for show. He was genuinely emotional about what he was about to say. He collected himself and raised his head.

"You don't have to infer or imply anything in this case. You don't have to worry that there is more than one way to interpret the evidence you were presented. Because Reed Karl told you exactly what happened. Believe him.

"Megan Lewis was in love with Reed. Their relationship was toxic and doomed from the start. I think even Megan knew that. Maybe Reed did too. I can believe that they found each other at a time when both of them needed something. Some change. He was lost in his marriage. He'd suffered an unspeakable loss when his young son died. Megan was frustrated in her career. Her life. Whatever it was, they found something in each other. Solace. Comfort.

"But the simple fact remained, Reed was never going to leave his wife. He strung Megan Lewis along. He kept secrets. He never wanted Dahlia to find out about his sins. And yes, maybe he even tried to do the right thing and end things with Megan.

"Ladies and gentlemen, none of that matters. None of it. How Reed treated Megan during their relationship, how Megan treated him. It's a smoke screen. It's irrelevant. No matter how much the defense wants to tell that story, it's nothing more than a diversion tactic to draw your attention from the cold, hard truth that Reed Karl left his home in the middle of the night when he knew his wife and daughter were sleeping. He drove to Megan Lewis's home. Let himself in. Stood over her while she was sound asleep, and beat her to death.

"You will receive instructions from the judge on premeditation. Because first degree murder requires it. Pre-planning. But what you need to understand is that premeditation can happen in a moment. Reed didn't need to go to that house with the intention of killing Megan Lewis. He only needed to form a plan in the moments before he actually killed her. The facts of the case are irrefutable that he did. Because the medical examiner told you, Megan was asleep. She had no defensive wounds on her body.

She was lying in a natural sleeping position, on her back, with her hands above her head. She quite literally didn't know what hit her. Which means Reed stood over her. We don't know for how long. It doesn't matter. Seconds. A moment—that's all it takes for premeditation. Reed wasn't provoked at that moment. Megan was silent. Sleeping. Not a threat. And Reed beat her. Caved in her skull. Broke most of the bones of her face. He ended her. Premeditation can happen in a second. But we have evidence that Reed formed a plan before he even walked into Megan's house.

"I want you to listen very closely to what Reed said to Detective Patel. When he walked into that police station on June 8th, he had already worked out how he was going to spin this. You know how we know that? Because he lied about one critical detail. He said he hit Megan Lewis with her bedside lamp. Why would he say that? Because he knew the truth would make it irrefutable that he walked into that house with a plan to kill. He wanted Detective Patel to believe he grabbed the closest thing he could to hit her with. In the heat of the moment. But we know that's a lie. That lamp never moved. There was no blood on it. Nothing. It was a cowardly lie to cover up the fact that Reed Karl walked into that house with his weapon already in hand. Cold. Calculating. With a plan. That's first degree murder, ladies and gentlemen. Plain and simple.

"The defense wants you to believe it matters why Reed went to the house that night. That it somehow mitigates its actions. It doesn't. Don't be fooled or swayed by that. It doesn't matter. It only matters that Reed went to that house with the intention to kill Megan Lewis. And it doesn't matter even if he formed the intention at the moment before he actually carried out his plan. It just doesn't matter. Except we know he didn't. We know because there is no other plausible explanation. He had the murder weapon with him. He left with it. It's never been found because he disposed of it. Covered his tracks. Planned.

"It doesn't matter if Megan Lewis was a flawed person. It doesn't even matter that Reed was. His grief for his son. His fear about the collapse of his marriage and break-up of his family. None of that matters. Quite frankly, I could argue that you shouldn't have even been allowed to hear about it. But it doesn't matter. The only thing that matters is that Reed intended to kill Megan. He told you he did. He voluntarily walked into the police station and confessed to Detective Patel. So take him at his word. He is guilty of first degree murder. What happened to Megan Lewis was not her fault. She didn't deserve it. Reed Karl is guilty. He admits it. He wants to be held accountable. He said that in his interview. So please, hold him accountable by delivering the only verdict that makes any sense in this case. I ask that you believe Reed and find him guilty of first degree murder. I ask that you give Megan Lewis the justice she deserves. Thank you."

Shaking his head, Rafe left the lectern. Reed was in tears beside me. Slow, silent rivers fell down his cheeks. I couldn't tell from the jury's expression whether that was helpful or hurtful.

At the judge's beckoning, I made my way to the lectern and faced the jury. I felt my heartbeat quicken. Everything I had planned to say when I took on this case didn't help me now. I knew the truth. In some ways it had been so much easier when I didn't. When I believed that Reed had actually carried out this crime. Now, I could not, would not say that Reed did this. I could not say he had lied during his confession. I could not say I knew who killed Megan Lewis.

"Thank you," I started. "You have been tasked with a responsibility I wish I could take from you. I wish I could go back in time and compel Reed Karl to make a different choice. But the choice he did make, he made out of desperation. Not premeditation. Not by some grand design. Reed was a father, a husband, who felt like he had no other choice. And he believed his family was at risk."

The back door of the courtroom opened. Kim Baker walked in. Behind her was Dahlia. The door made enough of a noise to draw Reed's attention. His face went white as he saw his wife. Dahlia and Kim took a seat along the wall. Dahlia looked even smaller and more frail since the last time I met her. She shuffled when she walked. Kim put an arm around her and whispered something. Dahlia nodded, then focused on me.

God. I wanted to point to her. I wanted to call out and make the jury look at her. The eyes of all the Taney County deputies were on me as well. They knew what I was about to do. What I had to do.

"Megan Lewis is the victim in this case. I will not stand up here and try to make you think she wasn't. Mr. Johnson was right. She didn't deserve what happened to her. It was horrific. And I wish different choices were made.

"Mr. Johnson is also correct that you'll be instructed on the legal definition of first degree murder. Its elements. Its requirement for premeditation. But I put to you that it's the wrong focus. You'll also be instructed on the legal defenses to murder. Self-defense and the defense of others.

"Mr. Karl admits his failings. He regrets that he pursued a relationship with Megan Lewis. That he fell in love with her. And he did love her. But something happened. Megan Lewis was a troubled woman. She suffered from mental illness. There is no dispute about that. And in her case, it manifested in deep paranoia, perhaps delusions. And ladies and gentlemen, the evidence has shown she acted on that paranoia in the most horrible way. She saw Dahlia Karl as a threat. She resented that Reed wouldn't leave Dahlia for her. She admitted that to her friends. To her therapist. But she hid things from them too. She mixed powerful antidepressants that exacerbated her paranoia and delusions. Then she mixed them with alcohol. She needed help. Among all the tragedies in this case, that she wasn't able to get it ... breaks my heart as well.

"Megan Lewis terrorized Dahlia and the Karl family. She broke into their home. Took photographs of Dahlia while she slept. While she was alone in the house. She preyed upon Dahlia's grief. She went into Dahlia and Reed's dead son's room, took his beloved toys, and made a gruesome display for Dahlia to find. And if it wasn't clear what Megan's intentions were, she put that to rest when she taped a note to the Karls' home. She threatened to harm Dahlia. These were not idle threats. We know that because she broke into their home! She slashed those toys. She hung them from nooses above Dahlia's bed. Her violent behavior was beginning to escalate. We know this. It was only getting worse.

"Reed Karl should have handled things differently. My God. That's an understatement. We all know it. But he tried to get help. He went to the police after the break-in. He wasn't taken seriously. Megan Lewis was a cop. He felt she was being protected. Nobody even bothered to interview his neighbors and find video evidence of Megan's presence at that house. Look at it. You don't have to assume. You can see it with your own eyes."

I pulled up a still of Megan Lewis in profile, her hood pulled up, her bleach-stained CMU hoodie. I put it side by side with her social media profile wearing the same sweatshirt.

"Reed Karl wanted to protect his family. Megan Lewis was a real and imminent threat to them. If Reed could go back in time and make a different choice, I believe he would.

"He acted to protect his family. Mr. Johnson is right. You should believe him. That is what he told the police. He did what he had to to protect his family."

I looked straight at Dahlia. At that moment, I felt every word I spoke was meant only for her. I was no longer talking to the jury.

"He went to the police to protect his family. He said what he had to to protect his family. He believed Megan Lewis was a real and imminent threat to his family. Because she was. We don't know how this would have ended if Reed hadn't done what he did. Did he make the wrong choice? Yes. Absolutely. But is he guilty of premeditated murder? No. He is not. I do not envy your task today. I do not wish to be in your shoes, ladies and gentlemen. But ask yourselves, what would you do to protect your family? Would you defend it against all odds? The state must prove Reed Karl committed first degree murder beyond a reasonable doubt. Planning. Premeditation. No. Reed Karl acted in defense of his family. He is not guilty of first degree murder. I trust that once you weigh the evidence. All the evidence. You will agree. Thank you."

Reed had fallen apart at the defense table. He sat slumped over with his head buried in his hands. Dahlia was rigid at the back of the courtroom. She didn't cry. She didn't tremble. For the first time since I'd met her, she kept her back straight. Her eyes locked with me. I couldn't help but wonder if that was the last thing Megan Lewis saw as well.

Chapter 25

I took the next day off and spent it curled up, watching the first early snowfall with my two dogs, Marbury and Madison. Every year, Marby acted like he'd never see this flaky white stuff before. He bounced through it, trying to eat the flakes while his mother, Madison, did the equivalent of a doggie eye roll. But twenty-four hours went by, then thirty-six, and the jury had not come back with a verdict. At eleven o'clock the second day after deliberations began, I dragged myself back into the office.

Jeanie and Emma were down in Jeanie's office. Jeanie had a bitter divorce trial coming up. Emma would act as her paralegal during it. She'd been invaluable to me during the Karl trial. I knew Jeanie would find her the same. I tried to slip upstairs without anyone hearing me. The creaky stairwell had other ideas. Within a few minutes, Emma and Jeanie had joined me in the conference room, a giant pot of coffee in tow.

"No word yet?" Jeanie asked.

I shook my head.

"What do you think that means?" Emma asked.

"It means Cass gave them something to think about," Jeanie answered. "It means they probably took a vote early on and not everybody on that panel was in agreement. You ask me, that's good news. Miraculous news for a guy who confessed to the crime."

"Or," I said. "It means they know a first degree verdict means Reed Karl's never getting out of prison. So they want to make doubly sure before they send him up the proverbial river."

"Have you talked to Dahlia?" Emma asked. "I got a call from Kim Baker this morning. She was hoping you'd stop by the house and talk to her. Dahlia won't eat."

"I can't be responsible for feeding the woman!" I snapped, then instantly felt like a jerk.

"Sorry," I said.

"It's okay," Emma said. "It's been a really rough two weeks. And a rough couple of months before that. You've taken a lot of heat on this case that you don't deserve."

"Don't I?" I said.

"You didn't kill Megan Lewis," Jeanie said. "You were hired to do a job. You did it. Anybody who can't handle that, well, they can suck it."

The stairwell creaked again, then fell silent. I didn't have to turn to know who was standing there. With impeccable timing, Eric had walked up just as Jeanie spoke. Of course he heard everything she said.

Jeanie turned around. She scowled when she saw him. "I'm including you in the category of people who can suck it, Detective Wray."

"Jeanie ..." I started.

"No," she said. "He's been walking around here all morose and broody. Well, broodier than usual. I know you're mad at us for taking the Karl case. I'm saying ... get over it. It wasn't personal."

"Jeanie, why don't we let Eric and Cass talk alone," Emma said. "You were going to get me up to speed on your financial witnesses in the Keller divorce. And I've got to set up a deposition for that accountant. Let's look at your schedule."

Jeanie stood up. Eric was more than a foot taller than her but I swear he shrunk a little as she glared at him. "You behave," she said to him.

Eric lifted his palms in a gesture of surrender. He smiled at Jeanie but this time, it didn't seem to be doing its usual charming magic. She kept her scowl in place. But she left with Emma. I waited until I heard the last of their footfalls down the stairs before closing the conference room door and reclaiming my seat at the long table.

"I didn't come here to pick a fight," he said.

"Good. Because I'm tired. No. I'm exhausted, actually. Despite what you and everyone else with a badge in this town thinks, this hasn't been fun for me."

"I hope not."

I set my jaw. Eric looked sad. But I meant what I said. I was too damn tired to fight.

"Are you kidding?" I said. "Please tell me you're kidding."

"I am. A little. I just ... I wanted to see how you were doing. That's the God's honest truth."

"Fine," I said. "I'm just fine."

"Jury's not back yet?"

"No."

He walked over and took the chair beside me. "That's ... interesting, I guess."

"I don't know what it is. But I'm ready for all of this to be over. I'm ready for things to get back to normal. And I'm ready for you to come back to work. I miss you. And not just around the office."

"Cass ..."

"Can you please be done punishing me?"

He let out a sigh. "I'm not punishing you. I just ... I just can't be around this, Cass. I know you understand that. You have to understand that."

I wanted to tell him that yes, I did. That I knew he was just trying to give me space. That I knew he was trying to respect my decision. But I couldn't help it. I *did* miss him. And part of me was angry even though I didn't have a right to be.

"I need you," I said. "I hate that I do, but I do."

He frowned. "Why do you hate that you need me?"

"Because I don't want to need anybody. It's just easier that way."

"Is it? Do you really believe that?"

"Well, it sure makes it easier not to have to explain every damn decision I make. Or justify what I do for a living."

"You don't," he said. "You don't have to explain anything. Not to me. But I shouldn't have to explain myself either. I told you, I just couldn't go down this path with you. You can say all the things about Reed Karl's constitutional rights. And how we're both part of the same system. How not so very long ago, I was the one who needed help when everyone thought I was guilty of something I didn't do. But Cass, it's not the same. And you know it isn't. Because Reed is guilty. He killed my friend."

"And you can't forgive me for being the one to make sure he got a proper defense in court."

He grumbled. "I didn't say that. It's not that you need to be forgiven. Not by me."

"By whom then?"

"That's not ... I don't mean ... ugh. Don't put words in my mouth. And don't put this back on me. I'm allowed to hate this. I'm allowed to be on Megan's side, dammit. She was my friend. And that ... monster ... because that's what he is. There's no debate about it as far as I'm concerned. But it's over. That's why I'm here. Because it's over. You don't have to have anything to do with this case once that jury comes in. So we can put it behind us."

"Until the next time someone needs my help that you don't approve of."

"That's not fair. This wasn't about my approval. I just said it. Megan was different. Megan was my friend. More than my friend. My colleague."

He held my eyes. Eric was hurt. In his heart, he was hurt. Not just because I took Reed's case. But because he lost a friend. Because he believed I'd spent the last few months fighting to protect the man he thought killed her. God. This was killing me in its own way too. I could never tell him. And because of it, Megan Lewis's murderer would go free. I wanted to be mad at Eric, but he wasn't the problem. I was. No. Dahlia was. And Reed was. But I was trapped by both of them. Duty-bound to never say a word.

"I'm sorry," I said. It was the only thing I could say. "And you're right. Soon enough, this case will be over. On paper anyway. But what if the jury comes back with a verdict you don't like?"

"They won't acquit," he said. "Cass, you never really believed you'd raise reasonable doubt, did you?"

"Maybe," I said. "It's been almost two full days of deliberation. They're not back yet. You and I both know what that could mean. And that's what we really need to talk about, isn't it? Because you're not just angry with me for taking the case. You're angry because you know if anyone could secure an acquittal for Reed Karl, it's me."

He squeezed his eyes shut for a moment. "Yeah. It *is* you. And yeah. That pisses me off. I know it shouldn't. But it does."

"Well, I can't apologize for that one."

He smiled but it didn't reach his eyes. "God, Cass. What are we doing? We've let this thing tear us apart. I can't do this anymore."

The air went out of my lungs. I felt a little lightheaded. "You're leaving me, then. I had a feeling we would end up here."

"Cass ..."

"Just say what you mean. Don't drag it out."

"Cass," he said. His face went pure white. He came to me, took me by the shoulders and crooked his finger under my chin. "I'm not breaking up with you. I don't want to break up with you. Just because we don't agree on everything doesn't mean I'm ready to bail. And yeah, I'm pissed at you. I was hoping my feelings would be enough to make you turn a client ... a paycheck ... down. It wasn't."

"Eric ... it's not that simple. And I told you. I asked you. I said if it was a deal-breaker for you, you needed to tell me."

He put a hand up. "I'm not breaking up with you, dammit. But I'm breaking up with this." He gestured to the room around us. "I can't work for you. Because Reed Karl is one thing. A big thing. But there will be others. I know that now."

"You're going to listen to everyone else? Every other cop who thinks you sold your soul to the devil to come work with me? Not for me, Eric. With me."

"I'm not listening to everyone else. I'm listening to me."

"What will you do?"

"I don't know. I can't not work."

"You don't have to. You have your pension. You ..."

"I'm forty-six years old. I'm bored. I'll go out of my mind."

"Are you going to go back to being a cop?"

"No. I don't know. I'm not sure. I've had some offers. The Feds. A couple of private security firms. But none of them are within a good commuting distance. I've got a lot of things to decide."

"Am I part of that decision?" God, I hated how needy I

sounded. But screw it. Maybe I was needy where he was concerned.

"Of course," he said. "But you took the Karl case. You take all your cases because you want to. Because there's something in it that speaks to you. I can respect that. Truly. I can. Even if I hate it half the time. But I have to do something that speaks to me too."

I reached for him. "I really am sorry. I didn't want this thing to drive a wedge between us."

"It hasn't," he said, only I didn't believe him. And God, it was killing me not to be able to tell him the truth. I hadn't chosen a guilty man over him. But on some level, he would believe that forever.

"I love you," I said.

"And I love you. You should go home. Or get back to work on something other than fucking Reed Karl. I'll see you later."

"Promise?"

"Yes," he said. He kissed me. I still saw pain in his eyes. I hated my part in putting it there.

After he left, Emma came back up. She looked worried. "You okay?" she asked.

"I've been better. But yeah. I'm okay."

"He'll get over it," she said. "He loves you."

"I know."

"And you don't deserve what people are saying about you."

I smiled. "Do me a favor and never tell me what people are saying about me, Emma."

"Sorry. And look, I wasn't eavesdropping. I swear. These just aren't the thickest walls."

"I know."

"But Eric is right about something. What you did in that courtroom was nothing short of incredible. I don't think this case was the slam dunk Rafe Johnson thought it would be. I think he realizes that now and it's ruining his damn day. His damn year."

"Maybe."

"You wanna grab some lunch?"

"Yeah. Actually, I do."

Emma lingered by the door. She had a scowl on her face. One I recognized from when she was the tiniest baby. A small crease formed between her eyes she only got when she was deep in thought, trying to work something out.

"What is it?" I said. "I know that look."

She straightened and smoothed her expression. "No. It's just ... your closing. It ended up being different from what you planned. You rehearsed it. We went over your notes together."

I gathered my purse. "I thought it was pretty much what I outlined."

"No," she said. "It wasn't. You didn't talk about Reed's confession. You never admitted to the jury that Reed was the one who killed Megan that night."

"Didn't I?"

"No. And it was subtle. I mean, I wonder if I was the only one who noticed. Except I think I wasn't."

"Emma, don't overthink."

"You never said Reed killed Megan to protect his family. Not those words. That he killed her. Was that on purpose?"

I said nothing, because there was nothing I could say. Emma paused for another moment, regarding me. I tried to find a light smile for her but knew I failed. So I moved in front of her and started down the stairs. She followed. I said a silent prayer of thanks that she didn't seem to want to ask me any more questions about my closing. And if she had, the moment passed as soon as we walked into the lobby. Miranda stood there with the desk phone at her ear, her face sheet white.

"Cass," she said. "You need to get over to the hospital. There's been an incident. It's Reed. Someone tried to kill him."

Chapter 26

THERE WAS nobody but me in the surgical waiting room of Windham Hospital. I'd fallen asleep on my coat on one of the couches. Emma had come with me, but she'd long since left after spending half her paycheck in vending machine coffee for us.

"Ms. Leary?" A soft voice and a hand on my arm woke me up. For a moment, I forgot where I was. Or what day it was. Sitting up, I tried to smooth back my hair and breathed on my hand. Ugh. I felt fuzz on my teeth. Emma left promising to bring me a toothbrush and a change of clothes. I didn't even know why I stayed.

"Ms. Leary?" I didn't recognize the nurse. He stood wearing surgical scrubs and a mask patterned after the American flag hanging around his neck.

"What time is it?" I asked.

"Just past eight. Mr. Karl's out of surgery. Do you know if his wife is here?"

"No," I said. "I mean, no, she's not here. It's just me."

The nurse frowned. "We really need to contact his wife. She's written on his paperwork as …"

"Is he dead? He died?"

"I haven't …"

I sat fully upright. The elevators down the hall opened. Eric stepped out. His face fell when he saw me. Emma was with him. He said something to her then the two of them strode toward me. I got to my feet.

I read the nurse's ID badge. "Paul, is it? I'm Reed Karl's attorney. Whatever it is, you can tell me. His wife isn't in any condition to make decisions for him. She's not even here."

Eric and Emma got to my side.

Paul the nurse looked uncertain. The pit in my stomach grew. This couldn't be happening. After everything else, Reed had been stabbed in the exercise yard. He'd been in surgery for hours. Now …

"You have to tell me whether he's alive," I said to Paul.

"I'll get the surgeon," Paul said, still not answering my question.

Emma handed me a small plastic bag filled with toiletries and a change of clothes. I thanked her.

"I talked to Sheriff Lubell," Eric said. "There's still a lot of confusion about what happened."

"No, there isn't," I said. "This is retribution. This is Reed getting punished."

"Trust me," Eric said. "The other inmates don't care that he's a cop killer. It makes him a hero."

Paul came around the corner along with a woman wearing purple scrubs and a surgical cap. She pulled it off and said something quietly to Paul. He nodded and excused himself.

"I'm Cass Leary," I said. "Reed Karl is my client. I'm his lawyer. And I'm the only one who's here for him. Please. Tell me his condition."

"I'm Dr. Martin," she said. "Mr. Karl is out of surgery. He's lost a lot of blood and he won't have use of his left shoulder for a while, there was significant tendon damage, but no major arteries. The blade went in just above his left shoulder blade in the back, but he was very lucky. It could have been a lot worse."

"Has he said anything?" Eric asked, going into detective mode. "Was he able to tell you or anyone who did this?"

Dr. Martin shook her head. "He was pretty out of it when they brought him in. He's still waking up from the anesthesia. Is this your case? I was told to come find Detective Bradshaw."

"I'll find him for you," Eric said. Dr. Martin nodded. Eric touched my elbow, then took off down the hall in search of the investigating detective for the Sheriff's Department.

"Ms. Leary," Dr. Martin said. "Mr. Karl is asking for you. Well, first he was asking for his wife. But I understand she isn't well enough to be here. So, he wants to see you. I can take you to him. But keep in mind, he's very groggy. I don't want him getting overexcited. He needs to rest. I'm going to tell the cops the same thing. My patient needs to stay calm. Having his blood pressure spike won't do him any good while he's in recovery."

"I appreciate everything you've done," I said.

Emma promised to stay back and wait for Eric to reappear. I followed the doctor through the security doors into the surgical recovery room. She led me to the patient cubicle at the very end of the hall. She peeled back the curtain and I stepped inside.

Reed looked terrible. If I didn't see his monitor chirping away with his heart rate and oxygen saturation stats, I might have thought he was already dead. His eyelids fluttered as he recognized me.

"Cass," he croaked out.

"Mr. Karl," Dr. Martin said. "You had a little bit of an ordeal there. I was just telling your lawyer, you were very lucky. Everything wrong with you was pretty much soft tissue damage. I've got you sewn back together but your left arm is going to take some time to heal. You won't be able to move it for a while, okay? Please don't try."

Reed's left arm was heavily bandaged. His right wrist was handcuffed to the bed.

"Is that really necessary?" I said. "Where do they think he's going to go?"

I peered around the curtain. Sheriff Lubell had ordered a deputy to stand guard near Reed's bed.

"Don't worry," Dr. Martin said. "The cuffs won't interfere with anything. He's also on some pretty powerful pain meds that'll kick in once the anesthesia wears off. Mr. Karl is going to be floating pretty high for a while."

"Thank you," I said.

"We'll want to keep him here in recovery for an hour or two, then he'll be moved to a regular room. Assuming there are no complications, which I don't expect, he should be ready for transport back to the jail infirmary by tomorrow afternoon."

She touched Reed's toe. His eyes snapped back open. "I'll check back in with you later this evening," Dr. Martin said. "You just work on getting some rest."

Reed tried to raise his good hand. The cuffs clanged against the bed railing. He scowled through his oxygen mask, but settled back into the bed. Dr. Martin closed the privacy curtain as she left. I pulled a stool up to the side of the bed and sat down.

"Hey, Cass," Reed said. He pulled his oxygen mask away from his mouth. "I think I look worse than I feel."

"I imagine that's true for now. They've got you on the good drugs."

"You have to tell Dahlia that I'm okay. I don't know what they told her. If they told her anything. I don't want her hearing about all of this from anyone but you."

"Well, I can't promise she hasn't already heard. The jail called her. I came as quickly as I could. You've been in surgery for a few hours."

"Don't let her come here. I don't want her getting upset. Dahlia can't be in this hospital. There are too many bad memories."

He meant their son, Ian. He'd been DOA, but I knew Dahlia had been in this very building when a different doctor told her that her son was gone.

"I'll call her," I said. "I'll let her know you came through surgery okay."

"Thank you."

"What happened? Who did this, Reed?"

He turned from me and stared at the wall. "It doesn't matter."

"Yes, it does. Somebody tried to kill you. You need protection."

He smiled then turned back to look at me. "You can't protect me. Nobody can."

"Who did this?" I whispered. The deputy was a good distance away, but I couldn't be sure what he could overhear.

"I don't know," he said. "I was just trying to mind my own business. There was a whole group of guys taunting me. I don't know most of them. I kept my head down. I don't want any trouble."

"Well, trouble has a way of finding you. Where were the guards during all of this?"

Reed's eyes clouded over. He wouldn't answer.

"Reed, where were the guards? You said you were being taunted. Did they see?"

"Just forget it," he said.

"Well, there are cameras. They'll pull the footage."

Reed let out a bitter laugh then winced in pain. "There won't be any footage," he whispered.

"They let this happen," I whispered. "Are you telling me the guards looked the other way?"

"I'm not telling you anything. And for the love of God, don't make an issue out of this."

"An issue? Reed, somebody tried to kill you. And you're telling me the jail guards didn't do anything about it?"

"I'm not telling you anything other than leave it alone."

"You'll be dead. We have to get you out of there."

"Any word on the jury?"

I sat back. "Not yet." We were heading into the third day of deliberations. It felt like an eternity.

"That could be good, right?"

"It could be anything. But we've got a much bigger, more pressing issue. I'm going to file an emergency petition requesting you not be returned to the jail. I want you staying right here in the hospital under guard."

"It doesn't matter."

"Yes, it does. Dammit, Reed. You're a sitting duck in that jail if every guard in there thinks you killed Megan Lewis. Or if they think you're about to get away with killing her. What is it going to take to get it through your head you have to tell the truth. Now. Before it's too late."

He smiled, but didn't answer. I felt my anger rising.

"You're not safe in jail, Reed."

"File the petition then," he said.

"And you'll tell the truth? You'll recant your confession and tell the cops what really happened?"

"I'm done talking to the cops. I'm at peace with letting the jury decide my fate."

"Except they're *not* going to decide it. It sounds to me like the guards are going to decide it. Somebody in there has decided they can win points by hurting you. Or worse. If you don't come clean, I can't guarantee your safety."

"I'm not asking you to. I'm asking you to finish the job I hired you to do. Relax. Soon enough, you'll be free of me."

"What good does this do anybody?" I said, trying not to shout. "If you get killed in prison. If you stay in prison. Dahlia needs help. Real help. You think you're doing the right thing for Clara letting her stay with her mother. But you're not. And I cannot just sit by and ..."

"Yes you can," Reed said, rallying. "And you will. I can take care of myself. Dahlia needs to take care of Clara. They need each other. That's the only way this works."

"She's not taking care of Clara. Clara isn't even in the house right now, Reed. The Bakers have her. Kim was worried about what she saw. Dahlia won't get out of bed. She won't eat. Won't shower. She's not taking care of Clara because she can't even take care of herself. You think you're protecting her. What you're doing is denying her the help she needs. Please ... please reconsider."

"No," he said. "And I'm done talking."

The curtain opened. Eric and Detective Bradshaw walked in.

"My client isn't up for an interview," I said.

"Yes, I am," Reed said. "You can go now, Cass. Thank you. Just let Dahlia and Clara know I'm all right."

"I'm not going anywhere," I said.

"Cass, leave," Reed said. "I'll talk to Detective Bradshaw. I don't need you here for that."

I rose. Blood boiling, I wanted to rip into Reed, even as he was chained to his hospital bed.

"You heard your client," Detective Lou Bradshaw said. "I just need his statement."

"Just need his statement," I said. "So then you can look the other way too. You know exactly what happened. If anything else happens to Reed ... if so much as a hair on his head gets touched, I'll have your badge."

"You sure about that?" Bradshaw said. He puffed out his chest and took a step toward me.

Eric got in the way. "You need to take a step back, Lou. Cool off. Interview your prisoner. Do your job."

Eric and Bradshaw squared off. For a moment, I thought it might come to blows. But Eric finally took a step back. He put a hand on my arm and led me back down the hall. We passed the deputy; he glared at me, his eyes filled with contempt. I wanted to scream. I wanted to punch something. Eric got me back to the waiting room. Emma was nowhere to be found.

"You need to cool off," Eric said.

"Cool off? You know what happened. Reed got jumped ... got stabbed in a yard full of inmates and guards and security cameras. Only nobody intervened. Nobody is going to admit to seeing a damn thing. They're going to let him die in there. And you know it's not right."

"I'll see what I can find out," Eric said. "See if we can arrange for Reed to get some protection. They're going to want to put him in solitary but that might not be a bad thing."

I shook my head. I was fuming. It seemed I would forever be surrounded by stubborn, pig-headed men. Reed's truth was bubbling inside me. I felt like a volcano ready to erupt. Except I couldn't. My hands were tied. I was muzzled. And at the rate things were going, Reed Karl was going to pay for his secrets with his life.

Chapter 27

By the next morning, Thursday, Reed had stabilized enough to be moved to a private room. My emergency motion to keep him from being transferred back to the jail was on Judge Niedermayer's desk. She refused to enter it without a hearing. We were set to appear in front of her Friday morning at eight a.m. I spoke to Kim Baker on the phone and she promised to relay all the information to Dahlia. For my part, I didn't think I could be in the same room with the woman.

I had moved most of Reed's files to my home office. I sat in the middle of the floor staring at the pages of witness statements. All of them meaningless. All of them presumed that Reed himself had carried out this crime.

I had my laptop in front me. I pulled Dahlia Karl's Facebook profile picture up. It was taken five years ago. A formal portrait of Dahlia, Reed, and their two children. A younger, more round-faced Clara smiled at the camera. She held her then four-year-old brother Ian on her lap. They looked like carbon copies of their parents. Clara had Dahlia's blonde hair. Ian was dark, like his father. He had the same deep green eyes.

Dahlia looked like a different person. Vibrant. Happy. Reed sat behind her. The picture was taken outdoors in a field of sunflowers. Dahlia had a hand up, touching Reed's cheek.

It was all a lie. An illusion. Maybe they had been happy then. Maybe the photographer had captured the brief moment in time before everything started to fall apart for them.

There had been no movement from the jury. Only a request to the judge to be able to replay Reed's confession in its entirety. Then later, they wanted to see the text of Judge Niedermayer's jury instruction on the elements of first degree murder. It would be easy to take hope from that. If they had reasonable doubt about premeditation, they could not vote to convict Reed of the most serious charge.

Dahlia. Her eyes seemed to follow me everywhere as I moved around the room.

She was guilty. Mentally unstable. Fearing her own life or the life of her remaining child, she had made a decision to end Megan Lewis's life. The thing was, had Dahlia been my client, I don't believe Rafe Johnson would have even attempted to charge her with first degree. I would have had a winnable case for second degree and felt certain a psychological evaluation would have led to a recommendation for in-patient treatment, not jail.

But here we were. Because of my stubborn client and an oath I couldn't break, I might very well watch Reed Karl go to prison for the rest of his life.

I wanted to throw my laptop and Dahlia's grinning face through the window.

There had to be something. Some way to prove that Dahlia committed this crime instead of Reed. There was his word, of course. But there was no physical evidence at the scene. Which meant she'd been careful. No hairs. No clothing fibers. No DNA other than Megan's.

I pulled the cell phone forensics report. Reed's phone remained on its charger the entire night when Megan was killed. So had Dahlia's.

"How did you get there?" I whispered to Dahlia's photograph. "Did you drive your car?"

She could have walked. It was certainly possible. They lived less than two miles apart. The newest plat of the Eden's Edge subdivision was just one open field away from Pine Circle, Megan's neighborhood. She could have easily slipped out and not been seen or heard by Reed if he slept soundly enough.

Could I prove it? Could I somehow build the case against her Rodney Patel failed to make? And then what? I couldn't even feed Patel the information anonymously without violating confidentiality. Without turning my back on everything I believed as a lawyer.

"Cass?" Vangie knocked on the door and poked her head in. "Sorry to interrupt you."

I quickly closed the laptop. I didn't want Vangie or anyone else to know what I was working on in here.

"It's okay."

"Matty and Tori are here," she said. "Everybody's downstairs. We're just waiting for you."

The newlyweds had just returned from their one-week honeymoon. Matty had taken Tori on a cruise of the Western Caribbean. It was my wedding present to them. Matty hadn't wanted to accept it. But what was the point of Reed's money if I couldn't use it to bring some joy?

I heard laughter downstairs. Little Sean's squeal of delight. He'd stayed with Vangie and Jessa all week. He missed his parents deeply. Marby and Madison helped with the excitement. Matty was one of their favorite people.

I dusted off my jeans and followed Vangie back downstairs. Joe and Emma had arrived bearing boxes of pizza and two liters of pop. The only person missing was Eric and nobody asked me about him. I hadn't seen him since the hospital yesterday. He promised he'd see what he could find out about Reed's jailhouse assault. But I held out no hope he would get anywhere.

"Cass!" Tori came toward me, open-armed. She looked amazing. Tanned. Healthy. Happy.

"I missed you!" I said. And I did. Matty was next. He was seated on the chair by the window. I leaned over him and hugged him. Then the Leary clan descended on the pizza.

I grabbed a couple of slices of pepperoni and went out on the porch. Matty brought his tablet and was busy showing everyone pictures of their trip. I would look at them later. For now, I just wanted to sit by myself and sulk.

My brother Joe was never going to allow that. As everyone settled inside and listened to Matty and Tori's stories, Joe came out and sat beside me. Late November and it was almost sixty degrees again. It had snowed four days ago.

"This is the last one of these," Joe said. "Temps are gonna drop twenty degrees by tonight. It's only supposed to get up to forty as a high tomorrow."

"Sounds about right," I said, taking a big bite of my last slice.

"You okay?"

I could have lied. I could have changed the subject. But it would have done no good. Not with Joe. Never with Joe.

"No."

"Where's Eric today? He knew about this, didn't he?"

"He knows."

Joe nodded. "Yeah. That's not an answer."

"I know."

"Is there anything I can do?

"There really isn't."

"I figured. Emma's been walking around in the same kind of funk. It's this case, I know that much."

"You know I can't talk about it."

"Yeah. Only I think you better. Maybe you can't with me. But Cass, you gotta talk to somebody. It's making you sick."

"What do you mean?"

"You," he said. "When's the last time you stepped on a scale?"

"What? When's the last time you thought it was okay to comment on a woman's weight?"

"Yeah. Knock it off. You know that's not what I mean. Look, whatever's going on. Is it worth it?"

"What do you mean?"

"I mean ... Eric's AWOL. And he's been AWOL for weeks now. You're doing crazy shit like spending a night in the hospital waiting room for some guy who's not even family."

"He's my client. And he almost died."

"He didn't almost die. Emma said it wasn't serious."

"He was stabbed. Somebody tried to kill him. That's serious."

"Is it really such a big deal if you lose? It's just a case. You've tried hundreds. I don't know, maybe thousands. You don't always win, do you?"

I smiled. "Most of the time."

"Are you ... um ... into this guy?"

"What?" I turned almost violently to face my brother. He immediately put his hands up in surrender.

"Sorry. Sorry. My bad. I guess not. I'm just trying to figure out what's going on. You're not acting like yourself and we've all noticed. We're all worried. I'm just the guy everybody voted to come out here and check on you."

"You all voted?"

"Well, it wasn't formal. Like we didn't draw straws."

"I don't need to be checked on."

"No. I know." He stopped. "Except you kinda do. Cass, I haven't seen you like this since you were about to finish law school and take that job in Chicago. You were single-minded like this. Refusing to talk to anybody. Then you made a choice that ended up being the exact worst thing for you."

"This isn't that," I said. "The case just got under my skin. That's all. I don't want to lose this one."

"Yeah. But he killed that girl, didn't he?"

I didn't say anything. I just stared out at the lake. A flock of geese had gathered near the shore. We would have open water for a few weeks yet. They were getting hungry. If anyone came out here and tried to give them their pizza crusts, I'd brain them. The geese and I had an understanding. They were welcome to swim out there, but could not go on the lawn.

"I get that he's allowed to have his day in court. I get why he'd want you in his corner. But he killed her. He admitted it. Only ... you're acting like ..."

"Like what?"

"Like you think he's innocent."

My heart froze. The desire to unburden myself on my brother swelled within me. We'd shared everything over the years. Kept no secrets. Not the big ones, anyway.

"Quit trying to read into things. Yeah. This one got under my skin. I just admitted that."

"Hmm."

"What do you mean, hmm?"

"I just mean ... I don't know. Never mind what I mean. Just come inside and have some more pizza. Come back to the land of the living."

"You're a pest, you know that?" I said.

Joe stood up. He tossed a piece of his crust right in the middle of the geese.

"Joe!"

He gave me a mischievous grin as he turned toward me. "Great," I said. "One piece of crust. I'm going to spend the whole summer chasing them off the lawn again."

"Isn't that Marby and Madison's job?"

"They suck at it. And Madison's getting too old. She can barely hear."

"She hears fine. She just doesn't listen." Joe put his arm around me. I felt myself go rigid. I couldn't get emotional. I didn't have the luxury. Not yet. Not until ...

As I opened the door, Emma rushed forward. She had her cell phone in her hand. "Aunt Cass," she said, breathless. "That was Miranda. She's at the office catching up on billings. She got a call from Niedermayer's clerk. They want you in court in an hour. The jury's back. I think the verdict is in. Can I ... do you mind if I come too?"

I was halfway up the stairs, headed for my closet. I'd have just enough time to throw on a suit. "Start the car," I called down. "Have Miranda call the court and tell them we're on our way."

Chapter 28

SHERIFF LUBELL and Rafe Johnson stood outside the courtroom. Lubell jabbed a finger in Rafe's chest. By his posture, I worried for a moment that the two men would come to blows.

I'd bypassed three local news reporters on the way in. Emma raced to keep up with me. As I approached, Lubell took a step back.

"You're another one," he muttered.

"You can believe whatever you want," I said, feeling my anger rising. But I was damn tired of being everyone's villain in this. "You wanna talk to me about what happened to my client under your watch?"

Lubell's jaw clenched.

"Enough, Sheriff," Rafe said. "Let's just get through the damn day, all right?"

Lubell glared at him, but backed off. He opened the courtroom door and went inside. Emma followed behind him, heading for the table.

"Rafe," I said. "You understand what happened. There has to be an impartial and full investigation into Reed Karl's attack. He's not safe in Woodbridge County. Lubell's people looked the other way."

"Cass, let's not jump to conclusions."

"It's not a jump. It's a fact."

Emma poked her head back out. "The judge is about to take the bench. They need you both in here."

Rafe and I exchanged a look. He reached out and held the door for me. I felt my stomach churn. Three and a half days. The jury had deliberated for three and a half days. It could mean anything.

I walked up to the table and remained standing. Rafe's paralegal waited for him. The kid looked as sick as I felt. Behind me, the deputies filed in and lined the wall. There was nobody here for Reed. Just me.

"All rise!" Judge Niedermayer's bailiff stood in the center of the courtroom. Her court reporter sat poised with her fingers over her keyboard. Judge Niedermayer herself stormed into the courtroom, her robes flying behind her. Her cheeks were flushed.

She rifled through the papers in front of her.

The bailiff took his post beside her bench. Niedermayer whispered something to him, then nodded to her court reporter.

"All right," she said. "We're back on the record. Counsel for the state and the defense are here. I would note that the defendant is not present."

"No, Your Honor," I said. "The defendant is still recuperating from the attempt on his life."

"What is his condition?"

"Stable," I said. "He was stabbed in the upper back. Just below the shoulder. The surgeon indicated he was very lucky that no major arteries were damaged."

"I would say so," Judge Niedermayer said. "All right. I have been in communication with the jury foreman all through the morning. I'm just going to cut to it. I have been informed that the jury is hopelessly deadlocked. I have asked them ... I have implored them to keep trying over the course of the last several hours. However, they remain at an impasse. At this point, we have a hung jury."

It took a moment for her words to sink in. Hung jury.

"Your Honor." Rafe spoke first. "Can you order them to keep at it?"

"We're beyond that now, Counselor. They're done. I have no alternative but to declare a mistrial."

The air in the room got thick. Hung jury. Mistrial. Not a conviction. Not an acquittal. Just ... nothing.

"Your Honor," Rafe said; he too seemed out of breath. "I'd like to know the outcome. What was the vote?"

Niedermayer looked at the paper in front of her. "We have ten guilty votes on the first degree murder charge, one vote for voluntary manslaughter, one not guilty on all counts. It is my understanding that that is the way the vote broke down from the very beginning and it has remained that way through several subsequent votes and deliberation. They're hung, folks."

I couldn't believe what I was hearing. It was a new kind of nightmare. This wasn't over.

Rafe slammed his pencil on the desk, earning an eye raise from the judge. He took a breath, attempting to compose himself.

"Your Honor," I said. "In light of the jury vote. In light of the events of yesterday at the county jail and my client's condition, I would like to move for his bail to be reconsidered. Mr. Karl is not safe in the Woodbridge County Jail. He is not receiving adequate protection."

"Your Honor," Rafe shouted. "Nothing has changed since this issue was adjudicated at Mr. Karl's arraignment. He is still charged with a heinous crime. He still poses a flight risk if he's let out."

"He's in the hospital recovering from a near fatal knifing," I said. "Exactly where do you think he's going to go?"

"Enough," Niedermayer said, banging her gavel.

"Your Honor," I said. "Mr. Karl has been in jail for six months. He has been a model inmate in that time. He has ties to the community. His young daughter lives here. His wife. He's not going anywhere. And the fact remains he is objectively not safe where he's being confined. If the state decides to retry this case ..."

"The state will absolutely be retrying this case," Rafe said.

"That could take months if not years," I said. "There needs to be an investigation into what happened at the jail. The county has a duty to protect Mr. Karl. They have failed. And he still benefits from a presumption of innocence until proven guilty. So far, the state has failed their burden. Mr. Karl deserves protection."

"Here's what we're going to do," Niedermayer said. "I agree that these are serious issues that need to be properly litigated. Ms. Leary has a point. Mr. Karl's safety is clearly a concern. However, he is still accused of murdering Megan Lewis. Of a violent crime. For now, he stays where he is. Ms. Leary will keep the court informed of when his doctors feel Mr. Karl is ready to be released from the hospital. Let's schedule a new bail hearing on this matter to take place in four days. I want briefs from both of you. For now, we're adjourned."

Her gavel cracked against the top of her desk. Niedermayer left the bench with the same twirling robe as when she stepped out. I stood there for a moment, not really knowing how to feel.

I turned to Emma. "Can you head back to the office and let everybody know what's going on?"

Emma seemed just as shell-shocked as I felt. She took my messenger bag from me, collected her own notebooks, and walked out of the courtroom with the rest of the spectators. It left just Rafe and me alone, staring at the empty bench.

"Congratulations," Rafe said, his tone bitter. I turned to him.

"This isn't a victory for either one of us, Rafe."

"It certainly isn't one for Megan Lewis. It's also not the end of this."

"Are you really going to fight me on bail for Reed Karl?"

Rafe shoved his notes into his briefcase. He walked over to my table. "What you heard out there with Lubell? That's the tip of the iceberg of the heat I've been getting. Sheriff Grover in Taney County is even a bigger hothead."

"You think I'm everyone's hero in this? You think I don't know Lubell and probably everyone at the Delphi Police Department has told your office not to deal with me on any future cases of mine?"

"So why'd you do it? Why dig your heels in on this case?"

I wanted to answer him. I wanted to profess my client's innocence. I couldn't. I couldn't say a damn word.

"Because it was worth my time," I said. "And worth the damage to my professional reputation."

Rafe's eyes narrowed. "I've got to hand it to you. You pulled a rabbit out of a hat with this one. I'd like to talk to those two holdouts."

"I won't stop you."

"You know I still can't offer your client a plea deal."

"I wasn't asking for one."

Rafe shook his head. "You're impossible. This was a gift you got handed today. A damn miracle."

"Except my client is still incarcerated. Oh, and he's recovering from somebody shoving a four-inch shiv into his back. There's that. It happened in front of a yardful of people and yet nobody claims to have seen anything. He's gonna get killed in there. How will that serve anybody?"

Rafe slipped the strap of his briefcase over his shoulder. "You do what you have to do. I'll do what I have to do."

"You're halfway out the door. I know you don't want anything to do with this case after you walk out of here. Between you and me, I'd rather deal with you than anyone else. You've let Lubell and Grover pull your strings too much on this one. You've been too worried about whatever legacy you want to leave here. And you know Rodney Patel handed you a hot mess with this case. You know his interrogation was deeply flawed."

"Karl wasn't coerced. It was a good interview. The next jury will understand that."

"Are you going to stick around long enough to be the one to make that argument?"

Rafe's nostrils flared. "I don't know yet. But this feels like unfinished business. I'm not sure I want to leave it for the next guy."

"I'll see you around, Rafe."

He slumped his shoulders as he turned his back on me and walked out of the courtroom. For some reason, I couldn't bring myself to leave. Not yet. I stared at the empty jury box.

Someone believed me. Two of those twelve people understood that Reed Karl wasn't guilty of murder. Rafe was right about one thing. After everything else Reed had done, that alone was a damn miracle.

Chapter 29

"So what does it mean?" Reed winced as he pushed himself further up in his hospital bed. I handed him his plastic cup and held the straw for him. He took a slow sip of water and settled back against the pillows.

"It means we're back to square one. Your case will have to be retried."

"You really think the prosecutor's office will go through it again?"

"I absolutely do. Megan was still murdered. They will seek justice for her. As they should."

"Thank you," he said. "I never would have made it this far without your help."

"My help? How have I helped you, exactly? Reed, you're still facing a murder charge. You're still not the one who killed Megan. And you're still protecting the person who did. This is a second chance. Recant your confession. Let me work on getting your charges dropped."

"We've been over this. I'm not changing my story. I'll stand trial as many times as they make me. I'm doing what I have to do. If you don't want to be involved anymore, I can respect that."

I let out a bitter huff. "You say that like it's easy. I *am* involved. I'm chin deep in this, Reed, and drowning right along with you."

His face changed. I wanted to swallow the words I'd just uttered. Drowning. It was a careless thing for me to say.

"I'm sorry," I said.

"What happens next?"

"Immediately? You work on getting better. The judge has agreed to revisit your bail. With any luck, I can argue to get you sent home. On a tether, maybe. But home. Only, I'm not sure that's the best place for you either. I don't like the idea of you being with Dahlia."

"She's my wife."

I bit my tongue past everything else I wanted to say about her. She was a killer. She was a liar. If anything, Reed living in the same house with her again would only strengthen his resolve to take the blame for her sins.

"I'll do what I can to secure your release pending the second trial. Beyond that, I don't know what my role will be."

"Will you tell her? Will you go see Dahlia and explain all of this to her? I think it would be best coming from you."

"Sure."

"And Clara. Do you think it would be possible for me to see her? Can she visit me while I'm in the hospital?"

"I'm not sure that's a good idea."

"I didn't want her coming to the jail. I talked to her on the phone a couple of times, but I didn't want her in that environment. But here. Maybe while I'm here, she could see me. If she wants to. Only if she wants to. Do you think you could talk to her? Tell her I love her?"

"I'll check in on her," I said. "Beyond that, no promises."

"Okay. I appreciate that. I appreciate everything. I'd be dead without you, Cass. I mean that figuratively and literally. I know you're the only person on the planet who believes in me."

"You're innocent of this crime," I said. "That doesn't mean I think you're innocent of wrongdoing. You're still protecting Megan's killer."

Reed sank back deeper into the bed. His eyelids fluttered. They had him on powerful painkillers and I knew they were starting to kick in.

"I'm sorry," he whispered. "I know I've made such a mess of everything. And I know I'm not worth all of this. But Clara is."

"I agree," I said. "Leaving her with Dahlia isn't the right answer, Reed."

"It is. You have to trust me on that. It just is."

"She's staying with the Bakers now. Maybe … well, I think maybe you should start thinking longer term. If I don't succeed in getting you released on bail. If the Bakers are willing."

"Dahlia needs her, Cass."

Dahlia needed Clara? What about what Clara needed? I was too tired to argue with him. The last thing I wanted to do was see Dahlia. But Reed was right. I was the only person who could explain any of this to her. So I would go. I would look that woman in the eye and not say the truth we both knew. Afterward, I would need a stiff drink.

"Get some rest," I said. "We'll talk tomorrow."

"Thank you, Cass," Reed said, but he was already drifting off. As I gathered myself and rose to leave, a strange thought popped in my head. The minute I had it, I knew it was true. Reed Karl would not survive prison. Never mind the stabbing, he seemed to be wasting away in front of me. As if he'd stopped fighting. Lost the will to live.

God. Clara would have no one. She would have worse than no one. And I felt powerless to stop it.

Chapter 30

DAHLIA DIDN'T COME to the door when I knocked. I knew she was home. I could see both cars in the garage from the side window. Three packages were stacked on the porch.

"Dahlia?" I called out. Her driveway and sidewalk had been shoveled and salted. I knew Sawyer Thompson, her neighbor, had been doing his best to take care of the outside of her property. Sawyer had waved to me from his own porch as I pulled up.

I knocked once more, then tried the doorknob. It turned in my hand. "Lord," I muttered. "She isn't even locking her front door?"

"Dahlia!" I called out as I entered the home. More packages were stacked in the foyer. A layer of dust coated the hallway table. Something smelled sour in the kitchen. I could hear the faucet dripping. As I moved through the house, I saw dishes stacked up in the sink.

"Dahlia, it's Cass Leary!"

I heard rustling coming from the first floor primary suite toward the back of the house. Thank God, I thought. She's not dead. That would have been the last thing I needed.

Feeling a little angry, I made my way to the bedroom and gently opened the door, ready to jump back to the hallway if Dahlia were indisposed. She wasn't though. She sat up in bed, absently switching channels with her remote control. She barely acknowledged me as I walked in.

"Dahlia, I'm sorry to barge in on you. Your front door was unlocked. I've just come from the courthouse. And from seeing Reed."

Her eyes widened. She looked at me but it seemed like she was having trouble focusing. Her skin was ashen, her cheeks sunken in.

"When's the last time you ate?" I asked.

Dahlia put the remote down. The woman looked like a bona fide zombie. I noticed a couple of pill bottles by her bedside. Screw it, I thought. I picked one up and read the label. She was taking Xanax. A lot of it.

"When's Reed coming home?" she asked.

"I don't know. I'm working on that. Dahlia, the trial is over. That's what I came here to talk to you about."

Dahlia adjusted the covers. She wore a dingy white tank top. One strap hung loose off her shoulder.

"The jury couldn't decide," I said. "They were deadlocked. It means it was a mistrial. We're going to have to start all over again. I'm working on trying to get Reed released pending the outcome of the next trial. It could take months though. If not longer."

"Oh," she said. It was as if she heard me, but wasn't listening. I sat on the edge of the bed.

"Dahlia, do you understand what I'm telling you? Your husband wasn't found guilty, but he wasn't acquitted either."

"Like a do-over," she said. "No. I heard you the first time. That's good though, right? I mean, he wasn't found guilty."

"I mean ... sure," I said.

"I have to tell Clara. Is she in her room?"

"What? No. Dahlia, Clara isn't here. She's at the Bakers. Don't you remember?" Good heavens. She was gone. Vacant.

"Oh. That's right. Yes. Kim and Dean. They've been so kind to us. I don't know what I would do without them. I miss Clara though. She needs to help me here. She said she was going to help me here. I just can't seem to get anything done. Clara was supposed to take out the garbage. I had a list for her."

I bit my tongue. I wanted to shake this woman. Wanted to tell her her daughter was probably far better off where she was. Far away from her. Then I saw the teddy bear on the bedside next to her. She had sewn the hole in its neck closed. It was the same one Megan Lewis had slashed and hung off the ceiling fan in this very room. The toy that had belonged to Dahlia's dead son, Ian.

Ian.

The police report I'd read swam in my mind. Dahlia had fallen asleep. She hadn't heard her four-year-old son walk out the back slider. I looked at the bottle of Xanax. Had she been like this that day? Stoned out of her mind on benzos?

"Anyway," I said. "I just came to tell you what happened in court. Reed's on the mend. He's getting better. He asked about you. I think arrangements could be made for you to visit him in the hospital if you wanted to. He's asking for Clara as well."

Dahlia nodded. "That would be nice. It's been so long since she's seen her daddy. She's always been Daddy's girl. Ian was mine, but Clara is Reed's."

"Right," I said. "Well, I'll leave you to rest now."

Dahlia raised a hand as if to wave goodbye. Then she started to stare at her own fingers as if she'd forgotten she had them.

I couldn't stand to be in the room with her for another second. The idea that Reed thought Clara was better off with her infuriated me. I may not be able to disclose the truth about who killed Megan, but I could sure as hell intervene to keep Clara safe.

I walked back to the kitchen. The sliding door was partially open, letting flakes of snow fly in. I went to the door and tried to close it. It was stuck in the track. I was able to open it wider. I stepped out onto the deck. There was a large dip in the yard where the swimming pool had once been. Reed said he wanted to tear out the deck itself someday.

I looked to the right. Sawyer Thompson was now in his backyard, shoveling a small path for his dog. The Karls' fence had a gate in the middle, leading into the woods beyond. Reed had put it there when they built the pool so Clara and Elyse Baker could cut through to each other's yards.

"How is she today?" Sawyer called out. I turned and pulled the slider shut. I'd just go around the side yard rather than back through the house. I just wanted to get out of there.

I stepped off the deck and walked to the fence. Thompson's security camera was mounted on the side of his house. I saw the path Megan Lewis walked the night she broke in.

"She's not great," I said. "I have to be honest. I'm worried. She seems pretty out of it."

Sawyer sighed and nodded. "We think the same thing too. She won't get out of that damn bed. Lettie asked her if she could come over and help her clean up. Take her out to lunch. Get her hair done. Something. She just keeps saying Clara's going to take care of everything."

"She's not here," I said, pointing to the back gate. "She's staying with Kim and Dean Baker, still."

"Good," Sawyer said. "They're good people. They'll watch out for her. I saw the verdict on the internet. Hung jury, huh?"

"Yep."

"Tough break, kid. Though I suppose it's better than a conviction. I mean, for Reed. Not better for that girl he killed. Man, I don't know how to feel. She was a whack job. But this whole thing has ripped that family apart. Clara's the one who's gotta pay for it."

"Yes. She is."

"Well, you tell her if you see her. Uncle Sawyer and Aunt Lettie are thinking about her. She's welcome over here anytime."

"Thank you. I think she'll like that. I'm going to try to go over and see her now. Explain to her what's going on."

Sawyer whistled. "Yeah. Good luck with that. I don't know how you explain any of this. To anybody."

"Thanks again for all of your help. Your testimony at trial is probably one of the core reasons the jury couldn't reach a unanimous verdict. It helped explain the whole picture, you know?"

"I just said what I saw. Doesn't mean I think what happened was good for anybody."

"I know. But you told the truth. That means a lot."

"Well, I'll say this much. If I'm ever in trouble. Or anybody I care about ends up in a fix. You're the one I want in my corner. And I'll tell anybody who asks. Keep your chin up, kiddo. Don't let the bastards getcha down."

"Thanks," I said. I felt a lump in my throat. I hadn't expected to need to hear those words so desperately today, but I did.

"You can still cut through there to get to the Bakers," he said. "Elyse and Clara don't use that pathway so much anymore, but it's still there."

"Thanks," I said. "I've got my car. I'll just drive."

Sawyer gave me a wave then went back to his shoveling. I walked around the side of the house closest to where my car was parked but realized I couldn't get through that way, the gate was on the other side. It forced me to walk all the way around the deck again and wave to Sawyer once more. The gate itself stuck. The latch was almost rusted shut. I supposed nobody had much occasion to use it anymore now that the pool was gone and winter set in. I gave it one more good shove and pushed my way through.

Chapter 31

A FEW MINUTES LATER, I pulled up to Kim and Dean Baker's house on the other side of the Eden's Edge subdivision. They had chosen the exact same builder's model as the Karls' home. A two-story, four-bedroom with a wraparound porch and half-acre yard in back. Kim Baker saw me from her front bay window and waved.

The Baker home was like night and day from the Karls'. Warm light, the heavenly scent of dinner cooking, spotless shelves, and gleaming countertops. There was life here. Peace. Normalcy.

"I just came from Dahlia's," I said, peering around the hallway. I heard muffled voices upstairs.

"The girls are in their bedrooms," Kim said. "There's been a little bit of girl drama. I think Elyse wore the same shirt Clara was going to wear to school today or some other tragedy. Don't worry, it'll peter out and they'll be inseparable again in a second."

"I assume you've heard about the verdict?"

Kim set her teeth on edge. "Yes. What does that mean for Clara?"

"Nothing so far. Kim, when's the last time you went over to Dahlia's?"

She let out a sigh. "Two days ago. I can't get her out of bed, Cass. I'm worried. I'm wondering if maybe there's some way to get a social worker in there or something. She's just wasting away. But to be honest, my focus has been Clara. I can't do anything for Dahlia. But I can make sure Clara has a roof over her head. Clean clothes. Good meals."

"You're doing great," I said. "But ... are you in this for the long haul?"

Dean Baker came around the corner. He was still wearing his work overalls. He was a tool and die maker at the Ford plant in Wayne. He carried a small black lunch box and set it on the counter. Kim opened it and started to clean it out. He came to her side and kissed his wife's cheek, causing her to blush.

"I was just telling Cass," Kim said. "How good it's been for Elyse to have Clara here. She's never had any siblings. We tried a long time ago, but it just wasn't in the cards. I've worried about Elyse being an only child, you know? She's never had to share. I'm not saying there haven't been challenges, but this isn't just about us doing something for Clara. It's good for Elyse too."

"I'm sure it is."

"Hmm," Dean said. A man of few words. He went over to the stove and opened the lid on the stew pot. He sniffed his wife's concoction. Beef stew. Smiling, he closed the lid.

"How do you feel about having Clara here, Dean?" I asked. Kim shot me a look, but I needed to know. If I was going to make a push for Clara, I had to be sure the entire family was on board.

"She's a good kid," Dean said. "Does her chores and her homework without complaining too much."

"That's good. Though having one teenage girl in the house is enough drama. How do you both feel about having two?"

"We're managing," Dean said. "Though it's mostly Kim. I'm working sixty hours a week these days."

"We're doing fine," Kim added. "Chaotic, but fine."

"I don't know for sure if I'm going to be able to secure Reed's release pending the outcome of another trial. There's a good chance he'll have to remain in jail for the foreseeable future. And Dahlia ... well ..."

"She can barely take care of herself," Kim finished my sentence for me.

"Yes," I said. "Clara is my concern. I'm wondering, how would you both feel about Clara staying with you on a more permanent, more formal basis?"

"You mean a guardianship," Kim said. She reached out and touched her husband's arm. Dean's face was unreadable.

"Yes. Guardianship."

"If we don't take her in. If Reed doesn't come home. If Dahlia can't get better ... what will happen to Clara?" Kim asked.

"She has no other family that's local," I said. "As I understand it, Dahlia's next closest family members are cousins that live in England. Most likely, that means Clara would go into foster care."

"No," Kim said forcefully. "Absolutely not. We can't have that."

"I don't want to put you on the spot. Obviously, it's a big decision for your family. For your whole family. But if ..."

"She can stay with us," Kim said. "Whatever paperwork needs to be prepared, can you do it?"

I looked at Dean, waiting for him to chime in. When he saw me looking, he put an arm around his wife.

"Kim's the one here all the time," he said. "I'll go along with whatever she wants to do."

It wasn't really the full-throated support I was looking for, but I'd take it.

"Well, I meant what I said. I was just trying to lay out what options there are for Clara. Take some time. Discuss it as a family. Elyse may have strong feelings as well."

"Fine!" A shout came from upstairs. Then a slammed door. A moment later, Elyse stomped into the kitchen. She stopped short when she saw me.

"Everything okay?" Kim asked.

"It's great." Elyse smiled. "Clara's just ... Clara-ing."

"Honey," Kim said. She went over to her daughter and tried to pull her into a side hug. Elyse recoiled. "We were just talking with Ms. Leary about Clara's living arrangements. Cass, we talked to Elyse about this the other night. About the guardianship. Honey, Mr. Karl may not be getting out of jail for a while. So the good news in all of that ... Clara will get to stay with us maybe for the rest of the school year. At least. I was just telling Ms. Leary that we're all on board with that."

Elyse moved out of her mother's embrace and grabbed an apple from a bowl on the counter. "That'll make Clara happy."

"What about you?" I asked.

Elyse bit into her apple. "It's fine. Whatever."

Elyse certainly didn't seem fine. But she turned on her heel and disappeared down the hallway. I resisted the urge to push Kim too hard. It wasn't for me to tell her how to handle her own daughter. At the same time, if we moved forward with the guardianship and custody agreement, I needed to make sure everyone was comfortable with it. I didn't want to move Clara from one volatile situation into another.

"She'll be fine," Kim assured me. "Elyse is just moody."

"I get it," I said. "I just want to look out for Clara's best interests. As I know you do."

"Of course," Kim said. "Clara will always have a home here as long as she needs it. Dinner will be in an hour. Cass, why don't you stay?"

Heavy footsteps bounded down the stairs. Clara walked in. She looked good. Radiant, actually. She wore a red sweater and blue jeans. Her hair was styled differently than the last time I saw her. She'd cut maybe six inches off the bottom. It curled around her face in a stylish wave. She had a healthy glow to her cheeks and it looked like the weight of the world had been lifted from her shoulders.

God. It was that house. The Karl house was cursed. It seemed to suck the life out of everyone who entered. But here. Here at the Bakers, things seemed healthy. Even the teenage moodiness Kim described seemed normal in its way. I made a vow to myself then and there. If I couldn't get through to Reed. If he refused to tell the truth and hold his wife accountable, maybe I could facilitate a permanent change for Clara.

"You look great, Clara," I said. "I like your hair."

"Thanks," she said, "Kim took me to her salon last week. I donated my hair. It feels good."

"I'll bet."

"Did you see my dad?" she asked. Kim whispered something to her husband. The two of them excused themselves and went into another part of the house.

"I saw your dad." Then, as simply as I could, I explained to Clara what happened in the trial.

She didn't react at first. She seemed pensive. "So he has to go through trial again?"

"Yes."

"But some of the people on the jury didn't think he should go to prison?"

"Well, they didn't agree that the prosecutor proved his case all the way. He'll have another chance. It might be harder next time."

"You told my mom?"

"I did."

"Did she ... understand?"

"I think so. Clara, your father is asking about you. He ... he was wondering if you'd like to visit him while he's in the hospital.

You don't have to. And you don't have to feel pressured. But if you wanted to, I could go with you."

She bit her lip. "I'm not sure. Is that okay?"

"It is absolutely okay."

"I'll think about it."

"That's all you have to do."

She walked around me and went to the stew pot. She picked up Kim's ladle and began to stir.

"Needs more salt," she said. She picked up a salt grinder and added some to the stew. She looked so grown up to me. So ... responsible. I had to remind myself she was only fourteen years old.

"Clara," I said. "Are you happy here with the Bakers?"

She put the salt shaker down. "It's ... it's easier here. They don't yell. Everybody gets along. And they're like ... happy to see each other. Nobody's sad."

"Would you like to stay here?"

"Doesn't my mom get to decide that?"

"Partly. Maybe."

"I can't stay here, Cass. Not forever. Somebody has to look after my mom."

"You're right. Somebody does. But it's not your job. You understand that, right?"

She shrugged. "Who else will if I don't?"

"I don't know," I said. "But you're allowed to be a kid, Clara. And it's okay for you to say what you want."

"Do they know? I mean … do the Bakers have a say?"

"Of course. But if they're willing, and I can't make you any promises … but if you want to stay here and the Bakers want you to stay here, I think there are options. Ways we can try to make it more permanent."

Clara'eyes traveled to the ceiling as another door slammed shut up there. "Elyse is gonna throw a fit."

"About what? You staying here?"

Clara rolled her eyes. "She just … she doesn't know how good she has it. You know? Things are easy for her and she doesn't even get it. She doesn't do anything around here. I mean, she still lets her mom pack her lunch. She's all wrapped up in boy drama and stupid school stuff. I love her like a sister. But she's a baby. I don't feel like a kid. I never did. I think I relate more to Kim than I do to anybody my age."

"Well, you've had a heck of a lot thrown at you at a young age. It's forced you to grow up faster than you should have."

"You know what that's like?" She leaned against the counter, folding her arms in front of her. She *did* look like a grown-up. Even the hair. It was similar to the way Kim wore hers.

"I know what that's like. My mom passed away when I was right around your age. My dad just wasn't around."

"I'm sorry for your loss," she said.

"Thanks. But it's been a long time. And Clara, I'm sorry for yours."

She went very still. Her eyes misted but she quickly wiped them away. "I wonder what it would be like to just worry about boy drama. Or whether I was going to get an A in Algebra."

"You're doing okay, kiddo," I said.

"You think my dad is going to end up in prison forever, don't you?"

"I think he might," I said. It was an honest answer. Clara frowned, but she didn't break down. Not completely. Her eyes welled with tears again.

"I'm sorry," I said. "I know that's hard to hear. But your father is facing very serious charges still. And there are no guarantees that ..."

"No," she said. "It's not him. I mean, yes, it's him. But ... is it wrong? Is it okay that I want to stay here? With the Bakers?"

I went to her. Clara folded against me as I hugged her. "Shh," I whispered. "Yes. It's okay, Clara. It's more than okay. We'll do what we can, okay?"

"She's not okay." Clara sniffled. "My mom isn't okay, Cass. And I don't think she's ever going to be okay again. I think she ... I think she's not telling the truth. I think ... she ..."

Clara looked up at me. As quickly as she started to cry, she made herself recover. She pulled away from me.

"Clara," I said. "What do you mean? About your mother not telling the truth?"

"Nothing," she said quickly. "I just mean ... if she says she's doing fine, she's not. That's all."

Except it didn't seem like all. It seemed like something was burning its way through Clara Karl that afternoon. A secret. A truth that was far too heavy for her to carry. She knew something. I felt it in my bones. Had she seen something? Heard something?

I desperately wanted to press her. And once again, I knew I couldn't. I could only try to fulfill the promise I made to her. I would fight to keep her from having to go back to that awful house again.

Chapter 32

"You're a worthless piece of crap. Cop killer. I hope you rot in hell!"

Miranda sat at her desk, chin in hand, as the voicemail message played.

"How many more are like that?" I asked. I held a mug of coffee in each hand. I set Miranda's in front of her.

"Oh, better than yesterday," Miranda said. "There were about six like that last night. Yesterday there were twenty."

"Don't sweat it, kid," Jeanie said, coming out of her office. "People will forget. It'll blow over."

Ever since the trial outcome, the hate mail and messages started ramping up again.

"Cass, it's not just the messages," Miranda said.

She handed me two folded pieces of paper. Letters. I scanned them. Two of the firm's long-standing clients were informing me they wanted to take their business elsewhere. Jeanie looked over my shoulder.

"The Hollands? Are you kidding? We've been handling their real estate stuff for years."

"I'm sorry," Miranda said. "This is partially my fault. I saw dollar signs when Reed Karl came in. It was short-sighted of me."

"It's not your fault. It's nobody's fault," I said. "If I made business decisions based on what's going to make me popular, I'd never be in court at all."

"How's Reed holding up?" Jeanie asked.

"He's improving. The doctors say he'll be ready for discharge probably the day after tomorrow. The same day as his new bail hearing."

"They cannot possibly think he can be kept safe at county," Miranda said. "Every cop in town has it out for him. And for you, unfortunately."

"It'll get better," I said, sipping my coffee. "It can't get worse. Right?"

Jeanie and Miranda shared a discouraging look, but didn't answer.

"Jeanie," I said. "The more pressing matter is Clara Karl. I paid a visit to her at the Bakers. They're willing to make her living situation more permanent. She seems happy there. It's good for her. What do we need to do to facilitate that?"

"They'd need to apply for guardianship. But it'll make things a lot easier if her parents consent."

"Reed won't be a problem," I said. "Especially if his bail hearing doesn't go our way. As far as the mother ... she's in no condition to parent that child. She's gorked out of her mind on medication. It may even come to getting adult protective services involved."

Not to mention the fact she was a murderer. But even now, I couldn't unburden that secret. Miranda wasn't bound by confidentiality the way I was. Jeanie though ... maybe the time had come to bring her in. The weight of the truth felt heavy on my shoulders this morning. As I thought it, another call came in. Miranda picked up the phone. She barely got her greeting out before she slammed it down again.

"Never mind," she said. "Wrong number." Though I knew she was lying.

"So," Jeanie said. "I can prepare the paperwork for the Bakers' guardianship."

"I'll prepare the fee agreement," Miranda chimed in.

"No," I said. "This one's pro bono. We'll do it for Clara. Consider this me paying it forward. Somebody stepped in for me, for my little brother and sister when I needed it."

"Softie," Jeanie muttered, but I knew she was teasing. That someone was Jeanie. I would be forever grateful she'd come into my life when things were about as dire as they could get. If I could be that person for Clara Karl, it might make the last three months truly worth it.

"I'll get the signatures," I said.

"If Dahlia Karl is as messed up as you say," Miranda said, "is she even competent enough to consent?"

"She has her moments," I answered. "It's what Clara wants. I'll take her to see her mother and we'll get it done. As far as Reed, I think I can convince him this will all be in Clara's best interests."

"Let him think it's temporary," Jeanie said. "And it will be, from a legal standpoint. At least at first."

"Right," I said. I didn't want to give voice to the real meaning of her comment. Let him *think* it's temporary. That presumed I wouldn't be successful getting Reed out of prison. And maybe I wouldn't. But I couldn't think that far ahead.

I went up to my office and pulled out my cell phone. Clara would be in school still, but Kim Baker was home. I punched in her number. It rang three times and went to voicemail.

"Hey, Kim," I said, when prompted to leave my message. "It's Cass Leary. I'm working on getting the paperwork together for the custody arrangement we talked about. If it's all right, I'd like to pick Clara up after school and go talk to Dahlia. Then I can bring everything over to your house for signatures. We can have things filed by tomorrow morning and go from there. Just let me know if that works for you. Talk to you soon."

No sooner had I clicked off the call when it rang again. It was Kim.

"Cass?" She was breathless. "So sorry. I couldn't get to the phone in time."

"It's okay. I was just leaving a message. If you and Dean are sure this is how you want to proceed, I can start preparing the paperwork for Clara's guardianship."

She let out a sigh. "That would be such a relief. Cass, I'm really worried about Dahlia. She just keeps getting worse and worse.

Do you think you could arrange to have her go visit Reed in the hospital? It might help. It might do something. I don't know."

I wasn't sure I could stand being in the same room with both Dahlia and Reed. I might snap.

"I don't know," I said. "He's still in the custody of the county. I'd have to get permission. At the moment I'm the only one with visiting privileges. They're worried about his safety."

That last part was a lie. It *should* have been true, but I knew it wasn't. I didn't think there was a sheriff's deputy in the state who would care if Reed Karl died today.

"Well, there has to be something."

"You are doing something. You're making sure Clara is safe. That's the only thing that matters. Truly. She'd be lost without you guys. So thank you. And like I said. I'll do whatever I can to help. I want to pick Clara up from school and take her over to Dahlia's this afternoon if that's okay. She can pack up more of her things and we can explain to Dahlia together what the plan is going forward. I'm hoping if Clara is the one asking, Dahlia will just sign the consent forms."

"I hope so. I hope this isn't the thing that finally breaks her. I just ... I don't know what I'm doing. I'm trying to do the right thing. I just ... I know it's horrible to say this. Horrible to even think it. But I'm starting to feel like Clara is the only one of them who has a chance, you know?"

"I know," I said. "I feel the same way a lot of the time. And it's not nothing, Kim. Trust me. I've been where Clara is. Having someone like you and Dean and even Elyse to be there for her. It's going to make all the difference. I promise."

I couldn't say it. I could barely even think it.

"It's just for now," Kim said. "Until we can get Dahlia the help she needs. Get her back on her feet. Then she and Clara can be reunited. And it's not like I would ever keep Dahlia from seeing her daughter. Please let her know that, okay? I will too. But I think coming from you. You can explain the legal parts of it. I think she'll listen to you. She trusts you. She's told me that a million times."

"She has?"

"Of course. She knows you're on her side."

Her side? I had to swallow what I really wanted to say. Her side. No. I was not on Dahlia's side. If it was within my power, and I thought it might be, I would keep Clara as far away from her mother as I could. As I thought it, I knew I had the makings of a real conflict of interest brewing. But I couldn't unknow what I knew. I also could not in good conscience facilitate Clara going back to live in a home with a murderer.

"I'll make sure the school and Clara knows you're the one who'll be picking her up today. Elyse has to stay after for volleyball practice anyway."

"Thanks," I said.

"No, Cass. Thank you. For everything."

I hung up. I tried not to think too much about Dahlia Karl. Or even Reed for that matter. But for the first time in a long time, I felt I was doing something positive for the Karl family. Then it occurred to me it would involve breaking it apart once and for all.

Chapter 33

"You sure you're okay with this?"

Clara hadn't said much when she climbed into my car. She stared out the window as the rain began to fall. We were lucky. The temperature stayed above forty degrees today. Otherwise we'd have several inches of snow on the ground.

"I'm okay with this," she said.

"You're handling a lot, Clara. You seem fine. But you don't have to be fine. You know? And if you don't want to do this. If you want me to talk to your mom without you, I can do that."

"No," she said. "I have to do it. She won't listen to anybody else but me. Just ... when we go in there. Just give me the papers and let me talk to her by myself."

"Okay," I said. "If that's how you want it. I'll be there to answer any questions."

Clara nodded. We pulled into her driveway. More boxes were piled up on the front porch. They were soaked now. Though somewhat protected under the overhang, the rain was blowing sideways. As I put the car in park, Clara ran out and punched the code into the garage door panel. It jerked upward.

I pulled my coat over my head and raced up the driveway to join her. Clara opened the side door and went inside. The kitchen was in even worse shape from two days ago. It smelled musty.

"She needs to take the garbage out," Clara said, pinching her nose.

"Mom!" she yelled out.

"She's probably in the bedroom," I said. A stab of fear went through me. I grabbed Clara's arm and held her back. If something bad had happened to Dahlia, I didn't want Clara to be the one to find her.

God, this was a mistake. More than that. It had the makings of a Greek tragedy.

"Wait here," I said. I went down the hallway to the primary suite. I knocked softly and poked my head inside.

Relief flooded through me. Dahlia was sitting on the edge of the bed holding her remote control. The television was on but no sound was coming out. By the looks of things, she hadn't gotten out of bed since the last time I was here.

"I can't get this damn thing to work," she said absently, not turning her head to look at me. "Reed was going to buy us a new one."

"Dahlia. How are you feeling today?"

She was still wearing the same loose tank top I'd seen her in two days ago. Her hair looked greasy and unkempt. There were piles of used tissues on the nightstand. I could see the bathroom garbage can was also piled high.

"Mom!" Clara shouted. She came in behind me. "You look awful. When's the last time you took a shower?"

Dahlia put the remote down. She smiled at her daughter. "Baby! Come give me a hug. We can watch *The Price is Right* together."

"It's three o'clock. It's not on now."

Dahlia looked confused. "It can't be. Did you skip school today?"

I had serious concerns whether Dahlia was even mentally competent enough to sign consent forms today. I had to be sure.

"Dahlia," I said. "Do you know who I am?"

She looked at me and frowned. "Don't be ridiculous, Cass. Yes, I know who you are."

"Okay. So Clara has some things she'd like to talk to you about. Some paperwork she's going to ask you to sign. I'm going to give you a few minutes to talk. But then I have to ask you some questions too. And if you have any questions for me, I'll answer them. Okay?"

"You're talking to me like I'm a child. Okay. You don't have to stay. I am perfectly capable of having a conversation with my own daughter."

"Mom, stop. Cass is trying to be nice. She's trying to help us. To help you." Clara turned to me. She gave me a wide-eyed look I interpreted to mean she was ready for me to leave the room.

"I'll go pack some of your things," I whispered. "I'll just be down the hall."

339

Clara nodded then turned back to her mother. God, I hated every second of this. Hated watching that girl go from fourteen to forty again in the span of five minutes.

I started upstairs to Clara's room. She'd told me it was the second one on the right. Across the hall was her brother Ian's old room. I paused there.

It wasn't a shrine. Reed and Dahlia had moved boxes and other things inside of it for storage. There was a dusty treadmill in one corner. But Ian's youth bed was still set up along one wall. It had been stripped, but his race-car-themed bedding was folded neatly on top of it. From the window, I could see down to the yard. To the place where this poor kid had died.

It felt haunted, this house. Though I had a thousand reasons to be angry at Reed and hold him accountable for the downfall of his family, I could understand what he was trying to escape.

I went to Clara's room. Hers was messy in a normal teenager way. The surface of every dresser was piled with things. Jewelry, hair ties, candy wrappers, pictures. She still had dirty clothes piled on the floor. Her closet was open, the laundry hamper filled to the brim.

"Lord," I thought. I may have to pack her clothes dirty and see if Kim could throw them through the laundry.

I went to the closet and picked out a handful of sweaters. Clara told me she had a suitcase against the back wall. I found it. It was pink with glittering gold handles. I opened it and laid the clean sweaters on top of it. She kept her jeans on hangers in the closet. I packed as many as would fit.

Clara's framed photos on her desk caught my eye. I went to them. There were pictures of her and Elyse riding the Maverick at Cedar Point. They were both smiling and laughing, their arms raised high in the air. There was a photo of a much younger Clara holding her newborn baby brother. He was still wearing the blue cap the hospital gave him. Clara's feet stuck straight out on the hospital couch. She was too short to touch the floor. I don't know why I did it, but I packed that photo in Clara's suitcase too.

Now for socks and underwear. Those were in the top two drawers of her dresser. She also asked me to find her black leather combat-style boots. I saw one of them poking out of the dirty clothes pile in the closet. The other was going to be a search-and-rescue mission.

I pulled the hamper out. I thought about just dumping the contents of it in the suitcase or finding a large garbage bag. That actually made more sense. I saw what I thought were the laces of her other boot under a pile of clothes and pulled.

A sweatshirt came along with the boot. I picked it up.

Maroon with gold on the inside of the hood. CMU was embroidered across the back in gold letters. Central Michigan University. The Chippewa logo was sewn onto the front to the right of the zipper.

I stared at the sweatshirt. It was as if my body processed what I was seeing before my mind did. I broke out into a sweat. My heart started to burn in my chest.

I sank back to the floor, clutching the sweatshirt to me. Where did she get this?

Clawing at the closet door, I got myself to my feet. Like a zombie, I walked over to the window. Clara's room faced the backyard as well. I could see the Thompsons' yard clearly from here. Sawyer was outside, puttering in his yard again, even in the rain. The black solar panel of his security camera faced me.

No. No. No.

When I closed my eyes, I could see the video Sawyer had of Megan Lewis leaving Reed's house, running across the yard until she went out of frame. She had been wearing her CMU sweatshirt. Just like the one I held in my hand. There were bleach stains on the right sleeve. I held the sweatshirt out. Absently, I slipped my arm into the sleeve, stretching it out. The bleach stains ran all the way up to the elbow. I jerked my arm out of it, as if I had been burned by acid.

It felt like the walls were closing in on me. What was Megan Lewis's sweatshirt doing in the back of Clara's closet? A million other questions swam in my mind.

Why had Megan Lewis left the Karl house through the back slider that night? There was nothing back there but the woods. The other day, I had trouble getting around the house as the gate closest to the street stuck. Sawyer's camera had picked her up heading in the direction of the back gate. The gate Reed Karl and Dean Baker had agreed to put there so Elyse and Clara could get back and forth to each other's houses through the connecting woods.

Megan Lewis couldn't have known about the gate. Could she? Did she?

The pictures on Clara's desk stared back at me. Her grade school softball trophies lined a floating shelf Reed had probably installed for her. In one photo, Clara smiled at the camera in her softball uniform, clutching a pink bat. I picked that photo up, my eyes transfixed on that pink bat. My head swam. It got hard to breathe. I don't know how long I stood there. A million scenarios ran through my head. I heard footsteps in the hall, but somehow couldn't tear my eyes off that photograph, then the sweatshirt I held in my other hand.

"Cass?"

I jumped. Clara stood in the doorway, smiling. "My mom is ready to talk to you. She's agreed to sign whatever needs to be signed."

I looked at Clara. Pretty. Thin. Blonde. Until she'd cut her hair last week, she'd worn it long and straight. Not unlike Megan Lewis had. I still clutched the CMU sweatshirt in my hand. Clara saw it. Her smile faded a bit.

"Is this yours?" I asked. "Where did you get it?"

She didn't answer.

"Clara," I said. "Where did you get this? This is Megan Lewis's sweatshirt, isn't it?" I walked toward her, holding the sweatshirt out so she could see the bleach-stained sleeve.

"Don't," Clara said. Not a denial. Not an explanation.

"Honey," I said. "What happened? You can tell me."

Clara shook her head.

"Did you take this from Megan's house?" No. That couldn't have happened. She couldn't have. Things slammed into place in my brain. Reed found more and more reasons to be away from the house in those last few months. Little by little, Dahlia had checked out. Clara was left to her own devices for so long. Who would have noticed if she slipped out of the house?

The pink softball bat in the picture. It wasn't here. No one had ever found a bat in the Karls' house. Had the police ever searched Clara's room? My heart racing, I scanned all four corners.

Sawyer Thompson's video kept replaying in my head. The sweatshirt. There had been no denying it belonged to Megan Lewis. She was wearing it in her social media profile picture. It was distinctive. The bleach stains ...

I looked at Clara again. She was roughly the same size, same build as Megan Lewis. Her hair ... God. If she wore this sweatshirt. If she kept the hood close around her face. In profile ... in a grainy video where she never turned to fully face the camera.

All this time I had assumed. We had *all* assumed the figure in that video was Megan Lewis.

"Was this you?" I said, my voice breaking. "Oh honey ..."

"Cass, just stop," she said.

"Honey, did you go to Megan's house? Were you angry with her because she was close to your dad?"

Clara began to cry.

"Clara, it's okay. You can tell me."

I heard a thumping sound in the hallway. Clara took a step further into the room.

Why? If that was Clara trying to make it look like Megan had broken into her parents' house, why would she do it? Could she have done it? The police report from Megan's break-in. Ian Karl's toys had been stored in a box in the back of his closet. How would Megan have known that unless Reed told her? I never asked if he did.

Clara had Megan's sweatshirt. Clara knew where her brother's toys were stored. Clara knew where Sawyer Thompson's cameras would trigger if she went out the back. She'd run along the fence. Clara had been staying at Elyse Baker's for a sleepover that night.

"Clara," I said. "I know you were scared. You knew your father was dating another woman, didn't you?"

The tears stopped. Clara made a sideways move. She picked something up off her dresser. I saw a flash of silver. She was holding a pair of scissors.

"Clara!"

"Stop," she said. Every trace of vulnerability gone. Her voice went flat. "Just stop. You don't know anything."

"I think I do. Honey. What happened? Let me help you."

"You can help me by shutting your damn mouth!" She yelled the last words so loudly, my ears rang.

She curled her fist around the scissor blades. Would she lunge at me with them?

Megan Lewis denied breaking into the Karls' home. She swore in her texts to Reed she hadn't left any sort of note for Dahlia taped to the door. All this time I had assumed it was Megan who had snuck into this house and done all those things. But what if …

"You're ruining everything," Clara said, the tears coming back. "Just go away and leave us all alone."

"Clara, please. Just tell me what happened. Tell me what you did."

"You can't do anything," she said. "You don't know anything."

She took a step toward me. Clara's jeans darkened. As she calmly spoke, she stabbed at her own leg with the scissors.

"Honey, put those down. You're hurting yourself. We can talk about all of it. I can help you figure it all out."

"No!" she said through gritted teeth. "You want to fuck it all up. You want to take everything away from me. Just like Megan did. Just like Ian did. I'm not going to let you. I'm happy now. I have Kim and Dean. So just fix all the paperwork so I don't have to deal with these people anymore. Do your job."

More blood began to soak through her jeans.

"Clara, please. Honey, give me the scissors."

"Stop calling me honey."

"Okay. Okay. Clara. Just tell me. I understand. I understand that you had to have been so angry with your dad. Maybe your mom too. You found out your dad was having an affair with Megan. Is that what happened?"

"No," she said. "We're not doing this. You're not going to mess things up for me. You're not going to be just like *her*. He was going to leave us. With *her!*"

"With Megan," I said, my throat going dry. "You didn't want your father to leave your family for Megan. He was going to, wasn't he? You could see it. He stopped coming home for lunch. He just ... stopped. You wanted him to hate Megan, is that right? You wanted him to think she was trying to hurt you and your mom?"

Clara kept stabbing her thigh and walking toward me. The Pine Circle neighborhood was just a short walk from here. How many times had she gone there? Spied on her father and Megan? Is that what happened?

"Did you take your brother's toys, Clara?" I asked. "Did you try to make it look like Megan was going to hurt your mom?"

"She didn't care!" Clara screamed. "She only cared about Ian! He only cared about Megan!"

Something was moving in the hallway. I heard a door creak open then close. Clara took another step closer to me.

"Honey," I said. "You're bleeding. Let me help you."

Clara shook her head. Her eyes went wild. "You can't help me. You're only going to get in the way!"

I felt my heart ice over. "Megan got in the way, didn't she?"

"I take care of everything!" Clara's words were little more than a hiss.

"Who did you take care of, Clara? What did you do?" I asked.

"Clara!" The shriek cut through the air. But it didn't come from me. It came from Dahlia. She stood behind Clara in the hallway. "Baby?"

Clara didn't take her eyes off me. "Go back to bed, Mom. It's what you're good at."

"No more, Clara. No more!" Dahlia sobbed. She took a step into the room. She had something in her hand. With horror, I realized what it was. Dahlia had a pink bat coated with mud in her right hand. Clara saw it as I did.

"Where did you get that?" Clara cried out. "Put it back! Put it back, you stupid bitch!"

Dahlia sobbed. "You hurt him," Dahlia whispered. Him? "Oh God. You hurt him. You hurt him. You hurt him!"

Dahlia raised the bat and lunged at her daughter.

"No!" I shouted.

Clara threw herself forward, scissors raised in the air. I got my hand up just in time. I curled my fingers around Clara's wrist. She was as tall as me. She was strong. But she was only fourteen. Clara brought the scissors down, and as we tumbled to the floor, I felt the blades slice into my shoulder. I slammed her right hand against the floor before she could raise the scissors again.

I twisted her arm until the scissors fell out of her grasp. I threw my arms around her, pinning her arms to her side. I sat on her. Blood poured from the stinging wound on my shoulder.

"Dahlia," I said. She stood there, wide-eyed, holding that filthy bat high in the air. She turned and looked at it. Fear widened her eyes. She dropped the bat. She took a step back, pressing her back against the wall. Then she sank slowly to the ground.

Clara squirmed beneath me, struggling to get up.

"Dahlia!" I shouted. Dahlia snapped back into the present. She crawled forward and sat on her daughter's legs. Clara started to cry.

I reached into my back pocket and pulled out my cell phone. I punched in a number and raised the phone to my ear.

"9-1-1, please state the nature of your emergency ..."

Chapter 34

"How bad does it hurt?" Rafe Johnson stood next to me, eyeing the blood on my sleeve.

"Thanks," I said. "I'm fine. I'll get checked out in a few hours if I feel like I need stitches."

My arm throbbed. I'd bandaged it myself. But I'd refused medical attention at the scene. So had Dahlia. She sat in the room next to this one, answering questions from a junior detective working with Rodney Patel.

Patel sat at the table in the room in front of this one. We were separated by a one-way mirror. Clara sat in the chair against the wall, her knee bent, one foot resting on the edge of the chair. She had a Mountain Dew in front of her. It was the only thing she'd asked for.

The door opened behind me. Eric rushed in. He took one look at my shoulder and his face fell.

"I'm all right," I said, keeping my voice low. The room was soundproof, but it was still unsettling sitting so close to Clara, even though I knew she couldn't see us. She knew we were here though. From time to time, she would smile, and seem to look straight at me.

"I'm trying to understand, Clara," Patel said.

"What's to understand?" Clara said. "I mean, unless you're stupid or something. Are you stupid, Detective Patel?"

"No. I'm not stupid. But for the last six months, your dad's been sitting in jail. Only he didn't kill Megan Lewis. You did."

Clara smiled again. "You ever hit somebody in the head with a bat? It's oddly satisfying. Maybe you should try it sometime." Clara looked back toward me again.

"Cass," Eric said. "Let me take you to the hospital."

"I'm staying put."

"When did you find out your father was seeing Megan Lewis?" Patel asked.

"Seeing? You mean screwing her. It wasn't that hard to figure out. He always goes out in the backyard when he wants to get away from us. He knows my mother won't go back there. He would talk to her on his phone. My mom was oblivious. She just let it all happen. She never knows anything. She just sleeps her life away and leaves it to me to handle everything. Well, I handled it. I did the thing she was too weak to take care of. I defended my family. I got rid of the problem neither of my parents had the balls to deal with."

"Megan Lewis was the problem?"

Clara tapped her temple. "Now he's catching on."

"Clara, did you write this?"

Patel had a copy of the letter found on Megan Lewis's computer, the one she had sworn she never wrote. The one Reed later said he'd found taped to the front door.

"Yes, I wrote it."

"How did it get on Megan Lewis's laptop?"

Clara pantomimed typing on the table. "Like this, genius. Do you need me to spell it out for you?"

"Yes," Patel said, his tone hard. "I do need you to spell it out for me."

"Does he have consent?" Eric said. "She's still a minor, Rafe. There can't be any mistakes with this one. The kid's smart."

"Dahlia signed parental consent about an hour ago," I said. "She's being interviewed too. She's cooperating fully. I mean ... she's shell-shocked. But I think on some level, Dahlia suspected there was something going on with Clara. Among other things, she said she saw Clara bury her softball bat in the backyard. I just ... I ... didn't."

"It's okay," Eric said. "How could you have known?"

"They've got it now," I said. "Eric, I saw it. Dahlia came into the bedroom with it. It was filthy. Covered with mud but ..."

"If it's the murder weapon," Eric said, "they'll be able to determine it."

"Crime scene lab has it now," Rafe said.

"She wouldn't leave us alone!" Clara shouted. "She was driving by the house. Calling my dad all hours of the day and night. She wouldn't take the hint and get on with her life. She wanted to destroy mine, so I made sure my dad saw her for what she really was. A psycho."

"How'd you do that, Clara? How'd you make sure your dad saw who Megan was?"

"You know, for a cop ... for somebody who was trying to be a detective, I can see why the Taney County Sheriff's Department didn't let her do anything more important than write traffic tickets. No alarms at her house. She kept a friggin' key under the mat at her back door. Half the time she didn't even lock the garage. She did it so my dad could come and go as he pleased. Well, so did I."

"You broke into Megan's house?"

Clara slapped her hands on the table. "You really are stupid. I just told you. I didn't have to break in."

"You composed this letter on her laptop?" Patel waved the letter. "What about the pictures on her computer? The ones of your mother. You know, we never found those on her phone. That always bothered me. I couldn't figure out what camera she'd used to take them. But there they were. It was a nice touch."

"You like that? I didn't do anything Megan wasn't about to do herself. I told you. She kept driving by the house. Looking at us. She was trying to screw with my mom. So, I did what my parents were too spineless to do. I gave that bitch a taste of her own medicine. Got my dad to open his eyes finally."

"What do you think would have happened if you hadn't opened your dad's eyes?"

"He would have kept on screwing her. Would have left us. He

would have left me alone to take care of my mom. Which I did anyway."

"Yes, you did. What about June 6th? What happened, Clara?"

"She would not stop hounding my dad. He told her over and over, I heard him. He said he wanted her to leave him alone. That he was going to try to fix things with my mom. We were going to be a family again. Just me. Just my mom and my dad and me. But Megan was going to screw all of that up. So I fixed that too."

"How did you fix it?"

"You know, this is ridiculous," she said. "You're sitting there thinking you're some great interviewer. I'm telling you what I want to tell you, idiot. I know how this works."

"How does it work, Clara?"

"I'm fourteen! I'm a baby. You'll send me to some youth correctional center. They'll babysit me for four years and then I'm out. I'll write my book. I'll be on all the talk shows. I bet they'll even make a movie about me."

Eric pounded his fist against the chair beside him. "She's probably right," he muttered.

"What did you do to Megan on June 6th?" Patel calmly repeated.

Clara leaned far forward. "I walked into her house from the garage. I went into her bedroom. I smashed her stupid face in until she couldn't get up again. Period. End of story. That's it."

"Is it?"

"Yes."

"Megan's not the only person who ever got in the way of you and your parents, was she?"

Clara sat back hard and rolled her eyes. "I can't believe my father actually thought my mom was capable of doing what I did. That she had the spine to go over there and fight for her family. Give me a break. He thinks he's being noble. Thinks he's protecting her. She doesn't deserve to be protected. She deserves to keep on sleeping until she never wakes up again. She's not a good mother."

"Did you help your mother fall asleep?" Patel asked.

"Did I try to kill my mother? No. I didn't try to kill my mother."

"But you drugged her. She told my colleague she believes somebody was giving her more medication than she was supposed to take. She said she felt drunk. Stoned. Did you drug her?"

"It's not like it was hard," Clara said. "She didn't exactly try to stop me. She just took the pills I handed her when I handed them to her. Mother of the Year, right?"

"I'm sorry you were put in that position," Patel said. "Is that what happened the day Ian died? Did you give your mother her medication that day too?"

"She should have taught the kid how to swim," Clara said. "He was four years old. I knew how to swim when I was four."

"Cass," Rafe turned to me. He was looking at a text on his phone. "The Bakers have reached out. Elyse Baker has made a statement to the police. She's saying the day Ian Karl drowned, Clara asked her to lie."

"She went back and forth from the Bakers to her house," I said, already able to piece together what Elyse probably said. "Dean and Reed put that gate in their fence when they built the pool. I've read the report. Clara was supposed to be playing at Elyse's that day."

"Elyse is now saying she disappeared for a while. They were supposed to be playing dolls or something in the basement, but Clara said she was going to run home to check on her mother. She was gone for maybe an hour. They were just kids. Just ten years old."

"Jesus," Eric said. "Why wouldn't a little kid like Elyse think to come forward with something like that?"

"Why would she," I said. "She didn't think her best friend had gone off to murder her little brother. My God."

"They don't thrash around like you think," Clara said. "That was so weird to me. He just sank to the bottom. Poof. It was almost like it was meant to be."

"You let your mother believe it was her fault," Patel said.

"It was her fault. She went to sleep. All sorts of things can happen when you're asleep."

"Rafe," I said. "Are you going to drop the charges against Reed? Are you going to fight my petition to have him released?"

"Cass," he said. "We don't know how deep this goes. I'm not convinced Reed and Dahlia Karl weren't complicit in this. Dahlia knew about the bat. She should have come forward."

"You have the murder weapon," I said. "When the labs come back, you're going to find Megan's blood on that bat. She's admitted to being the one who killed her. You knew from the beginning Reed's confession was problematic. Now we know why. He thought he was ..."

I couldn't finish the sentence. Even now. I couldn't break his confidentiality. He thought he was protecting Dahlia. Would he have done anything different had he known it was Clara the whole time?

"He didn't kill Megan Lewis," I said. "He wasn't there."

"He gave a false police report," Rafe snapped. "I can make a case for obstruction ..."

"Fine," I said. "But he's been in jail for over six months already. He's paid the price."

"Cass," Eric said. "There's nothing else you can do here. Let me take you home."

"Dahlia needs representation," I said. "It can't be me. I'm still Reed's lawyer. But ..."

"She hasn't asked for one," Rafe said. "Dahlia Karl is fully aware of her legal rights. She's signed a Miranda waiver she didn't need to. She isn't being charged with anything. Yet. She gave consent for Patel to interview her daughter. I'm not trying to destroy these people."

"I know," I said.

"Are you sure you're okay?" Rafe said, his tone softening. "That had to have been pretty terrifying."

"I'm okay," I said, rising. I took Eric's offered arm. I did feel a little dizzy once I got to my feet. "But I need to go talk to my client. And I'd like to tell him what's going to happen to his wife."

"I told you. As long as she continues to cooperate, nothing."

Nothing, I thought. I looked back into the interrogation room. Clara was absently chewing on her thumbnail. She seemed bored. Remorseless. Cold.

A shudder went through me. I'd missed it. All of it. I saw myself in Clara Karl. She'd been alone. Seemingly taking care of all the broken grown-ups in her life. Just like I had when I was her age.

"Come on," Eric said. "I'll drive you to the hospital. I insist you get checked out."

"I need to talk to Reed first," I said. "Then okay. I'll do whatever you want me to."

We walked out together. I wanted to feel as if a weight had been lifted. I'd proven Reed Karl was innocent of killing Megan Lewis. I'd done it despite his confession. Despite a trial where all the evidence pointed to him. And yet, the gravity of the truth threatened to pull me under. Or it would have. If I didn't have Eric's steady hand guiding me back into the light.

Chapter 35

TEN DAYS LATER, I sat in my car as Reed walked out of the Woodbridge County Jail. There was nobody else to be there for him. There was only me. He slipped quietly into the passenger seat and for a moment, we both stared straight ahead, not knowing what to say.

I put the car in gear. "Where do you want me to take you?" I asked him.

He let out a bitter laugh. "Home. I don't have anywhere else to go."

Dahlia hadn't come to visit him. She wasn't there in the courtroom when Judge Niedermayer passed sentence on him. Rafe had made good on charging Reed with obstruction of justice and making a false police report. Reed had pleaded guilty to all of it. He'd been given credit for time served and would do six months of probation.

Dahlia faced no charges. Rafe gave her immunity for her cooperation with Clara. Plus, there was no evidence that she knew anything about Clara's stalking of Megan Lewis, or her eventual murder of her. There was the bat she saw her daughter bury, but no real proof Dahlia had anything but suspicions. She'd been in denial, not wanting to believe how deeply her daughter's problems went.

The murder of Ian Karl was another matter. The cloud of it still hung over Dahlia even though she now knew it wasn't her fault. Clara spelled out how she had crushed Xanax into Dahlia's orange juice at lunch. She knew Dahlia would put Ian down for his nap about an hour after that. She went to the Bakers for a playdate, then ran back home, convincing Elyse not to tell anyone she wasn't in the basement playing with her.

All while her mother slept, she took her brother down to the pool and threw him in the deep end where he sank like a stone. She watched the whole thing. Made sure to do it the week the Thompsons were away, visiting their son. There would be no witnesses.

Then later, she knew the one thing she could do to finally make her father hate Megan Lewis. She admitted to being the one to slice her brother's toys and hang them from the ceiling fan, then run out the back door in Megan's sweatshirt. It was the one part of her plan that didn't work out as she hoped. She thought the police would question the Thompsons and ask to see their security footage. She thought Megan Lewis would be arrested.

But it never happened. Nobody asked for the footage until I got involved. By then, Clara had already decided the only way to get rid of Megan for good was to kill her. And so she did.

"Will Dahlia be there?" I asked.

"No," Reed said. "Kim said she's already moved most of her stuff into storage. She's going back to England for a while. She has a cousin there she's still close with. She's offered to let her come live with her for a little while until she figures out her next step. Dahlia told me she can't be in that house anymore. She never wants to see it again. She doesn't care what I do with it."

"I'm sorry, Reed."

"No. I know it's what I deserve. I know she blames me for all of this."

"Reed, Clara is mentally ill. It's not your fault. The shrinks are going to say she has sociopathic personality disorder. It's not something you or Dahlia did. It's just something she was born with."

"Is there help for that? Therapy. A pill?"

"I don't think it's that simple."

He dropped his chin to his chest and cried. "She took Ian. God. She thought I didn't love her enough after he was born. That's what she told the police."

"Reed ..."

"How could she think that?"

"Reed ..."

I made the turn down his street and pulled into his driveway. The house next door was quiet. The Thompsons had left for Florida for the winter. Reed really would be all alone at his end of the cul-de-sac for now.

"Thank you," he said. "I know what this case has cost you. I know what people said about you. If it helps ... I release you."

"What?"

"Or … if you need me to sign something. I'm sure there were people you wanted to tell. People who thought you were representing me even though I was guilty. You can tell them whatever you want to now. It doesn't matter. The truth is out."

"Thank you," I said. "But the people who care about me understand what my job is."

"Still, as I said. I know my case cost you."

"I'm sorry things weren't different, Reed. What do you think you'll do now?"

He looked back at his empty house. "Is there something wrong with me that I still love my daughter?"

I let out a breath. "No. I don't think it's wrong that you still love her."

"I know what you're saying. I know what she is. What she did. But I'm the only person she has now. I don't know if Dahlia can ever forgive her. I don't know if I can. But I think I still have to be her dad somehow. I mean, if there's even a sliver of a chance that sweet little girl I knew is in there somewhere. I don't know. I just …"

"It's okay," I said. "I think I understand. Or at least, I can try to."

"Maybe I'll sell the house. Dahlia thinks it's cursed. As if that's the reason all this happened. Maybe she's right. It was our dream house. We didn't know it would bring something evil."

He put his hand on the door handle. "Take care of yourself, Reed," I said.

He looked at me. He seemed to have aged twenty years in the last six months. I wondered if he could survive what had happened. He got out and started up the sidewalk, shoulders slumped.

I found myself staring at that house for a moment after Reed disappeared inside. Its white-washed brick, and tall chimney. The oak trees in the front were bare now. Their crooked branches stretched out toward the roof, almost as if they were all pointing an accusatory finger.

My whole life, I had been raised to believe this neighborhood was a utopia. The kind of haven I could never afford. Never be part of. Now I knew all the unspeakable things that happened here at Eden's Edge. Now, to me it would forever be the edge of hell.

Chapter 36

THREE SWANS SWAM near the sea wall. A mother and father along with one of this past spring's cygnets. He still had some of his gray feathers and was almost as big as his mother. They'd chased off four other cygnets a few weeks ago but this one remained, needing some extra attention perhaps.

Eric tossed some of Marbury and Madison's dog food to them. They gobbled it up and stretched their necks, waiting for more.

"They like you," I said. I threw an Afghan over my shoulders as I walked down to join him. He had more dog food sitting on the stack of dock sections beside him. I grabbed a few pieces and tossed them toward the mother swan. She gave me a short chuff in gratitude, then scooped up the food.

"I'm thinking of naming them this year. I've almost got the male eating out of my hand."

Marbury barked inside, protesting the purloining of his food.

"Oh, pipe down," Eric yelled back. "There's plenty for you and you don't have to freeze your ass off out here scrounging for it. Your mother puts yours in a heated bowl, for Chrissake."

I nudged Eric with my shoulder. "He's worth it."

"He's spoiled." But Eric was smiling.

"Eric," I said. "I'm sorry about the last few months. That I couldn't tell you what was really going on."

He shook his head. "You don't have anything to be sorry about. I should have known you had a reason for sticking with Reed Karl. If I wasn't acting like it, I need you to know that I trust your decisions."

"Eric, when I took Reed's case, I *did* think he was guilty. I need you to understand that. I need you to be okay with what I do for a living. I need to know you understand that just because I defend somebody in court, it doesn't mean I condone their crime."

He turned to me. "I do understand that. I also understand that if it weren't for you, nobody would have ever figured out what really happened to Megan. And I blame myself a little for that too."

"Why?"

"Because maybe if I hadn't been so stubborn, I could have gotten over myself long enough to help you. Maybe I could have done more digging. Looked harder at Rodney Patel's police work. Because you were right. He did botch Reed's interrogation. He didn't search Clara's phone. His warrants weren't broad enough. Maybe I would have been the one to find that sweatshirt in Clara's closet. Or the softball bat she buried. I talked to him this morning. They were able to retrieve all the pictures Clara took of her mother. The ones she uploaded to Megan's laptop to make it look like she was the one who took them. They tracked her GPS too. Cass, the phone pinged the tower close to Megan's at two a.m. the night she was killed. It was all right there. Patel missed it. If it weren't for you, the wrong person would be in prison for killing her right now."

"Hey," I said, smiling. "I had another crack at it, remember? What makes you think I couldn't have gotten Reed acquitted the second time around?"

"Ya know, knowing you, you probably would have. That'll teach me to ever bet against you again."

"Were you betting against me this time?"

I meant it as a joke, but Eric's face grew serious.

"Eric," I said quickly. "I'm sorry too. I know I had a one-track mind with this case. It was wrong of me not to take your feelings into consideration. I know that. I just got so laser-focused. I don't want to do that again. I don't want to risk losing you over something like this ever again."

I took a breath. Everything my brothers tried to tell me flooded through me. I didn't want to lose Eric. The thought of it made my stomach twist into knots. A rush of heat went through me.

I wouldn't lose him. I wouldn't leave things to chance or tomorrow. I grabbed Eric's hand.

"Eric," I said. "I love you. I know you know I love you. But maybe I haven't been clear enough how much. You're it. Okay? My partner in this life. The last few months have been awful. I thought it was just this case. Just the absolute soul-sucking evil of it. It was that, but that wasn't all of it. The rest of it ... the majority of it ... was because I didn't have you at my side. So I want to fix that. Right here. Right now. Eric Wray, will you … will you … marry me?"

Eric took a step back. He misjudged his distance to the edge of the seawall. He lost his balance and cartwheeled his arms. I reached for him but his momentum was too strong. I pitched forward and we both ended up falling into the frigid water.

It was only shin-deep this close to the shore, but we landed on our asses. Eric sprang up and pulled me to my feet. The swan family rose up and flapped their wings and hissed at us. They moved off out of reach.

"Are you okay?" Eric asked. He pulled himself back up to shore then helped me up behind him.

"Just wet. And you didn't answer me. I asked you to marry me."

"I remember," he said.

"Well?"

"No." He smiled.

"What? What do you mean, no?"

"I mean, no. Not yet. I won't accept a proposal based on fear or guilt. I'm not going anywhere, babe. Haven't you figured that out by now?"

"You don't want to get married?"

"Do you?"

I opened my mouth to answer, then realized I didn't have one. Not exactly.

"I'm not sure."

"Well, there ya go. That's my point. And I feel like we've already had this conversation. Yes. I do want to marry you someday. But you're not ready."

"I'm not ready?"

"Nope."

"Are you sure?"

"Completely sure."

"Are you planning on telling me when I *am* ready?"

Eric smiled. God, he killed me with that. All devilish, sexy, smug. He reached down and picked up the Afghan I'd dropped. My teeth started to chatter.

"I'll think about it. Come on. Let's get you out of those wet clothes." His tone was filled with sin that sent heat shooting through me. Then I started to follow him up to the house.

"Wait," I said, stopping. "I meant what I said. I don't like it when you're not around. If you don't want to work for me, fine. But ... I want you here, okay? All the time."

He froze, back to me, his shoulders squared. Slowly, he turned around to face me.

"So we don't get married. Not yet. But move in with me. Live here. With me. Sell your condo. You're barely there as it is."

"Cass ..."

"I want you to. I'm not just saying this out of guilt or fear, Eric. I want ..."

He put his hands on my shoulders. "Cass," he said, softer. "Okay."

"Okay?"

"Yes. Okay. You are definitely ready for me to move in with you."

"I am?" I laughed.

"Definitely."

He brought me close. Kissed me deeply. Then Eric Wray swung me off my feet and carried me across my threshold. Behind us, the swan family honked and flapped their great wings before gliding off to the center of the lake.

NEXT UP, Cass is called on to represent an innocent client who refuses to break his silence and betray a friend. If Cass can't get through to him, he'll spend the rest of his life in jail and set a killer free. Don't miss Code of Secrets, the next spell-binding novel in the Cass Leary Legal Series.

A Note for Legal Thriller Fans!

HAVE YOU READ THEM ALL YET?

Get caught up with the Cass Leary Legal Thriller Series today!

What readers are saying...

"...like old school Grisham with a strong female lead..."

"Taut legal mystery that will keep you up at night turning the pages."

"Whatever Robin James writes, I'm going to read. These books are *that* good!"

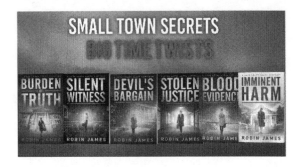

Available for Kindle, Print, Hardcover and Audio!

DID YOU KNOW?

All of Robin's books are also available in Audiobook format. Click here to find your favorite! https://www.robinjamesbooks. com/foraudio

Want to know how to nab a FREE novella in the Cass Leary series and see what these characters really look like? Turn the page for more information.

Newsletter Sign Up

Sign up to get notified about Robin James's latest book releases, discounts, and author news. You'll also get *Crown of Thorne* an exclusive FREE bonus prologue to the Cass Leary Legal Thriller Series just for joining. Find out what really made Cass leave Killian Thorne and Chicago behind.

Click to Sign Up

http://www.robinjamesbooks.com/newsletter/

About the Author

Robin James is an attorney and former law professor. She's worked on a wide range of civil, criminal and family law cases in her twenty-five year legal career. She also spent over a decade as supervising attorney for a Michigan legal clinic assisting thousands of people who could not otherwise afford access to justice.

Robin now lives on a lake in southern Michigan with her husband, two children, and one lazy dog. Her favorite, pure Michigan writing spot is stretched out on the back of a pontoon watching the faster boats go by.

Sign up for Robin James's Legal Thriller Newsletter to get all the latest updates on her new releases and get a free bonus scene from Burden of Truth featuring Cass Leary's last day in Chicago. http://www.robinjamesbooks.com/newsletter/

Also By Robin James

Cass Leary Legal Thriller Series

Burden of Truth

Silent Witness

Devil's Bargain

Stolen Justice

Blood Evidence

Imminent Harm

First Degree

Mercy Kill

Guilty Acts

Cold Evidence

Dead Law

The Client List

Deadly Defense

Code of Secrets

Seasonable Doubt

With more to come...

Mara Brent Legal Thriller Series

Time of Justice

Price of Justice

Hand of Justice

Mark of Justice

Path of Justice

Vow of Justice

Web of Justice

Shadow of Justice

With more to come...

Audiobooks by Robin James

Cass Leary Series

Burden of Truth

Silent Witness

Devil's Bargain

Stolen Justice

Blood Evidence

Imminent Harm

First Degree

Mercy Kill

Guilty Acts

Cold Evidence

Dead Law

The Client List

Mara Brent Series

Time of Justice

Price of Justice

Hand of Justice

Mark of Justice

Path of Justice

Vow of Justice

Web of Justice

Made in United States
Orlando, FL
17 January 2025

57410512R00228